SHADOWS OF RED EARTH

Suzanne Cass

S C

STORM CLOUD
PRESS

Shadows of Red Earth

Storm Cloud Press, Perth Australia

Copyright © 2019 by Suzanne Cass

Cover by Vikncharlie

All rights reserved.

Dedication

To Andrew, Chris, Cath and Bev.

CHAPTER ONE

The sound of a two-stroke engine buzzed in the distance, breaking the quiet of the desert. Rose lifted her head and concentrated. It was coming toward her. Excitement bubbled in her veins. This could be her ticket out of here. She got to her feet and stood beneath the wizened desert oak, the only tree to offer any shade for as far as the eye could see along the deserted stretch of road.

A small plume of red dust floated into the sky, broadcasting the motorbike's path. Rose craned her neck to see over the scrubby salt bush, trying to determine what kind of bike it was. And more importantly, who was riding it. She'd been hoping for a car or truck, something with a bit more room. It wasn't ideal. But she could sit on the back of a bike just as easily as in the seat of a car.

She grabbed her backpack and snatched her straw hat off the top, squashing it firmly on her head as she slipped the straps over her shoulders. Then stepped out into the middle of the dirt road and stood, legs akimbo, waiting. The road ran dead straight off to the horizon behind her, but in the direction she faced, a sweeping bend curved away to the left. The plume of red got closer, the droning louder. The sun beat mercilessly down on Rose's head, even through the straw hat. It was hot out in the blasting midday sun, but she waited.

This might be her only chance. There may not be another vehicle along here for hours, or even days. And she couldn't wait that long, they'd already be out looking for her. It wouldn't take them long to find the car she'd ditched a few miles over.

The bike appeared as a red blur around the corner. The buzzing rumble of the engine reverberated from the road and came up through the soles of her boots, making her legs tremble. She raised her hand in a command to stop.

Rose had her story straight in her head. Tourists were always doing stupid things. Thinking they were a match for the desert and then paying the price. The person on the motorbike couldn't in all conscience leave her here if he thought she was lost and clueless. Nobody who lived or worked out here would ever leave someone stranded by the side of the road.

The rider changed down through the gears and slowed to a crawl, coming to a stop a few meters in front of her. She waited for the fine dust to clear before she walked toward him. The guy wasn't wearing a helmet, instead he had on a black cap, turned backward and a pair of dark sunglasses.

'Hey,' he called out.

'Hey,' she called back, squinting her eyes against the sun and dust to make out the figure atop the bike. Wild black hair fell in curls over his ears and down the back of his neck. He had dusky skin, the color of the unsweetened black tea her grandmother loved to drink. Then he raised his sunglasses, and she caught a glimpse of dark eyes appraising her warily.

'Can I have a lift?' It was the only question that mattered, so she may as well dispense with the pleasantries.

'What you doin' out here, all on your own?' He sounded rightfully suspicious.

'My car broke down. Way over there.' She waved a vague hand over her left shoulder.

'You shouldn't leave your car, you know, if you get lost.' He was still glaring at her.

'Yeah, the guy at the car hire company said the same thing.' Rose added a slight, high-pitched giggle, and his eyes narrowed. Good, her ruse seemed to be working. 'And my phone wouldn't work, either. This place is archaic, no reception for miles.' This time, she flicked her hair impatiently. 'The desert is not what I thought it would be.'

'Bloody tourists,' he mumbled, just loud enough for her to hear. 'Where you headed?'

'Back to civilization. Anywhere that's not here.' She reached around and pointed behind her. He continued to appraise her with that wary gaze, looking her up and down, taking in her well-worn hat, her backpack, blue chambray shirt, jeans and Blundstone boots.

'What about your car?' he asked, still looking unfriendly.

'I'll ring the hire company when we get somewhere with phone reception. They can bloody-well come and get it. I'm not going back there. I've seen enough of this country for a whole lifetime.' A trickle of sweat escaped from beneath her hat and ran down her temple. She ignored it. 'I'll pay for the petrol if you give me a lift.'

His face lit up in a slow smile that was wondrous to see. 'Okay.'

Finally, she seemed to have broken through that wall of distrust. White teeth flashed against dark skin and a bold dimple appeared in his left cheek. Rose's heart did a couple of extra-fast beats before she could stop it. Handsome. Definitely handsome.

The urge to delve into his mind was strong. But she'd made a vow to herself that she wouldn't do that. She wanted to be just like normal people. Wanted to prove she could live on the same level as a regular person. On the other hand, it'd be good to know whether this stranger was actually an axe murderer before she hopped on the bike with him. She narrowed her eyes and let a tiny ribbon of consciousness slip toward him, and…She hit a brick wall. Nothing. The shock made her take a step backward. She couldn't read his intentions.

And now she didn't know whether this stranger was a good guy or not. She'd have to work it out like anyone else. Have to read his body language and facial expressions. She'd have to trust a stranger.

A smile split her lips. Isn't that what she wanted all along? Now wasn't the time to back away, she needed to grab this experience with both hands and run with it.

'Hop on then.' He shuffled a little further forward to allow more room on the single vinyl seat. 'You been on a bike before?'

She nodded. She could probably ride the bike better than him, but he didn't need to know that.

'Sorry, no helmets,' he said as he put his sunglasses back into place.

She grimaced. It was an oversight, and her parents would kill her if they knew she was riding without one. But what her parents didn't know…

'My name's Koen. Koen Babroda, at your service.' He turned and flashed her that mischievous grin again.

'I'm Rose. Thanks for stopping.' She didn't give him her last name. The Simmonds family was well known around these parts, and she wasn't going to take the risk.

'No probs. Hang on.' The bike had been modified for traveling, with a bar behind her, as a kind of backrest. And two satchels were fitted to each side, which must be where Koen kept his bags. It meant she could hold on to the bar and didn't have to put her arms around him. Didn't have to touch him. He might be immune to her probing from a distance, but that didn't mean she wouldn't be swamped by his emotions

4

if she dared to touch him. Now wasn't the time to experiment. She settled her backpack against the metal bar and reached around with her left hand to grab on. At the last second, she swiped her hat off her head and tucked it into the front of her jeans. Wouldn't do to lose her second-most prized possession.

Koen faced the front, revved the engine a few times, let the clutch out, and the bike lurched forward and picked up speed. Wind whipped past her face and threatened to pull her hair from its ponytail. At least the rushing air cooled the sweat from her skin, and the hot midday sun didn't feel quite so scorching. A weight lifted from her shoulders as they flew over the red dirt road. Replaced by a freedom she'd never felt before.

The image of her mother's face hovered in her mind's eye. Her parents would be distraught. Her mother especially. And Rodney and Tallow would be missing her like crazy. They were like surrogate brothers to her and would be worried. Guilt gnawed at Rose's guts. This whole thing was so unlike her. It was so crazy and untethered. She'd never done anything like this in her life. Always been so dutiful and loyal.

Which is exactly why she was doing it.

* * *

Koen was only half-concentrating on guiding the bike over the rutted dirt road. What was he doing? Why had he let the woman on his bike? She'd just slow him down.

Because he was a sucker for a pretty face, that's why.

And she *was* pretty. Elfin almost. Blonde hair pulled back into a ponytail, slim hips beneath well-worn jeans. Eyes as blue as the sky. She wasn't any damn tourist either, or he was a monkey's uncle. No tourist he'd ever met had her air of assurance; that confidence. No tourist stood out here in the middle of the desert all alone and didn't shit themselves, thinking that they were going to die out here. No, she lived in the outback somewhere. Or had spent time out here, at the very least.

Koen cast a guilty glance behind him. No telltale plume of dust followed them. He laughed at his own stupidity. Of course no one was following. They wouldn't find him, not out here. They probably didn't even know the motorbike was missing. Yet. They would still be deeply immersed in their Sorry Business. In their grief, in the ceremonies and traditional rites that were part of the funeral for his cousin.

But soon, very soon, his uncle Billy would discover the motorbike was gone. And then he'd track down Koen's mum and find out that Koen was gone, too. And put two and two together.

It was all bullshit. But he wished he could turn back time to twenty-four hours ago. Wished he hadn't gotten so angry and let his fury carry him away. But he had to get out of there. The town already felt like a cage, the bars closing slowly in on him. Mack's funeral had been the last straw. The overwhelming emotions gripping the whole town, the outrage and despair at the waste of such a young life. A terrible sadness twisted through him at the thought of Mack. Only thirteen years old, and he'd felt as if life was no longer worth living. It tore at Koen's heart how the epidemic of youth suicide ripped through the fabric of community and family. If only he could've done something to stop it. But what?

The girl behind him shifted slightly on the seat, and he startled. He'd almost forgotten she was there. Rose, she'd said her name was. Well, she had a damn good seat on a bike, light and easy, flowing with the rider. As if she'd ridden many times before.

Koen slowed the bike and half-turned so she could see his lips move. 'Where you from?' He was almost shouting to make his words heard above the rush of the wind. It was still a long ride into the next town, where he'd have to stop and refuel. He may as well pass the time with some conversation. 'You an Aussie? Or a Pom or something?' She had that English rose complexion, pale skin with a smattering of freckles across her nose. Her thighs tensed at his words, and while he couldn't look back to see her face, he got the impression she was instantly on guard.

'Ah, here and there. Like I said, I'm a tourist, just wanted to come and see the desert for myself,' she shouted back.

'Yeah, but where were you born? That's what I meant.'

'Ah…Brisbane. I was born in Brisbane.'

'Really?' He didn't believe her. All it took was one bullshit artist to recognize another bullshit artist. But he'd play along with her game for now. 'Ain't that near the Gold Coast? I've always wanted to go to that theme park, Seaworld.'

'Yeah,' she replied, but said no more, and their conversation lapsed as the roar of the engine filled his ears.

Then she surprised him by shouting in his ear, 'What about you, where are you from?'

It was his turn to hesitate.

'Balgo.' Shit. Should he have lied to her? It wouldn't do, her having too much information on him. But she'd caught him unawares, and he hadn't concocted a ready story yet.

There was a second's silence, and he wondered if she'd figure it out. 'Is that where the artist community is? That world-renowned Indigenous art place?'

'Yep, that's the one.' Surely there was nothing she could do with that knowledge. She was a stranger. They'd part ways just as soon as she got wherever she needed to go. She wouldn't have the chance to give him up. To his uncle, or the cops, or anyone.

'So, are you an artist too?'

'No.' His hands tightened on the handlebars. Not him.

He'd never be an artist. Didn't want to be. He didn't have the skill, the finesse, the dreaming. His mum said he had it, but he never believed her.

'Where are you headed?' As she leaned forward to shout into his ear, her breasts brushed against his back. Her mouth was so close to his neck, he could almost feel her lips against his skin. Something squeezed tight deep down in his gut.

'Darwin,' he replied.

'Can I come with you?'

'All the way to Darwin?' He was shocked. 'I thought you just wanted to go to the next town, Halls Creek. You can phone the car hire company or a friend or whatever to come and help you.' He never imagined her sitting on the back of the bike all the way to Darwin. Could he do that? And if he let her come, what about his Uncle Billy? Did he want to embroil her in all his family's affairs? Their community didn't generally involve the cops in things like this. Domestic disputes. They preferred to sort out family matters themselves. Tribal retribution. Koen shivered. Shit, he was an idiot. It would be better if she wasn't involved.

'You know it's nearly two days' drive? I won't get there until tomorrow arvo. I don't ride at night, too dangerous, so I'll have to stop when it gets dark.'

'Yes, I know. If you let me come, I'll pay for our petrol all the way.' This time he did risk a quick glance backward. She had light blue eyes. So light, they reminded him of the pale color of the early morning sky, just as the sun peeked over the horizon. It was a tempting offer. He was damn low on cash. The less he spent on petrol, the more he'd have left when he got to Darwin. But was he prepared to put up with her until then?

'Please.'

If he wasn't mistaken, she almost sounded like she was as desperate as he was to get to Darwin. But what for?

'I'll think about it, hey.' He returned his focus to the road. There were still a few hours until they hit Halls Creek. He'd make a decision then.

CHAPTER TWO

'I need to get gas,' Koen shouted back to Rose, his words flowing past her, whipped away by the wind.

'Great.' She'd welcome a chance to get off and stretch her legs. Nearly three hours on the back of a bike was a lot more tiring than she'd imagined. Her neck ached and her arm was nearly numb from holding onto the bar at the back. Koen must be tired, too. He'd ridden the motorbike over the rough terrain and corrugations of the road with skill and made it seem almost easy. Which she knew it hadn't been.

The road had turned to asphalt a few kilometers back, heralding the upcoming town of Halls Creek. Rose knew the town and was familiar with the layout and shops. Her family came here a few times a year to pick up things they couldn't get in their local township of Smokey Creek, now three hundred kilometers behind them. A long way to go for a bit of shopping. God, she hoped she didn't happen across a familiar face here. It was unlikely, but she still needed to be careful. The last thing she wanted was word getting back to her parents while she was still so close to home.

The first house appeared along the edge of the road. Ramshackle, with the front yard full of dead weeds. A standard sight out here. More houses appeared, and they were suddenly hemmed in on both sides, as outback suburbia formed around them.

Rose glanced away from the dusty houses and stared at Koen's back. The sight had become burned into her retinas for the past three hours. When she hadn't been staring at the dry desert racing past on both sides, she'd been looking at Koen's back. Trying to figure him out. His black curly hair became a snarl of tangles as the wind whipped through it where it poked out from beneath the backward cap. The curls just brushed the back of his collar. Her eyes traced the curve of his shoulders beneath the fabric of the red and white checkered shirt. Strong and straight. Broad, tapering to a narrow waist. He was athletic and agile, his movements reminding her of a nimble cat. The way he handled the motorbike with surety and confidence impressed her. Every now and then she caught his profile when he turned his head and she sketched out high cheekbones, firm, full lips and a strong jaw covered with a week's worth of growth of scruffy dark beard. A rough diamond.

The motorbike slowed, and Rose leaned with Koen as he turned off the road into a gas station. He put the kickstand down and stepped off the bike, stretching his arms high above his head as he did so. Dragging the cap off his head, he shook out the untidy curls.

'It's going to be a long way to Darwin.' He grimaced, and she silently agreed, not sure she was quite so keen to go all that way on the back of a bike now she'd experienced it firsthand. But then again, Koen still hadn't promised to take her yet.

She dismounted and did a similar stretch, dropping her backpack on the ground near the bike and rolling her shoulders.

Then she stepped backward to give Koen room to undo the gas cap on the top of the bike and, turning, stared down the road they'd just arrived on. Reflexively, Rose reached up and felt for her necklace, which lay against her breastbone, hidden beneath her shirt. This was her most prized possession. Her finger traced the familiar teardrop shape. Pure black, the necklace was made of jet, a semiprecious stone, set in fine silver. It was supposed to absorb energy, so when she was hit with someone else's emotions, the jet would draw the potency away from her body. Rose had only been little when her mum presented the jewelry to her, nestled in a beautiful black silk bag. But she still remembered that special day clearly.

'Damn,' she swore quietly. Thinking about her mother was not good. But she couldn't help herself. How would Jenna be feeling right now? Rose imagined her mother, standing at the kitchen sink of the old homestead, staring out the window. Her faithful dog, Jello, would be sitting at her feet. Jenna would be looking at—but not seeing—the vista of open rolling hills parading all the way to the horizon. This was what her mum always did when she had a problem. She said the vastness of the desert view brought clarity. Either that, or she'd be in the stables with her beloved horses. Talking to them, running a hand over their soft ears, listening as they talked back.

Her mum had an affinity with animals, especially horses.

It was an amazing ability, a gift similar to Rose's. But it was also one of the reasons Rose had never been allowed to stray too far from the station. Jenna was scared. Paranoid really, if you asked Rose. Kept telling Rose to be careful of strangers. Not to trust anyone. There may be people out there who wanted to hurt her.

Rose snorted out loud. She didn't hate her mother. Not really. But she had to leave. Get away from the station. Otherwise she would've suffocated. Some days on the farm it was like Rose couldn't breathe. No matter how much air she dragged into her lungs, it couldn't make it past the tight restriction across her chest.

She was nearly twenty. More than capable of taking care of herself. Hadn't she proved that over and over? She knew she was responsible, carried out her duties as a station hand tirelessly. It was time she took hold of her freedom.

She sighed. Her parents were going to kill her. That fact was set in stone. But they'd have to find her first.

'You okay?' A warm hand landed on her shoulder, and she spun around in surprise.

'Oh. Sure. Just thinking.' She gave Koen a quick smile. 'Have you finished filling up? I'll go and pay if you like?' He gave the nozzle one last shake, then turned and gave her the thumbs up.

She reached into her backpack and pulled out her wallet, opening it without thinking to grab some money. As she closed it again, she glanced Koen's way and saw his eyes follow her hand as she put it in her back pocket. He must've seen the large wad of cash in her wallet. Damn. She needed to be more careful. That money was her escape. Her freedom. She'd been hoarding it for months now in preparation for just this moment.

She went inside the shop, grabbed a bag of sweets, and quickly paid the man.

Koen had moved the motorbike off to the side of the shop and was checking the air in the tires.

'Shall we grab a meal? I'm starving,' she said.

He glanced up, a frown darkening his brow, and she thought he might say no. Then his brow cleared, and he said, 'Sure. Just let me put the bike around the back first. Wanna eat at the hotel?' Koen's face brightened visibly at the idea of a big hot meal, but Rose's blood ran cold at the mere mention. Koen meant the Halls Creek hotel, a little further down the road, with both a bar and restaurant. They had a quaint little beer garden in a walled courtyard to one side that was nice to sit in after sunset, and normally, she'd jump at the prospect. But she couldn't take the chance that the publican might recognize her. Whenever she came to town with her parents, they always went there for a meal as a treat.

'How about we just grab a burger from the roadhouse?' She didn't meet his eyes when she spoke. 'They do an amazing fish burger. And they put beetroot on them, my favorite.'

She crossed the road and walked down the footpath, keeping her hat on and her head down so her face was partially hidden, Koen a few paces behind her.

'Whatever. I'll eat anything,' he said with a shrug. 'So, you've been in this town before?'

She'd forgotten she was just a tourist driving through the area. 'Ah...yes. I ah...stayed here the other day. Why?'

'Because you know they put beetroot on the burgers at the roadhouse.' His shrewd gaze settled on her face. Damn. She really needed to be more careful. She wasn't very good at this covert running away thing.

'Ha, yes. I can't go past a good burger. It's a thing I do. Make sure I try the burgers in as many new places as I can. I can probably name each town I've been through by how good their burgers are. But I'm vegetarian. So, they have to have a veggie burger or at the very least a fish burger, if they're going to rate.' And now she was rambling. Making up lies. She'd have to up her game, or Koen would get suspicious. She needed him to take her to Darwin. Needed to keep him on-side.

Perhaps a bit of diversion by changing the topic might be in order. 'What about you? Have you been to Halls Creek before?'

'Yeah, plenty of times. It's the next biggest town after Balgo.' A row of dilapidated shops edged the footpath in front of them. They passed a pharmacy and then there was the roadhouse, which also doubled as the local Greyhound bus stop, with a few laminated tables and benches squatting beneath a low patio roof. Two locals sat at one of the tables, eating fish and chips from a pile of butcher paper. They nodded to each other in acknowledgement. The smell of fried food wafted to Rose's nostrils as they pushed the door open, and her stomach gave a large rumble. Breakfast had been a muesli bar at three a.m. this morning. Shoved in her mouth hurriedly as she walked between the homestead and the sheds, on her way to steal one of the cars. Not steal, she corrected herself. Borrow. The Land Cruiser was one of three station cars, which belonged to her parents, so technically they belonged to her. They'd find the car, eventually; she'd parked it up under a large copse of casuarinas in a little back road a hundred kilometers or so from Smokey Creek. She'd hoped to get further away but hadn't counted on the car being so low in petrol, and she daren't fill up in Smokey Creek, as she would've been recognized immediately. She'd always planned on ditching the car anyway—it made her too easy to find—but her plan had entailed getting further away from home before she had to do so. And nearer a main road, where the chance of hitching would be high. She was lucky Koen had come along that back-road when he did.

It was now after four in the afternoon, and she was well and truly ready for some food. She ordered a fish burger and chips and bought two bottles of water, one of which she stowed in her backpack. Then she waited as Koen ordered his own meal. She didn't mind paying for the petrol, but she wasn't a charity. He could buy his own food. Koen didn't baulk at the price, and handed over a fifty-dollar bill, so he obviously wasn't short on cash. Which made her breathe a little easier. If he had his own money, then he wasn't interested in hers. She'd been imagining the look he'd cast at her wallet earlier.

When their burgers were ready, they took them to a nearby small memorial park and sat in one of the two rotundas to eat. A table and two rickety wooden benches in need of a good coat of paint huddled in the welcome shade of the hut, surrounded by a patch of green grass. Silence ensued as both of them satisfied their hunger. Goddamn, the burger was good. Beetroot really was her favorite.

'So, you've been to Halls Creek before. What about Darwin? Been there too?' Rose stopped eating long enough to phrase the question before she popped a hot chip into her mouth.

Koen looked up, and she had to stifle a laugh as a dribble of sauce and beetroot juice dripped down his chin. She picked up a serviette, and without thinking reached across the table to wipe it off. Her finger grazed the side of his jaw and a shot of heat went up her arm. Like touching an electric fence. She scrunched the serviette in her fingers, and he looked up in surprise, as if he too had felt that zing of something passing between them.

Belatedly, Rose realized that aside from the shot of electricity, she hadn't felt anything else. No emotions had come crowding through to her. He was truly immune to her touch. Very interesting.

'Ah, Darwin. Have you been there before?' she asked again, trying to cover her embarrassing reaction.

'Yep. I worked up there for about nine months a couple of years ago. I wanna see if I can get me old job back.'

That was good to know he could hold down a job. It was another tick on the score sheet that told her she could trust him. Without the help of her Empath talent, she needed to resort to old-fashioned methods to work him out.

'What kind of job?'

'I was working for a carpentry business. They're in the building trade, making stairs and roof beams, that kinda thing.' Koen's eyes glazed over, and he stopped chewing. 'I really liked that job. Was pretty good at it too. Sometimes they got contracts with the big mining companies and I got to fly out to the mines. That was cool.'

'What made you leave it?'

The nostalgic look disappeared, replaced by something akin to a flash of guilt, before Koen covered it up with another of his mischievous grins. 'Oh, this and that. Long story. I was stayin' with my cousin and his mob. He's got a place up there. But he kicked me out.'

'Mmm hmm,' she prompted. There was obviously a lot more to that story he wasn't telling her.

'I'm hoping my cousin, Jon, will let me go back and stay with him.'

'Can't hurt to ask,' she replied, and then took another large bite of her burger. She knew Indigenous family relationships were complicated at the best of times. They had a special bond, a commitment that was owed to family, which made it hard for them to turn a family member away.

Her surrogate brothers, Rodney and Tallow, were both Indigenous. Twins, three years younger than her and inseparable from each other.

So, she had more than an average understanding of the dynamics of Indigenous families, but without being born into it, she would never truly understand.

She missed those two. Scoundrels that they were. They'd probably be out looking for her right now. Wondering where she'd gone. Why she'd gone.

She'd left a note on the kitchen table, trying to explain, but they'd still look for her, even though she'd asked them not to. Out of habit, she reached up and touched the jet stone beneath her shirt as she thought of her family.

She glanced down at the table. Her chips were getting cold, so she popped one into her mouth. Much better if she concentrated on what needed to be done here and now. Not ponder what might be going on at home anymore.

'You said you'd think about taking me all the way to Darwin. Have you come up with an answer yet?' she asked, looking Koen directly in the eye.

* * *

Her question caught him off guard, and he coughed as a piece of hamburger stuck in his throat. He should've been expecting her to bring it up sooner or later. He already knew his answer. Had known it ever since she'd flashed that huge stash of cash in her wallet. But he needed to play it cool.

'Yeah, I did say I'd think about it, hey.' A truck roared past on the road beside them, and he took another bite of burger and pretended to be considering her question. 'It's a bloody long way. Do you reckon you can hang on the back that far?'

'Course I can,' she scoffed.

He liked her bravado. Even though he knew her back must be killing her from the past three hours on the bike, having her backpack pulling down on her shoulders all the way. Even if it was a relatively small backpack. But who was he to care about her comfort? If she wanted to come with him, then it was no skin off his nose, and he didn't need to worry about any hardships she might be going through. After all, he never cared before. Not about a woman, anyway. If they wanted to be with him, then that was fine. But don't let them start getting all whiney and clingy or he'd just up and leave.

Rose didn't strike him as either of these things. And she was tough. Well, at least her outer shell was. He still hadn't worked out what was going on inside her head. There was a secret there. That much he'd discovered in their short time on the bike together.

She was used to hard work, he could tell from her hands, callouses on the palms with fingernails short and practical. Right now, her long, supple fingers were wrapped around the remains of her burger. She dressed like someone from the bush as well, in her thigh-hugging jeans, sensible light-blue shirt and boots. Although that sensible shirt couldn't hide the generous swell of her breasts, or her narrow waistline. He could probably wrap his hands around her waist if he wanted to.

Which he didn't, he reminded himself. It didn't matter if he was attracted to her. He needed to control that impulse. He had many, many other things on his plate. And a white woman with problems of her own was one less thing he needed. He had to concentrate on getting to Darwin as soon as possible. Find his cousin and figure out a way to get the stolen bike back to his uncle. Try and explain how he hadn't wanted to steal the bike, but at the time it'd felt like his only option. His only way out. His mum was always telling him he needed to stop and think first, before he did something stupid. That was him, though, always acting on instinct. Spontaneous.

Rose was still looking at him with those big blue eyes. Instinct told him to say no. Leave her here to find her own way north. She didn't need the kind of trouble he was liable to bring. Didn't deserve it. But the money in her wallet called to him. He wasn't going to steal it. Maybe once he might've thought about it, but he'd changed, turned a corner. Was on the road to becoming a better man. At least he would be once he got to Darwin. Nah, he just needed her to pay for the petrol, that was all. He was down to less than ninety-five dollars, now he'd paid for this burger.

'Alright, you can come.'

She gave him a huge grin of thanks; her smile lighting up the small rotunda, her sky-colored eyes sparkling. And again, something stirred deep inside him, as if recognizing something inside her.

Shit, he really needed to control this attraction thing that was going on if he ever wanted to make it to Darwin in one piece.

'You finished? We need to get going. Got a long way to go before nightfall.' He made his voice gruff as he stood up and aimed his burger wrapper at the nearest rubbish bin.

CHAPTER THREE

Jenna stared out the kitchen window, hands resting lightly on the edge of the sink. Jello gave another long sigh, just to remind her he was there, lying next to her bare feet. The dog was her shadow; she couldn't go anywhere without him. And she didn't want to. It was nice having a faithful safety blanket follow her around, always there to lay a warm muzzle in her lap or give her a happy doggy-smile when she patted him. Having changed out of her jeans, boots and western shirt, she was now dressed in shorts and a t-shirt that hugged her slim frame.

'Yes, I know,' she said to the dog. His tail thumped the boards lightly. It was habit now, to speak out loud to Jello, even when she didn't need to. It was for Dan's benefit. And Rose and Ebony and Jay. And everyone else who knew she could hear what the animals thought. It was her gift. And now her daughter, Rose, had a gift, too. One she was still coming to terms with.

Where was Rose? That bloody stubborn, strong-willed girl. Dan said she was too much like her mother, but Jenna was sure she'd never been that stubborn. Or that determined to get her own way. Jenna turned her gaze back out the window to watch the last of the sun's rays leave the earth, the shroud of dusk turning everything black, almost like the flick of a light-switch.

It was her turn to give a long sigh. Please let them find Rose. And soon.

She could hear Dan's heavy tread on the floorboards as he came down the corridor, and she turned to watch him come through the door.

'I've been on the phone to Damien again.' He ran a hand through his unruly hair. He kept it shorter now, but it still curled enticingly whenever she ran her fingers through it. 'He said even though it's too early to put out a missing person report, he's made sure that all his guys at the station will keep an ear out for word of her. Someone has to be missing for at least twenty-four hours before they can make it official.'

At least that was something. Jenna knew Damien would do his utmost to help them find their daughter. Senior Sergeant Damien Potter was one of Dan's oldest friends, and it just so happened he was the officer in charge of Karratha Police station. He was a good guy, and it helped ease her mind just a little to know he was on the case.

'Can the police track her phone?' she asked. Rose must've taken her mobile with her. Jenna had looked everywhere for it after she left. They didn't use mobile phones much out here, because the reception was patchy at best. They only got good reception near the main towns, but there were large areas out here that weren't covered, Shiralee Station being one of them. Rose still had a mobile, however, as did they all, because, well, it was the twenty-first century and everyone had a mobile nowadays, especially teenagers.

'I'm not sure. I didn't ask,' Dan hedged. 'But if Rose is smart, and she's determined not to be found, she probably won't turn it on,' he continued. Jenna had to begrudgingly agree with him. Rose was smart. And determined. 'Anyway, Damo said he'd file the missing person report tomorrow morning, first thing.'

'We might not need it. Maybe we'll have found her by then.' It was false hope, and Jenna knew it. But it made her feel better to say the words out loud.

'Damo said the fact that Rose left a note also makes it less urgent. As well as the fact Rose is nineteen, nearly twenty. Technically, an adult and capable of making her own decisions,' Dan continued.

'No, she's not,' Jenna snapped without thinking. As soon as she uttered the words, she clamped a hand over her mouth. Eyes wide, she stared at her husband, trying in vain to keep the tears at bay.

'Oh, babe, come here.' He enfolded her in his embrace, laying her ear against his chest. He was so tall he could rest his chin on top of her head.

'I know you're worried about her. But she has a good head on her shoulders. And she's also more like you than you want to admit.' He pulled back so he could look into her eyes. Taking the end of her long blonde plait in his fingers, he toyed with the flaxen strands as he seemed to think about his next words carefully. 'You weren't much older when you had to go on the run from Liam, remember.'

The mention of Liam made her jerk back from him. 'That was out of sheer desperation, to save my own neck. Not out of some misguided need to run away from my parents to prove myself.' Crossing her arms over her chest, she leant back against the kitchen sink and swiped angrily at her drying tears.

'Yes, I realize that,' he said in a soothing tone. 'What I'm trying to say is that she has all your courage, tenacity and strong-will. And stubbornness.' A slow smile spread over his face. 'Which is one of the things I love most about you.' He reached for her again. How could she refuse him? They'd been married just over twenty years, and she loved him as much now as she had on the day of their wedding. She took a step forward, back into his embrace.

The sound of the front door banging open made her jump, and she and Dan swiveled to see who was coming down the corridor.

'Mum.' Jenna let go of Dan and went to meet her mother as she came through the door. Ebony's face was lined with worry, and the two women embraced, taking comfort in each other's arms. Some of the tension drained from Jenna's body. Her mother had a calmness around her, she always knew how to make the best of a situation.

Ebony was small in stature, much like Jenna, but with a few more rounded curves than her daughter. Her husband, Jay, often joked that Ebony embodied a French actress, with her creamy skin and wild, dark hair, left short to keep her disobedient curls under control. A few gray hairs spiraled at her temples, but the rest remained dark and lustrous. Probably after today, after the stunt Rose pulled, there would be many more appearing on both Jenna and her mother's head.

A low cough made them look up and Jenna said, 'Sorry, Jay, didn't see you there.'

The women moved out of the doorway to let Jay pass, and Jenna leaned in to give him a swift kiss on the cheek.

'Thanks for coming,' Dan said as he shook the older man's hand.

Jay returned Dan's clasp, then pulled out a chair and sat down at the kitchen table. Jay and her mother lived on the neighboring property, only a fifteen-minute drive from Shiralee. Many years ago, they'd moved to the outback from the small coastal town of Margaret River. Then turned their homestead into a youth center to help vulnerable kids, and Jenna knew they must be extremely worried to have dropped everything to come here.

Even at the age of fifty-two, Jay was still a good-looking

man. Tall and dark, with regulation short hair—a residue from his time spent in the army—intelligent brown eyes and a long straight nose that suited his angular face. He'd married her mother eighteen years ago and been her devoted partner ever since. Rose was glad her mother had found Jay. To help erase the horrible memories she had of her first husband, Jenna's father, Alexander.

'Of course, we're just as worried about Rose as you are,' Jay replied. 'You found the car she used to get off the station?'

'Yep,' Dan sighed. 'Moon found it parked under a tree, nice as you please, just up from Balmoral Downs Station. It was out of petrol. He found her footprints leading overland toward Padbury's Road. We think she hitched a ride from someone.'

'Hmm,' Jay mused quietly. 'You said she left a note. Can I see it?'

Dan took a bit of rumpled paper out of his back pocket and handed it to Jay.

'It doesn't tell us much,' Dan muttered.

'Read it out loud,' Ebony requested, taking a seat opposite Jay at the table.

Jay cleared his throat. 'Dear Mum and Dad, I need some time to myself. Please don't try and find me. And please stop worrying, I'll be fine. You worry too much. I'll call you in a few weeks and let you know I'm okay. Love Rose.'

'Ooh, that little…' Ebony pursed her lips, but didn't finish her sentence.

'She doesn't realize the danger she's in,' Jenna said quietly.

'No, she doesn't,' agreed Jay. 'She is a very stubborn girl. Much like her mother.' Jay cast Jenna a quick grin.

'What is it with you all? I am *not* that stubborn,' Jenna said indignantly.

No one replied, and Jenna let out an exasperated sigh. Okay, perhaps she was a tiny bit stubborn, but really, did they have to keep dwelling on it?

'But at least Rose has one advantage over everyone else out there.' Jenna looked Dan directly in the eye. 'At least she has her gift. Hopefully that'll help her figure out the good guys from the ones who mean her harm.'

'Maybe,' Dan admitted. 'But perhaps we've done it all wrong.' He ran a hand through his hair, leaving a few curls to stick up at random. 'Perhaps we should've given her more freedom, right from the start, rather than keeping her sequestered here on the farm.' He raised his broad shoulders in a shrug of uncertainty.

'But we were doing it for her own safety. For our safety,' Jenna cried. 'Corey is still out there. Just because he hasn't threatened us in years doesn't mean he's forgotten about us.'

'Hmm,' Jay muttered. Jay had never fully concurred with Jenna's fear that Corey was still biding his time until he could get back at them. It was true, Corey had stopped harassing them ages ago. It might even be as long as seven or eight years since they'd heard from him. The threatening phone calls had stopped. The clumsily written letters in the mail had ceased. And as the years passed and there'd been no more sign of anything untoward, Jay had begun voicing his thoughts more loudly. Telling them they should perhaps relax their guard a little, let Rose off the tight leash they were keeping on her.

Every time Jenna thought about Rose leaving the safety of the station, she broke out in a cold sweat. She'd lived through the nightmare of being hunted by Alexander, her own father, who'd sent out his son, her half-brother, Liam, to find her and bring her back. Dan and Jenna managed to defeat Liam and his band of thugs in a shootout in the desert—she'd killed Liam with his own knife—but the images never left her. The debilitating terror that Liam had come so close to taking Dan's life still haunted her.

Then, to compound her fears, a year later, Ebony also had to fight off an attack from Alexander, when he'd finally tracked her down to the small town of Margaret River. Deciding to do the deed himself rather than sending one of his henchmen, bringing his other son, Corey, with him to finish the job. Jenna had been there and seen it all unfold, sure she was going to lose the mother she'd only just reconnected with to the monster who was her biological father. Alexander was a psychopath, a rich man who thought he could control everyone with his money and power. Probably suffered from a narcissistic personality disorder. He'd physically and mentally abused Ebony while they'd been married, which is why Ebony finally got the courage to run away from him.

Perhaps Jenna had transferred those fears onto Rose. Perhaps she was an over-protective mother, who'd tried to keep Rose away from any kind of life outside that on the station. But it was the only way she could be absolutely sure she would stay safe.

Jello stirred uneasily at her feet, reacting to her swirling emotions. A wet nose landed in her palm as his expressive eyebrows raised in concern. She laid a calming hand on his black head, but she was too concerned about Rose to let the dog's usual steady way have an effect on her today.

'We know Corey hooked up with a biker gang when he got out of jail. What if he is still holding a grudge? He could use the bikers to attack us now.'

'Anything's possible,' Ebony agreed, turning and taking Jenna's hand in hers to give it a reassuring squeeze. 'But that private detective guy, Paul, is that his name? He assures us Corey only seems interested in his petty drug crimes. That and terrorizing as many people as he can. Poor kid.' Ebony's last statement was said so quietly that Jenna almost missed it and she had to stifle a sigh. Her mother had always felt responsible for Corey's plight. That's why Ebony had originally hired a private detective to keep tabs on him. As much to ease her own mind as to keep them forewarned. Corey was Alexander's other son, another half-brother to Jenna, and Alexander had brought him to Margaret River to help him abduct Ebony. But when things had backfired, Corey was arrested and sent to jail for his role in the kidnap and abduction. He'd spent four years in jail, but it hadn't helped him reform, instead it'd placed him even more firmly on the pathway to depravity and illegal pastimes. The provoking letters had started before he even left jail, telling Ebony and Jenna they were responsible for his father's death, and they would pay for what they did.

Jenna didn't see Corey as a *poor kid* at all. He'd lost his father when Alexander had died. Now he wanted his own kind of sick revenge on the two women he saw as having taken his father away from him. After much persuasion, Ebony had finally agreed to take out a restraining order on Corey, but it didn't stop the letters and calls. The incident that'd clinched the fact Corey was seriously dangerous in Jenna's mind was the day, a year or so after he'd been paroled from jail, when Corey had approached her in the local grocery store in Smokey Creek. Rose was with her, holding her hand and looking up at the strange man with curiosity. She was only five years old at the time. Corey had shouted something insane and vulgar, lunging at them, and Jenna had scooped Rose up in her arms and run for the door. Dan was waiting in the car outside. Corey backed down and walked away at the sight of Dan striding toward him. Jenna also took out a restraining order on Corey that day. But the confrontation had shaken her to the core. After that, she never allowed Rose off the station without supervision.

CHAPTER FOUR

It was so dark, Rose couldn't see her hand in front of her face. She also couldn't see the large expanse of water spread out in front of her. But she could feel it, like a large void. Quiet and serene. And she could smell it, an earthy, damp, musty smell. If she reached out her hand, she could almost feel the humid air rising up to meet the black sky. Her fingers fluttered up to touch the jet stone nestling beneath her shirt. Taking a last, deep breath, she turned on her phone torch app and made her way back to find Koen.

Koen had brought them to the edge of Lake Argyle. This was where they were going to stay the night. He said he didn't have enough money to stay in a hotel and he didn't like to camp too close to the highway. Too many *odd* people out there. She'd covered a laugh with her hand at that comment, but she was fine with sleeping rough. Sleeping under the stars was one of her favorite things to do.

Koen didn't want to ride at night. 'It's the roos,' he'd said with a grimace.

She agreed with him. Kangaroos were a menace to any driver on country roads, but especially dangerous to motorbike riders. Particularly riders without helmets.

The journey from Halls Creek to the Doon Doon roadhouse had taken a little under three hours. They stopped to refuel and buy a few supplies just as the sun was setting over the horizon. Rose saw the sideways look the shop attendant shot toward Koen when he thought he wasn't looking and had to tamp down on a flash of outrage. The shop attendant wasn't looking at *her* with suspicion. There were lots of small-minded people out there, and this shopkeeper was just one more.

Once they were back on the bike, Koen guided it down a rutted dirt track that wasn't obvious from the main highway. He said he'd been here before and knew the way and—perhaps naively—Rose trusted him.

They arrived just as the last of the light was leaving the sky, the low hills around the lake turning a dusky purple. The lake itself was like a piece of black velvet that'd been ripped from the sky, smooth and mirror-like. And huge. Bigger than anything else she'd ever seen before.

'It's amazing. Just…amazing,' she breathed, stepping off the bike as he brought it to a dusty halt next to a huge old boab tree. 'And so big.'

'Yep,' he drawled, dismounting the bike and leaning it onto its kickstand. 'It does something to your insides when you see it for the first time, hey.' They stood side by side and stared at the lake for many long minutes. Rose had seen the ocean before, when her mum took her to Perth, and once when they'd visited Broome. The ocean was vast and salty and wild. The big crashing waves had scared Rose back then, not that she told anyone of her fear. This man-made lake seemed nearly as big as the ocean, yet it was calm and peaceful. Full of fresh, soft, silky water, surrounded by the ochre red of the outback. Much more to her taste.

'Some of my people didn't want the dam built here. There were all kinds of protests and stuff. But right now, I kinda like it,' Koen muttered, casting her a sideways, cheeky glance. Her heart-rate skipped up a beat.

Both of them were too young to remember the time when the Ord River had been dammed. Which was probably a good thing, because Rose agreed with him. It was lovely, and she was enjoying the view. Perhaps it was that little more special, because Koen was standing beside her.

Koen was the first to break away from the lake, ambling back to the motorbike and unpacking one of the satchels strapped to the side. He pulled out a large jacket, a knit-cap and a plastic bag of food, then sat down with his back against the old pockmarked trunk of the boab tree. Its stark branches reached toward the sky, the base spreading out wide below them, like an old woman's backside.

She left the view and went over to get her own jacket out of her backpack. It'd get cold out here tonight, sleeping on the ground, and now she wished she had stuffed a jumper into her bag before she left. She dropped her bag on the ground and plopped down next to Koen, using her pack as a backrest. It was nearly dark now, and she used the last minutes of remaining light to find her own bag of food and set up a picnic, using the empty plastic bag as a tablecloth. There were crackers, some cheese, a few dried apricots, a packet of salty peanuts, a tin of tuna and two small apples, all smuggled from the pantry at home this morning. The muesli bars and ginger snap biscuits she'd bought back at the Doon Doon roadhouse were left in her backpack; she'd keep those for breakfast.

Suddenly, the last of the light disappeared, leaving them in complete dark. Rose fumbled for her phone and turned on the torch app.

'Wanna share?' she asked, directing the beam of light at her food.

'Okay, you can have some of mine, too.'

Rose shone the light on his pile of food and almost laughed out loud. Seemed like Koen might have a bit of a sweet tooth.

He had two bars of chocolate, a packet of chocolate chip biscuits, some Twinkies, and a bag of fruit jelly sweets.

She glanced up at his face and saw his dark eyes watching her in the torchlight. Watching her so intently that she drew in a quick breath. His features were all shadows and square lines in the flickering light, but this made him even more handsome, if that were possible. She'd almost forgotten how good-looking he was in the past hours she'd spent staring at his back. But now she was looking at him properly, her heart skipped a few beats, just like it had the first time she'd laid eyes on him. Locks of black hair curled over his forehead, and his mouth formed a sensuous line as he gave her a small smile. His gaze locked on hers and stayed there. Longer than it should.

'Shall we eat then?' Rose broke the silence between them before it became uncomfortable. She dragged her little pile of food closer to his and shuffled over in the dirt to sit next to him. Helping herself to a chunk of cheese and some crackers, she shoved them in her mouth and Koen snagged an apple and bit into it with relish.

'Where'd you get all this food?'

She couldn't tell him where it really came from. 'I bought it in Fitzroy Crossing when I was there a few days back.'

'Oh, right. You certainly get around, don't you?' It almost sounded like he didn't believe her. 'You know you were lucky today, don't you?'

'No, why?' Her fingers fumbled with the tin of tuna as she pretended to be only half-listening to him. Her hands were cold. Out here when the sun set, it took all its warmth with it.

'Because if I hadn't come along, you might have had to sit on that roadside for days before anyone else found you.'

'Pfftt.' Rose made a dismissive gesture. 'Nah, I would've been fine.'

He grinned in the torchlight. 'You tourists just don't get it, do you? How dangerous this country is?'

'I've been in worse situations.' She finally managed to pull the ring-tab open on the tuna, then sat, wondering how she was going to get the fish out of the tin with only her bare hands.

'Give it here, I've got a pocket knife.' Koen stretched out his hand for the tin. As she handed it to him, their fingers brushed against each other, and an immediate flare of heat flew across her skin. As if he'd just held a match against her fingertips. The same as before. Surreptitiously, she rubbed her hand against her jeans. Koen also pulled his hand back just a little too quickly, but then covered the move with the pretense of fishing around in his jeans pocket for his knife.

What was that? She'd never encountered this kind of physical reaction before. Because of her ability, she was used to reading people's emotions. She was always pre-warned if a man found her attractive. But even then, even if the attraction was mutual and she let them touch her, it'd never felt like this.

There were a few others before. Mostly seasonal jackaroos, who never stayed very long. Sam had been her latest. They'd dated—if you could call it that—for nearly six months. He was a local boy, and she'd met him at her nineteenth birthday party at the Smokey Creek pub, one of the few times her parents had given in and let her go into town. Rose's parents had practically forbidden her to see him when they found out, but he managed to sneak onto the property every now and then.

Sam said he loved her. And she thought he might've meant it. But then he was offered a traineeship to become a diesel mechanic in Perth, and he'd jumped at the opportunity to get away, leaving Rose more than a little miffed, but not heartbroken. But even on the few times when she'd snuck out of the house to meet Sam in one of the back sheds under the cover of darkness, she'd never felt any kind of sizzle when she touched him. More of a sense of curiosity and a vague gratification. It'd been nice, but that was about it.

Rose continued to rub her fingers on her jeans, and they ate the rest of their meal in silence.

After dinner, Rose pulled her jacket on and used her torch to walk back to the edge of the lake, then switched it off and stood there in the cold and dark, letting the enormity of the large body of water seep into her bones. She breathed in. And out. Slow and steady. It was the first time she could ever remember being without one of her family hovering nearby. It was liberating. And a little scary. Frosty tendrils curled around her as a light breeze brought cooling air in from the lake and she shivered and turned back toward Koen.

And now it was just the two of them stretched out on the blood-red earth beside the boab tree. The stars popped out in the night sky like a silvery blanket, and a sickle moon rose on the horizon. The night turned a little less black. She could make out shadows and outlines now. It was silent except for the sounds of the night animals waking up. A scuffle in the dry undergrowth off to her left, and a low mournful cry from some kind of water bird on the edge of the lake. But she was used to the silence of the desert, welcomed it. Then, for the first time, it hit Rose that she was completely alone out here with Koen. Isolated and alone. If he *was* an axe murderer in disguise, he had her exactly where he wanted her. And she'd let him lead her there like a lamb to the slaughter. She shifted a little on the hard ground, suddenly uncomfortable. If only her empathetic abilities worked on him, then she could be completely sure. It was disturbing that he was one of only three people who had this effect on her.

Perhaps if she found out a little more about him, she might be able to fathom why he was protected from her powers. Did it have something to do with that intoxicating jolt every time they touched? But where to start?

She asked him the first question that came to mind. 'So, what's it like to live in Balgo? I've never been there, but I've heard about it. Were you born there?' Her voice came out loud in the quiet night.

There was a shuffle in the dirt beside her. In the dimness she could make out his form as he leant up on one elbow so he could answer her question. Jesus, the ground was cold. It'd been a while since she'd slept outside, with no protection other than the branches of a half-dead boab tree.

'Yep, born there and grew up there. I lived with my mum most of the time. She's the head nurse at the health clinic.' Pride for his mother was clearly evident in his voice. 'Not a lot to tell, really.'

'Well, that can't be all true. Isn't the artist collective a big part of the town? I heard they bring in quite a bit of money. Surely it's one of the more prosperous communities?'

'I guess an outsider might think that.'

Okay, there was obviously stuff going on that Koen wasn't keen to talk about. Perhaps a change of tack was in order. 'What about brothers or sisters? Do you have any?'

'Yeah, two sisters. Daisy, the oldest, she lives in Perth now. She's a nurse too, just like mum.' Rose couldn't see his features in the starlight, but she could just make out his outline. Koen had tipped his head back and was staring at the sky. 'Bindi is in the middle. She lives up in Kakadu.'

He stopped talking and continued to stare at the sky. Okay, so he wasn't big on the small talk. It was almost like pulling teeth, getting personal information out of him.

'How come you left Balgo? I mean, I know you want to get a job in Darwin, but was that the only reason?'

'I just had to get away.' There was another long pause, and Rose thought he'd finished speaking. But then he said, 'It was my cousin's funeral the other day. And I…just had to get away.' Rose heard the slight hitch in his voice and felt a pang of compassion for his obvious pain.

* * *

Bloody hell. He hadn't meant to say that. Why did he tell her that? And now, like a typical woman, she was probably going to go all mushy on him and want to delve into how he felt about the whole thing. It was all bullshit, and the last thing he needed tonight was a touchy-feely woman. He was tired from over seven hours of riding that damn bike, and all he wanted was to go to sleep. Head still propped in his hand, he kept his gaze directed upwards to the stars.

'Hmm, I know a little how that feels,' she said softly. 'The need to get away from somewhere.'

He swallowed his surprise and gave a grunt in reply. What, no tenth-degree dissection of his innermost feelings? It'd been playing on his mind all day. The sight of Mack in that bloody pine box. Everyone crying and wailing. Maybe that's why he'd opened his big mouth, because his subconscious knew she might understand. Perhaps because he felt safe, cocooned in the dark of the night, where no one could see his face.

'I mean, it sounds like you had a good reason to leave. Funerals aren't fun for anyone,' she continued.

How true that was. He hated funerals. He liked fun and frivolity. Parties and good times. Always the joker in the crowd. And people loved him for it. A lovable larrikin, that's what his mum called him. He could admit to himself now, he probably hadn't coped very well with the Sorry Business. Of course he'd wanted to farewell his little cousin, but at the same time, he hadn't really wanted to believe it was true. That Mack was dead.

His mum made him go. Said he had to pay his respects. To his uncle and his family. And in some ways, she was right. Mack needed to know how much he'd loved him.

'I've got two Indigenous brothers. Bloody rat-bags, the

both of them. They're twins and they're always playing jokes on me.' She was just a blob of dark against an even darker background. He couldn't make out any of her face in the starlight. 'But I do miss them, even so. They're a couple of years younger than me.' The tone of her voice made him feel almost as if she was talking to herself, as if she'd forgotten he was there. 'I don't know how I'd cope if one of them died.'

Mack had been a bit like a younger brother to him. The closest of all his nine cousins. Only thirteen years old, but so full of life. Koen could still see Mack's cheeky smile as he showed him one of his finished paintings. A shy, humble smile that nonetheless told of how hungry he was for praise, no matter how small or insignificant.

'I was the one who found him,' Koen said. Rose shifted on the ground next to him, a dusty scratching sound, as she too propped herself up on her elbow. 'His mum, Aunty Teal, told me he'd been gone most of the day and she was getting worried about him. So, I went out looking. I knew all his favorite spots. He hanged himself in a tree.'

Her hand landed softly on his shoulder. It sent a spark of heat through him, so strong he felt it even through his own self-despair.

'I'm sorry, Koen. That's awful.'

'Yep. It's all so much bullshit.' A huge lump formed in the back of his throat. He wanted to shake that hand off, reject her consolation. But it was the first human contact since the funeral. And for some reason, it felt good. She was practically a stranger, and so her compassion, while a little awkward, wasn't stifling as it might've been if one of his family had tried to console him. His uncle had come up after the funeral and tried to hug him, and Koen almost punched the man in the face. That's when he knew he had to get out of there. Get away from all the cloying sympathy and self-destructive guilt and blame being thrown about. Guilt that burdened him most of all. He should've done something. He should've known how bad Mack felt. Should've been there for him that morning, instead of off with his mates, playing footy.

'I probably would've run away too.' Her hand still lay warm and heavy on his shoulder. She left a silence for him to fill, but he couldn't find the words. Couldn't force any sound past the tightness in his throat.

After what seemed like an eternity, where he kept trying to swallow the pain, but it wouldn't go, she said, 'But then again, if you hadn't left Balgo, you'd never have rescued me from the side of the road. I'd probably still be sitting there. Probably dying from dehydration or some such thing.' She gave his shoulder a little squeeze. 'And then you wouldn't have the pleasure of my scintillating company.'

'Yes, aren't I lucky.' He forced all those images of groups of men and women, brushing the ground near his Aunty's house with leaves to cleanse the spirits, weeping rivers of tears, heaving with sorrow and pain, back into that box in his mind. Time to think about something else.

'Your brothers are both pranksters, huh?' Koen asked, forcing his voice to lightness. He'd felt an immediate kinship with her siblings when she spoke about them.

'Yup. And they nearly always take it out on me.' Koen's heart lifted as he listened to her talk about her brothers. She buoyed his spirits, and he felt slightly less weighed down by the pressures of life. By the pressure of his dead cousin.

A cool breeze ruffled over the sand, bringing the musty smell of the lake to his nostrils. He pulled his jacket tighter around his shoulders. It had a sheepskin liner and was good on nights like tonight at keeping out the cold. Rose curled into a tight ball and shuffled around on the dry dirt. He noticed her jacket was a Drizabone, a good warm one. But if she wasn't used to sleeping rough like he was…

'It's getting cold,' he said after she finished talking about her brothers.

'Yes. Colder than I thought. Must be because we're so near the lake. Probably going to be a long night.' Her voice was muffled by her jacket, which she'd pulled over her nose.

Could he hear her teeth chattering? Surely not. It was cold, yes, the temperature always plummeted in the desert at night. But Koen didn't feel the cold like other people. As if he had a little internal fire burning that kept him warm.

It was his decision to come out here and sleep the night. But she'd gone along with it; hadn't demanded they find a hotel to stay in for the night like he'd half expected her to. Irritation warred with concern in his chest. Her comfort wasn't his responsibility.

Bugger it. 'Come over here, we can share my jacket and stay warmer.'

She stilled for a second, not replying.

'I won't bite, you know.' Did she think he was going to hurt her? He wouldn't do that. Women could be annoying, and sometimes downright infuriating, but he'd never, ever get physical with them. It wasn't right. And he wouldn't try anything on with her. Not tonight. He wasn't in the mood, with Mack's face still lingering in his conscience. Besides, he'd never force himself on any woman. His mum had taught him to respect women.

'Oh, I know,' she replied in a voice that was just a little squeaky. 'I was just—'

'If you want to freeze, go right ahead. It's no skin off my nose.' Damn right it wasn't.

He should never have said anything in the first place, and he was just about to turn over, when she replied, 'Sure, I'll share your jacket, if that's okay.'

He waited as she crawled the few feet that separated them and lay her Drizabone on the ground for them both to use as a blanket. Then she curled up with her back toward him, not quite touching him. Her whole body was ramrod straight, stiff as a board, and he stifled a gruff laugh.

'It's just body-heat we're sharing, girl. Nothing to get your panties in a knot about.'

'I wasn't—'

'Whatever.' Koen fluffed his sheepskin jacket up, so it covered her rigid shoulder, draped his arm over her midriff, and then pulled himself the last couple of inches, so their bodies met.

A fever flashed through him. As if someone had poured hot liquid into his veins. Like the previous two times they'd accidentally touched, only this time it was one-hundred times worse. Or better. Depending on your perspective. Every one of her curves fit into his body seamlessly.

She felt it, too. It was obvious in the way she sucked in a sharp breath.

Great, how was he going to get any sleep now? This was a bad idea. What should he do? He couldn't very well push her away, it'd been his idea they share his jacket. He willed his body to relax. She was indeed cold. Small shivers racked her shoulders. He grunted and took hold of one of her hands, tucking it in against her waist. It was cold against his warm palm. He was hot, burning up, and it was her fault. As if her presence stoked that small internal fire into a raging inferno in his belly. He eased his hips away from her. It wouldn't do for her to feel exactly what kind of effect she was having on him.

'Why didn't you tell me you were this cold?' he asked defensively.

She shrugged her shoulders against his chest in response. 'I didn't want to worry you. And I can take care of myself.'

Hmm, Koen wasn't sure how much of that statement he believed. He'd known her less than a day, and she did come across as a determined, strong-willed kind of woman. But there'd also been a few times when she'd almost looked bewildered, as if she wasn't used to dealing with certain situations. Like when the guy at the takeaway joint told her how much the burger cost, she'd glanced around as if someone else was meant to pay for it, before quickly whipping out her wallet. And a few times he'd caught her looking at him with speculation in her eyes, as if trying to figure him out. Her speculation was probably warranted. With his dirty, worn jeans, three-day growth, and grease from the bike beneath his fingernails, he was no oil painting. But she'd got on his bike, anyway. Her naivety amused him. But it also made him feel strangely protective. Which was bullshit. All he needed now was to get her to Darwin, then go and find Jon and the rest of his mob.

He could leave her then, be free of her. Never look back, not even once. She was obviously way out of his league. She said she was from Brisbane, but he didn't believe her. Clearly, she came from the land. You couldn't fake that kind of ease being on a bike or wearing those clothes. Some kind of rich bitch then, from one of those large cattle baron families with all that money nearly exploding her wallet. There would be plenty more where that came from. Probably on some stupid quest out here to find herself, using daddy's money. Yeah, that was it. He didn't need to feel sorry for her.

His body still burned from within, but he resolutely ignored the fire and closed his eyes. He would beat this, get a good night's sleep, and move on in the morning.

CHAPTER FIVE

Rose shook her head and reveled in the feel of the warm wind rushing through her hair. If this is what freedom felt like, then it was magical. Wondrous. Sublime. Why hadn't she done this earlier?

It was late afternoon, and they'd sat on this damn bike for most of the day. Her butt was completely numb and her legs cramped and stiff. But it was worth it, because they were nearly on the outskirts of Darwin. Low looping hills rolled by on either side as the bike sped along the asphalt highway. She wanted to stretch both arms out wide and pretend she was soaring and swooping, just like a bird on the breeze. But she daren't let go of the back of the bike, in case they hit a pothole. And Koen would probably think she was plain crazy if she did an imitation of the girl in the Titanic movie. So, she kept her arms at her side and let her soul roam free instead.

A year. That's all she needed. A year to explore this beautiful country. Perhaps even other countries as well. Prove she could live an independent life out in the real world.

Her mum was wrong. There was no one out there harboring ill intent for her.

Rose had heard the story of her grandfather and his evil doings many, many times. Had even believed them for a while in her adolescence.

Alexander Pallan. Corey Pallan. They were names that'd once tied her stomach in knots, brought a prickling sensation to the back of her neck.

But not anymore.

She didn't doubt her mother and grandmother had indeed done the things they said. Or that Alexander had murderous designs on both of them. But that was all long in the past now. Before she was born. Alexander was dead. His body had washed up out of the ocean two months after he tumbled over the cliff. And it was ridiculous to think that his son, Corey, was lurking out there, waiting to pounce on her and take his revenge. Sure, he'd sent nasty letters to her grandmother, and he'd sounded insane and menacing back then, but they'd stopped years ago. He posed no threat anymore. There were crazy people everywhere, you found them in every society, every corner of the world. And Rose would have to learn to look out for those kinds of people, just like everyone else. But there was no one hunting for her specifically. Of that she was one-hundred percent sure.

There were infinitely more good people than bad in this world. Just take Koen, for instance. He didn't need to stop and pick her up off that isolated road yesterday. But he was a decent, trustworthy guy, who couldn't leave a stranded woman out in the desert.

If only she could be as trustworthy. If only she didn't have to lie to him about her family and where she came from. She wasn't used to lying, and every time she uttered untruthful words, the weight in the pit of her stomach got heavier. Guilt. And it'd definitely gotten bigger last night, when Koen had talked about his family and his cousin's death. He'd opened up to her about his feelings, but she couldn't do the same.

The bit she'd told him about her brothers had all been true. They didn't need to be part of the lie. It was just that they weren't all the way over in Brisbane, Queensland, but only a few hundred kilometers back down the road they'd just travelled.

Hopefully, they were looking after her horses while she was away. Chantilly, her favorite quarter-horse mare, was the color of clotted cream; a Palomino and the best barrel racer in this part of the country. Then there was Dancer, her Australian stock horse gelding, who was the most gorgeous bronzed chestnut. Tallow liked to ride Dancer because he was gentle and responsive, almost knew instinctively where the rider wanted him to be. Tallow and Dancer had similar personalities in many ways. But Rodney liked to ride Chantilly, because she was bold and fiery and turned on a dime.

They could use any of the horses on the station, of course, which they did for the day-to-day work on the farm. But hopefully they'd find the time to make sure her horses got worked as well.

For a second, Rose worried at her bottom lip with her teeth, thoughts of how much her horses would miss her tumbling through her head. She hadn't given that as much thought as perhaps she should've, but there was no way she could take the horses with her and they'd be fine on the station. Her parents would make sure they were cared for in her absence.

Drat, she was thinking about her family again. She tipped her chin up and drew in a deep breath of the warm rushing air, and then huffed it back out again, letting it take all those guilty thoughts with it. She needed to stay strong and focused on what she wanted if she was to reach her goal.

The vast fields of red dirt and open woodland on either side of them gave way to the occasional softer shrub, and up ahead she could see a range of green trees materializing on the horizon. Even though she couldn't see it, the magical Kakadu, with all its waterfalls and pristine wilderness, was nearby as well. She couldn't wait to go and visit it.

Soon houses replaced the trees flashing past them. Some were tall houses on stilts, others squat bungalows hidden by jungle ferns, and some were surprisingly modern with big square windows and oddly angled rooflines. This city had become a bustling metropolis now, recovered from the deadly cyclone that nearly tore it apart over forty years ago.

Koen slowed the bike to the city speed limit and shouted back over his shoulder, 'I know a cheap hotel in the city, near the Esplanade. I'm going to head there for the night. Is that okay?'

'Sure,' she shouted back. As long as they stopped soon so she could get off this damn bike, she didn't really care where he took her.

As they neared the center, the city streets were wide and even, with green parks scattered amongst office buildings and tall jacaranda trees lining the edges. Rose swiveled her head from side to side, as if watching a tennis match, trying to take in everything about this city at once. Before she knew it, Koen was pulling up outside a two-story building that'd seen better days.

'Welcome to the Blue Lagoon hotel,' he said with a mocking flourish of his wrist.

Her legs were so stiff now she could hardly unclasp them from the bike and she stood on the sidewalk and stamped her feet in her boots until the feeling came back.

'I'm not sure what kind of hotel you're looking for, but this is the cheapest in town, and I need somewhere to crash for the night. There are nicer hotels further up the main street if you want.' He raised a questioning eyebrow at her.

'I'm fine with this one.' The straps of her backpack were digging into her shoulders, and she dropped it on the ground and rubbed her neck with a groan. 'God, it's so good to get off that bloody motorbike.'

'Amen to that one, girl.' He threw her one of his best grins. At the very least, they'd always have this shared bond of spending two days together on a motorbike riding through the desert at The Top End of Australia. It was quite a feat.

'I thought you were going to stay at your cousin's place.'

'Yeah, I am. Just don't wanna rock up unannounced, that's all. It's better if I go and see him in the morning. Anyway, I'm tired and feel like shit, and need a shower.'

Rose followed him through a glass-fronted door into a dingy reception office, filled with a peeling wood paneled desk, faded beige carpet and a woman wearing a bright pink kaftan.

'How much for a room?' he asked, and the lady fluffed her faded blonde hair and sat up a little straighter.

'That'll be seventy a night, handsome.'

'Bloody hell, that's gone up since I was here last.'

'It's the economy, baby. You know, the mining-boom bubble has burst and all that,' replied the woman, and Rose caught a glimpse of stained teeth when she grinned at Koen.

Koen seemed to hesitate for a second. 'Give us one room then, will ya?'

'What?' Rose was incredulous. But the woman didn't even glance Rose's way, just kept her gaze firmly fixed on Koen. Poor woman, she probably didn't get too many good-looking men in here. Rose could almost sympathize with her. Almost.

'I'll sleep on the floor,' Koen said, and for a second she didn't grasp his meaning. 'It'll be cheaper if we share a room.'

'Oh…Ah…' She hadn't been ready for that. But if they could share a jacket out under the stars, then why couldn't they share a room? And thinking about staying at Lake Argyle last night, he probably couldn't afford a room on his own. 'Okay, as long as you promise to stay on the floor.'

'Great.' Koen pulled out his wallet and dropped forty dollars on the bench, then looked at Rose expectantly. Oh, that's right. She reached into her backpack for her own wallet. She was so unused to paying for anything, her parents had always done that for her. Just one more thing to get used to.

Pink Kaftan lady stashed the money in an old-fashioned till and handed Koen a key, letting her fingers run over his palm as she did so. Rose might've been wrong, but she thought she caught Koen give a slight shudder at her touch and she had to hide a giggle under a cough.

'Room number eight, handsome,' the receptionist drawled, her eyes never leaving his face. 'Down the hall and to the left. There's a carpark out back if you've got a car.'

'Yeah, right. Thanks,' replied Koen, stomping off down the corridor without a backward glance.

Rose followed at a slower pace, taking in the peeling paint on the walls and flickering light bulb up ahead. The old saying was definitely true in this place. You got what you paid for. Still, it was a roof over her head tonight, and that's all that mattered. At least Koen was the one sleeping on the floor. It was possibly just as dirty as the desert floor they'd slept on last night. Probably with as many creepy crawlies as well.

* * *

Smoke hung thick in the air and music from the live band thrummed through his veins like a buzz saw. Koen chugged back the last of his pint of beer and contemplated ordering another one from the bar. The second beer of the night was starting to have an effect, and a mellow peace descended through his body.

'What's taking them so long, I'm starving.' Rose had to talk loudly to be heard over the band.

Even though they'd found a table right at the back, away from the little stage and the bar, it was still loud. The pub was only half a block down the street from the hotel. It was open-mic-night in the bar, and the latest band seemed to fancy themselves as some kind of heavy metal rock gods. Which they definitely weren't. Rose pushed a strand of hair behind her ear and took a swig of her own beer. It was the first time he'd seen her with her hair out of its ponytail. Her shoulder-length dark blonde hair was straight and sun-bleached at the tips. They'd both taken turns to have a shower, and he'd even had a shave and was feeling like a million bucks again.

Her light blue eyes regarded him from over the rim of her glass. They were serious, perceptive, and he felt like she might be able to see right through him. They were so pale. Almost the exact opposite of his dark brown eyes. Her jaw was heart-shaped, and she had that kind of English rose complexion you heard about in books. Her skin tone gave the wrong impression, though. It made her look almost breakable, frail. And he knew she was anything but. Her coloring was the complete opposite to his own. They were completely different in every way possible.

'Pub's pretty full tonight. They're probably working their asses off in the kitchen.' He took his tan-colored hat off his head and placed it neatly on the table. His mum always told him not to wear his hat at the dinner table. Once they'd got into the hotel room, he removed the black baseball cap and put on his trusty old Akubra, which he'd kept hidden in his bag. He loved this hat. It hardly ever left his head, except when he was riding a bike. Couldn't take the chance of it blowing off and being lost in the desert.

'Yeah, well, it's still been over half an hour since we ordered,' she huffed, and picked up the beer mat off the table and began to pick at it. His stomach rumbled, and he sympathized with her. It'd been a long time since their hasty breakfast this morning. They hadn't bothered stopping long enough for lunch, just filled up with gas, grabbed a bottle of Coke each and kept on motoring, both of them eager to get to the city before dark.

A large plate landed on the table in front of him, and another smacked down in front of Rose. The waiter disappeared as quickly as he'd appeared, looking harassed and sweaty, off to serve another table.

Koen cut into his large steak, mouth watering at the smell drifting up from his plate. He'd almost spent the last of his cash, but he couldn't resist the treat of a juicy steak. The meat was cooked to perfection, nice and pink on the inside, charcoaled on the outside. A dribble ran down his chin and he wiped it off with the back of his hand. Rose didn't bother with pleasantries either, lifting her veggie burger to her mouth and taking a large bite.

'This is actually pretty good,' she mumbled around a mouthful. 'It's got real chickpeas in the pattie. Not like the one in the Smokey Cr—' She coughed loudly as if choking on her food and grabbed her beer to take a large gulp of liquid.

'You okay?'

She nodded and flapped her hand in his direction while thumping her chest.

'Sorry, what were you going to say? Some other pub somewhere?'

'Never mind,' she croaked, and waved his question away. 'Doesn't matter. Wow, the band was pretty…interesting.'

They'd finally stopped making their distorted wailing sounds and were packing up, ready for the next victim of the night. There was scattered applause as they finished up. A young woman and two guys were next to set up on the stage, all dressed in brightly colored hippie clothes.

'Yeah, open-mic-night always brings in some of the more interesting people.'

'Can anyone get up there and sing?' Her eyes went wide as she checked out the trio setting up.

'Of course.' He glanced at her with confusion. 'That's what

an open-mic-night is all about. Wannabes strutting their stuff, hoping they sound better than they really do, so someone will *discover* them and make them millionaires.'

She cast him a disgusted look. 'Surely it's more about them having a voice, getting used to being up on stage. That kind of thing.' She was studying the new band thoughtfully. 'My mum thinks I'm a good singer.'

'Really?' He was shocked. She didn't look the musical type. But then again, he hardly knew her, so who was he to make a judgement. 'Maybe you should get up and sing. You just have to ask the owner, he'll put you on the list if there's an opening. Hell, they might even pay you to get up there. If you're any good.' He was intrigued now. What would she look like up on that stage? Was she any good?

'Oh no, I couldn't. I've never sung in front of anyone else but my parents and the other station—' She stopped abruptly. 'Anyway, I don't have my guitar. And I'd never be able to get up there and do that.' Tilting her shoulders in a shrug, she took another large bite of her burger.

'Fair enough.' It was no skin off his nose whether she got up and sang or not. 'What are your plans, now you're in Darwin?' he asked through a mouthful of steak.

'I'm not really sure. I want to go and see Kakadu, I've heard so much about it. But I probably won't stay in town for too long. I want to keep moving, see the rest of this wide brown land. You know, do the tourist thing.' As she said this, she cast a swift gaze around the pub. If he hadn't known better, he might've thought it was a probing gaze, as if checking for something. Or someone. Was she running away from someone? Like him?

'Ah yes, the tourist thing.' Koen raised an eyebrow. Was she really going to persist with that story? Again, it was nothing to him, whether she did or not. He could almost admit he'd enjoyed her company for the past two days, but he had more important things to think about than whether she was telling the truth or not. He'd be leaving her to her own devices in the morning, anyway. Probably never see the girl again.

The band struck a chord, and then the girl began to sing. She had a low sexy voice, reminded him of the singer Adele. Sounded like they were a cover band, as she was singing a song he recognized, called Me and Bobby McGee. His feet started tapping away under the table.

'I'm going to get another beer. You want anything?' he asked as he pushed his plate away and stood up.

She shook her head in reply, mouth too full of food to answer. A few minutes later, he was back. Rose had finished her food and was smiling at the band, her fingers drumming on the table to the tune. Now the band was singing What I Like About You, and doing a good job of it. The rhythm was getting right into his bones, and he suddenly felt like dancing. He loved to dance. Especially when there was a pretty girl at his side. The dance floor in front of the stage was small, but there were only a few couples up at the moment, most people still finishing their meals.

He downed most of his beer, slapped his hat back on his head at a jaunty angle, and held his hand out to Rose. Then gave her one of his roguish smiles, calculated to win her over. 'Come and dance with me.'

'What? Oh no, I couldn't.' She shook her head, and her hair swirled enticingly around her cheekbones.

'Why not? No one here knows you. No one's gonna care. Come on, girl, live a little.' His grin got wider as he saw her hesitate, her gaze flicking toward the dance floor, then back to him, and he kept his hand extended.

'Okay, why not. I came out here to try new stuff.' Her warm palm landed in his, and he pulled her up out of her seat. That tingle, the same one that happened whenever they touched, was still there. The buzz made him grasp her hand harder, put a little hitch in his step. Hell, he was going to enjoy this.

At first, she was reserved and awkward on the dance floor, tapping her feet together while she watched him shyly from beneath lowered lashes. But he knew he was a good dancer and he let his body flow with the music, twisting his hips and shaking out his boots in a toe-tapping rhythm as if he had no shame. Which he didn't. Taking her hand up in his, he pulled her expertly around in a twirl, and she laughed out loud. The sound did something to his insides. He liked it. So, he twirled her again, and she laughed again.

Another song started up. This time it was actually an Adele song, Set Fire to the Rain. It was a slower song, but one with a wicked beat.

'Wow, this band is really good,' Rose said, throwing an appreciative glance over her shoulder.

Still holding onto her hand, he acted on impulse, pulling her in closer and putting her hand on his shoulder, so they could slow-dance together. With his other hand, he grabbed her hip, feeling the soft round of her curves beneath the fabric of her jeans. Their shoulders bumped gently against each other.

Perhaps this hadn't been the best idea, now he thought about it. She was facing him, and he could smell the clean washed scent of the new western shirt she'd put on before they came out. And her perfume. It was sweet, like roses. Like her.

This was like it had been last night, when they'd spooned to keep warm. Only this was ten times worse, because they were facing each other. He could see the emotions flickering across her face. Eyes wide, like a startled rabbit, she stared up at him. There was a darker ring of blue around the light sky-color of her iris. Why had he never noticed that before?

She was small. He had to look down when he spoke to her. There was that flash of fire burning through him again, just like last night. What was it about her that set him off? Sure, he liked women. Liked to sleep with women, liked their pliable bodies and soft kisses. But he knew how to control himself around them, he never let his body's reactions run away with him. Until now. Did she feel it, too?

'I ah…' Her gaze was locked onto his, but then she looked down and pulled back.

'Yeah, let's wait for a better song, this slow-dancing is for the oldies.' His voice was brash and loud as he let go of her, plastering a smile on his face.

As they left the dance floor, the door to the pub swung open and raucous voices drifted in on the breeze. A group of men entered, pushing and shoving each other good-naturedly. They were all wearing plaid shirts and seemed as if they'd been hitting the drinks pretty hard already.

Koen groaned. This bunch was trouble, he could feel it.

But Rose was already winding her way through the tables, back to their own, so he followed her. The group of men moved right by them on their way to the bar. One of them whistled at Rose. Koen kept his head lowered, hat pulled down. But it didn't help. Another of the men shoved Koen's shoulder as they passed, knocking him off balance.

'Hey, arsehole, watch where you're going,' the man shouted.

'Sorry,' Koen mumbled, but kept going. It would do no good to interact with these dickheads. It would only give them more ammunition. He kept his fists balled tight, close to his side.

'Yeah, so you bloody well should be,' the man countered, as a few of the other men in the group laughed loudly at his back.

'Bastards,' Koen muttered just before he sat down at the

table with Rose. It was always the way. He seemed to attract trouble, no matter where he went.

'What did you say?' Rose had missed the altercation and was now looking at him, confused.

'Doesn't matter,' he growled and grabbed his beer glass, downing the remainder in one long slug. The waiter came past, and Koen waved him down and ordered another drink. If he couldn't dance with Rose, then he may as well just get drunk.

CHAPTER SIX

Rose tried to ignore the bunch of men lined up at the bar, but it was almost impossible. They were so loud, they had all the other patrons turning their heads to stare. One of them whistled at her when they first came in, a low appreciative sound that made the hairs on the back of her neck stand up. But not in a good way. She had a bad feeling about that bunch. Every now and then one of them would glance in her direction, muttering quietly to their mates.

Koen was glowering at them too, although he was trying to hide it behind the big schooner of beer he was drinking. Black eyes staring out from beneath that Akubra he'd donned when they got to the hotel. It suited him, gave him a more raffish air, if that were possible. But something had happened as they were walking back from the dance floor. She hadn't seen anything. It was just a vibe she was getting. And it made Koen simmer like a pile of hot coals about to erupt into a fiery inferno.

Or perhaps she was partly to blame for Koen's change in mood. Perhaps she shouldn't have jumped back so quickly when he took her in his arms for that slow dance. But she couldn't help it. It was almost as if whenever he touched her, a white-hot electricity buzzed between them. It startled her, and she still didn't know what to make of it. After all, she hadn't escaped from Shiralee just to fall in love with the first guy she met. She was out here to experience life, to find her independence. To be free. The last thing she wanted was any kind of romance. No ties, no commitments.

Even if he did have eyes so dark and deep, they reminded her of her mother's homemade chocolate fudge cake. And teeth so white and keen against his dusky skin, it made her want to smile in return every time he flashed them.

She glanced over at him, but he kept his eyes on the band, taking another large slug of beer. If he didn't slow down, he'd end up as drunk as the other men at the bar. She wasn't sure she wanted a drunk Koen sharing her hotel room. He'd been a complete gentleman last night when they'd slept next to Lake Argyle. Keeping her warm, wrapping his arm around her. But would he give her the same consideration if his judgement was impaired? She hoped she was a good judge of character, and while Koen was a natural larrikin, a joker, a clown, he also seemed to have a good head on his shoulders, was a decent bloke underneath all that bravado. But then again, she'd only known him for two days, and because she couldn't use her gift to read him, how the hell could she really know what he was like?

Staring broodily at the band on the stage, she remembered Koen's comment that anybody could sing at open-mic-night. The idea intrigued her. Her family all told her she had a wonderful voice. What would it feel like to get up there and sing in front of all these people? Butterflies tumbled inside her stomach at the mere thought of it. No, she couldn't do it. But still…

Koen's eyes narrowed suddenly and went brittle, like dark glass. Rose cast a glance in the direction he was looking. Oh shit, one of the loud drunken men had broken away from his friends and was coming toward them. She tensed, clasping her fingers tight around the arm of the chair. She didn't need her gift to figure out that this guy was trouble. Waves of arrogance, bigotry, and alcohol-fueled brutality oozed off him. If she touched him, she would probably be knocked backward by the violence of his raging emotions. Which she wouldn't be doing. There was no way she was going to touch this man. Her hand went automatically up to the necklace, the feel of the hard stone calming her slightly.

'Hey, beautiful,' the man slurred as he arrived in front of their table, swaying slightly. He had eyes only for her, totally ignoring Koen. The guy looked like he might've just stepped off a mine-site, he was wearing a plaid shirt, dusty jeans and workbooks. His mates were similarly attired, one even had on a Hi Vis shirt. She didn't look at Koen, but could sense him go rigid in his chair. 'What's a nice-looking chick like you doing with this lowlife?'

Rose was too shocked to speak. How dare he think he could come over and talk to her like that? Or treat Koen like that?

Mistaking her silence for consent, he continued, 'Why don't you come and join us instead?' He waved an arm in the direction of the bar, where the rest of his mates were leering at her. 'We'll show you a good time.'

Somehow, she managed to curve her lips into a smile. 'Oh, thanks. But no thanks. I'm fine right here.' Something told her not to antagonize this Neanderthal. Especially for Koen's sake. It was the same kind of discrimination she'd seen back in the gas station, where the shop assistant had cast suspicious glances in Koen's direction. Rose was hoping once they arrived in the big city of Darwin, this kind of racism would go away. They were a civilized country, after all. Surely this behavior didn't still exist anymore?

'Come on, luv, you don't need to be hanging out with no black bastard,' one of the guy's mates called out from the bar.

Rose gasped at the insult.

Koen shot to his feet, grabbing the table edge to steady himself. 'What did you just say?' Venom and anger dripped from his voice as he stared at the other man standing at the bar. The rest of the pub went eerily quiet as everyone turned to watch the spectacle. Rose noticed no one else seemed to be jumping to their defense. The band kept playing, but the girl stopped singing, watching with interested eyes.

'I called you a black bastard. What ya gonna do about it?' The guy started to make his way over to their table, leaving the rest of his mates sniggering to themselves. This was going from bad to worse, and Rose wasn't sure what to do to defuse the situation. She got to her feet as well. The drunk man still stood at their table, swaying gently, while his mate made his way quickly between the tables. Soon there would be two mean, drunk men hemming them into the corner.

'You take that back, arsehole,' Koen ground out from between clenched teeth, lifting his fists in front of him.

'Glen, get over here.' Rose heard a voice raised above the low rumble of the other patrons. Then she saw the barman come from behind the bar, walking quickly toward them. He was tall and very wide. The large man, called Glen, peeled himself away from the doorway he'd been leaning against and stalked over. The drunk man who'd first approached her table didn't seem to notice what was going on, he only had eyes for Koen. And Koen stared back at him, hatred burning deep in his eyes.

He took a menacing step toward Koen. 'No, he's not taking it back. Because that's what you are. Your kind don't belong in this bar.'

The man who'd called out the insult in the first place was almost upon them. But big Glen intercepted him just in time, stepping between him and their table, blocking his way.

'Well, that's where you're wrong, arsehole. There's a law that says I have just as much right to be here as you do,' Koen replied icily.

Rose was frozen to the spot, she didn't know what to do. This couldn't be happening, could it? Did racist pigs like this guy still really exist? The extreme emotions spilling from all the testosterone-fueled men was playing havoc with her senses, sending her gift into overdrive, threatening to overwhelm her and she had to fight the urge to cover her ears and hunker down under the table until it all went away.

The man still standing beside them lunged forward and snatched up a handful of Koen's shirt-front, shoving his nose right into Koen's face, snarling like a rabid dog. But the barman arrived and rammed himself bodily between them, pushing the drunk guy away.

'Quit it, right now,' the barman growled in a low, dangerous voice. 'I don't tolerate racism in my bar. And neither do I tolerate violence. If you want to fight, go and take it somewhere else. You're not wreaking havoc in my pub tonight.' He was so tall, he even towered over the other man as he scowled down at him. He was facing the drunkard, keeping his back to Koen. Thank God he'd worked out who the true aggressor was here. Koen's face was grim, suffused with red as he glowered at the barman's back. Still itching to finish the fight, by the look of him. Rose silently willed him to stay quiet and keep his cool.

'You guys can all leave. I won't be serving you any more alcohol tonight.' The barman glared over the top of the assailant's head at the three remaining men still standing at the bar. The men were all muttering and looked like they were about to do the exact opposite.

'Sammy, can you please escort the rest of these guys out?'

Another bouncer, bigger than Glen, if that was possible, stalked out of the door to what Rose assumed was a back office and was behind the guys at the bar before they could take one step toward her.

'Sure thing, boss.' Sammy gave a big, friendly grin and placed one enormous hand on the shoulder of the guy nearest him. 'This way, if you please,' he said sociably, as if these men were his best mates. But the steely look in his eyes belied the friendly tone in his voice.

'You, too,' Glen said to the inebriated man. 'Out you go.'

'I can't believe you'd serve scum like this over us,' he snarled.

The barman just smiled, but didn't budge an inch. Even he could see it was no use arguing with this bunch of imbeciles. He just pointed a finger toward the door and then followed the man out to join his mates all trooping through the back door.

'We'll never drink here again, you can guarantee that,' shouted one of the group. 'This bar is a heap of shit.'

'Good riddance,' Rose heard the barman mutter under his breath.

She let out a whoosh of air. Jesus, that was intense. Her first day in the big smoke and already she was in the middle of a bar-fight. It was all too much to take in. Her mum had been wrong on quite a few counts. But right on many others. There were big, scary men out there, intent on causing havoc, but at least they weren't hunting her specifically. Corey was a figment of her mother's very overactive imagination.

'You okay?' she asked Koen.

He stood there, stiff as a statue, a look that might've been revulsion mixed with defeat on his face.

'Those guys are useless imbeciles. Don't worry about them.' She really wasn't sure what to say to make the situation all right again. Her hand reached out to touch his shoulder, but he shrugged her off with a violent heave, his face twisting with anger.

'Don't,' was all he said.

The barman made his way back over to their table. 'I have

to apologize. I shouldn't have let them in here in the first place. They were all way too drunk when they arrived. I should've followed my instincts and got Glen to turn them away at the door.'

'Oh, that's okay. Never mind. No harm done,' Rose said with a smile.

'Yeah, no harm done.' Koen echoed her words, but his tone dripped with sarcasm.

'Look, mate, I dislike those sorts of guys and their bigoted notions as much as you do. But I—'

'Yeah, yeah, I know,' Koen snapped. He picked up his beer and sculled the rest in one huge swallow. 'I need to get out of here for a while. Go for a walk,' he said to Rose. 'I'll see you later.' He slammed his glass back on the table and stomped out.

'Koen, wait.' Rose didn't know whether to follow him or leave him be. She might make it worse if she went after him. Perhaps he just needed time to clear his head. He ignored her plea, and the door banged shut behind him.

'Again, I'm really sorry, luv.' The barman wiped his forehead with an old dishcloth slung over his shoulder. 'Can I offer you a free drink? To make it up to you?'

What the hell, she may as well stay for one more drink. She didn't know her way around Darwin, and she was just as likely to get lost if she went after Koen now. She'd see him back in the hotel room soon.

'That would be nice, thank you.'

'What'll you have? I'll bring it over to you.'

'A Bundy and Coke, please.' The girl on the stage had taken up singing again and the rest of the patrons went back to eating their meals and chatting between themselves. Rose sat down and was surprised to see her hands were shaking as she laid them on the table. Delayed reaction to the adrenaline. Wow, nothing exciting like this ever happened on the station.

She was getting more than she bargained for when she decided to leave Shiralee. A small smile played over her lips. But wasn't this exactly what she wanted, deep down? To experience life first-hand. Not to be locked up like a prisoner on the farm. Well, okay, not a prisoner. But with her parents always hovering nearby, never letting her off the station without someone accompanying her, never letting her go further than the local town, it was akin to being a prisoner.

She sighed. Her parents had her best interests at heart. They did love her, of that she had no doubt. But they were mistaken. There was no one out here hunting her and her family down. There was nothing to be scared of. They needed to stop being so overprotective and just let her lead her life.

Loud clapping broke out as the band finished their last set.

The barman came and placed her drink on the table. 'Enjoy,' he said with a smile.

On impulse she asked, 'How often do you have open-mic-night?'

'Oh, are you a singer?' He glanced over at the trio, now packing up their instruments.

'Well, ah…yes and no,' she hedged, but he wasn't really listening.

'Twice a week, on Mondays and Wednesdays. It's really popular, I always have musicians lining up to fill the spots. And the patrons love it, some of them say they even come especially on those nights.' He glanced down at her. 'I always audition my singers first. I don't want to scare my patrons away. So, if you're interested, come and see me and we'll have a chat.'

'Thanks.' But before she could say anymore, he was rushing back to the bar to serve three new customers who'd just come in.

Rose sipped her beer thoughtfully. There was no way she was going to get up on that stage. For one, she wanted her presence in Darwin to be as low key as possible. She didn't want to attract undue attention that might lead her parents to her. Because they would be looking for her, without a doubt.

But her fingers itched as she watched the next guy warming up, strumming his guitar. How good would it feel to play? She'd left her own guitar back at home, and she missed the feel of it under her fingertips. The way it seemed to come alive when she played, the wood warm and heavy on her thigh.

* * *

Koen wanted to punch something. Someone. He was so angry he thought he'd burst into flames from the sheer depth of emotion. Long strides took him down the footpath, passing stores closed for the day and other bars with music streaming out onto the street. He took hardly any of it in, so lost in his own thoughts that all he wanted to do was find somewhere quiet where he could vent his frustration. He wanted to shove his way through the group of people milling outside a restaurant, studying the menu, deciding if they wanted to eat there or not. Push them out of the way and rant at them, swear at them to keep out of his fucking way.

He crossed the street instead, barely reining in his feelings. Because if he did do what his instincts were screaming for him to do, snarl and swear and curse, then he would become no better than what the men in the bar had accused him of.

It was always the same. Where ever he went there were always people who looked down on him. Who called him names. Thought him less of a human being. Koen knew these men were ultimately responsible for Mack's death. How could they not be? It was this kind of daily subversion, a thousand little cuts, that made kids like Mack feel it wasn't worth it anymore. Fucking bastards, the lot of them.

And Rose. What had Rose thought of it all? She'd stood there like a stunned mullet. Either unwilling or unable to say much of anything. This kind of intolerance might be new to her, so perhaps he could excuse her reaction a little. But it wasn't new to him. How dare that guy say Rose was better off with them than she was with him? With a bunch of white men? How dare they?

He pounded his fist into the nearest wall and felt a welcome stab of pain shoot through his knuckles. He stopped and looked at his hand. It was bleeding now; the knuckles scraped raw.

Bloody hell, he was an idiot.

He needed to get out of here. This place was just like all the rest. What did he think he was doing, sharing a room with a girl he'd picked up on the road? A girl who was spinning him a dubious story. A girl he had no chance in hell with.

Turning around, he headed back toward the hotel room. He'd go and find somewhere else to sleep tonight, then head to Jon's first thing in the morning. This girl didn't need him. Didn't want him around. She was better off without him, and he was better off without her.

In the hotel room, he threw his few meagre belongings back into his duffle bag while casting a seething glance around the room. Then his eyes settled on Rose's bag. He'd watched her out of the corner of his eye just before they went out for dinner. She'd put most of the money from her wallet into a side pocket of her bag, obviously worried she might lose it, or have it stolen. Only kept a hundred or so in her wallet. Which was the sensible thing to do, there was at least a couple of thousand dollars there.

A couple of thousand dollars, sitting right there in her bag.

There was no safe available in this cheap dump of a hotel room to lock it in.

He didn't believe her tourist story at all. She was obviously from a well-to-do-family. Probably on a spiritual journey, perhaps running away to find herself, or some such shit.

There must be plenty more where that came from.

He needed that money. More than she did.

Those guys at the bar had made it bloody obvious Koen wasn't welcome in this city. That he would never really be welcome anywhere. His mother's disapproving face flashed into his mind. He shook his head to get rid of the image.

Fuck it.

He strode over to the bag before he could think any more about it. Felt around until he located the wad of money and pulled it out.

Without another backward glance, Koen strode out of the room, toward the carpark and his motorbike.

CHATPER SEVEN

Rose knocked quietly on the hotel room door. There was no answer. Koen must be asleep. After waiting a few more seconds, she fumbled, trying to get the key into the lock. Whoa, perhaps she'd had a little more to drink than she intended. But that was alright. When was the last time she'd been really drunk? Never, because her parents were always watching. Not that she was really drunk now, just a bit tipsy.

The room was pitch black when she opened the door. Bugger, it was too dark to see if Koen was curled up on the floor somewhere, asleep. She opened the door a tad wider, allowing the light from the corridor to flush the room. There was no obvious lump on the floor that might be Koen's slumbering body. Her gaze flicked to the bed. He hadn't reneged on his promise and taken the bed instead, had he? Nope, the bed was still smooth and perfectly unrumpled.

Rose bit her lip and then turned on the light switch. The room was empty. Where had Koen got to? Was he still out, walking off his anger? She'd stayed at the bar for another hour or so, got caught up talking with the girl from the band, Jewel, who'd just come off stage. Had found her fascinating. She had such an interesting lifestyle, traveling around the different pubs in the area, making a living from her music. Jewel encouraged Rose to get up on stage and try it out for herself. At the time, and after her third drink, Rose even started to think it might be a good idea.

Rose hoped Koen had his key on him, because all she wanted to do right now was fall onto that comfy looking bed and sleep for the next ten hours.

Sitting on the edge of the bed, she pulled off her boots with a sigh and leaned down to extract her toiletries bag from her backpack. Koen's duffle had been sitting right next to hers on the floor. But it was gone. Her head sprang up as she searched the room for signs of his bag. Had he moved it? She got up and took a quick look in the bathroom. No bag or any other sign of him in there, either.

Had he left without telling her? Without saying goodbye? Why would he do that? A leaden weight suddenly settled in her stomach as a horrible premonition flashed across her skin.

She dove for her bag and unzipped the side pocket. The money was gone. Oh Jesus. Oh fuck! He'd taken her money. Her vision whirled violently, and she had to sit on the floor before she fell down.

How could she have been so stupid? She trusted him. And he'd betrayed her. She was a poor judge of character, after all. Perhaps her parents were right, she didn't belong out here in the real world. But wasn't it partly their fault for keeping her locked up and away from everyday society so that she didn't know how to form a solid opinion of someone? Normally, she let her gift do all the hard work. She would know without having to evaluate why, what kind of person stood in front of her; whether they meant her harm or not. But with Koen, her gift didn't work, and she'd let him slip beneath her radar. And now he was gone. Hightailed it out of her life, with her money. The bastard. She pulled the necklace out from beneath her shirt and held it in the palm of one hand. But tonight it wasn't offering any of that familiar comfort.

Laying her head in her hands, she let out a low moan.

What in hell was she going to do now? Funnily enough, even though she should be dissolving into a torrent of tears, a strange kind of calm descended over her. She needed to think this through logically.

Reaching around stiffly, she retrieved her wallet from her back pocket and flipped it open. There was one hundred-and-seventy-five dollars in there.

Enough for about two more nights in this hotel, if she decided to stay here. Then what would she do? Koen told her he was going to stay with his cousin Jon and his mob, but she had no idea of his last name or even where he lived, so there was no chance Rose was going to track Koen down. Not in the immediate future, anyway.

That money had been her ticket out of Shiralee. A ticket to her continued freedom, at least in the short term. She'd planned on getting further away from Shiralee than Darwin. It was too close, too easy for her parents to track her down. The money wouldn't last forever, she wasn't that stupid. But once she'd got somewhere safer, say on the east coast, a city like Townsville or even Brisbane, then she was going to get a job.

She had money in a bank account, her parents paid her for working on the station, they'd been adamant about that. But Rose had watched enough cop shows on TV to know as soon as she used her card to withdraw money or make a transaction, they'd be on to her. So she'd squirreled away cash whenever she got the chance, until she had a tidy sum of three thousand dollars hidden away beneath her bed. That should've been more than enough to keep her going for a while. If Koen hadn't stolen it, that was. But already her anger at him was draining away. There was no point in staying mad at him. She didn't know much about his family or his history, but he obviously thought he needed the money.

Rose levered herself slowly to her feet and got ready for

bed. She probably wouldn't sleep, but maybe by morning she might have come up with a plan. One thing was for certain, she wasn't about to give up. She wasn't going to crawl back home, not just yet, anyway.

* * *

Koen rolled over in the dirt, hoping to find a more comfortable position. But it was no use, sleep eluded him. Opening his eyes, he stared up through the dark into the leaves of the milkwood tree above him. Its large branches were just dark smudges against the bright stars in the sky. After he left the hotel, he'd headed straight for the outskirts of town. To a stretch of natural bushland he knew from his previous stay in Darwin. The hum of cicadas was loud in his head.

He shouldn't have ridden the motorbike in the state he was in. If the cops had picked him up, he'd be in jail for drink driving. But in the heat of the moment, with his anger fueling his stupidity, it was the only way out of there.

Jon's place was the next suburb over. But he didn't want to show up in the middle of the night, drunk. Jon would immediately wonder what he'd been up to. And so would Jon's wife, Sally. They had four kids, with another on the way. The last person Koen wanted to piss off tonight was Sally.

Would Jon even be home, though? Jon had a job as a laborer in a building company. Sometimes the company contracted out to the mines, and Jon would be on a fly-in-fly-out shift of two weeks at the mine and one week at home. But most of the time he was able to come home every evening to his family. The job allowed him to rent a large house on the outskirts of Darwin and keep himself and his family clothed and well-fed. Indigenous families were usually big, and his was no different, so plenty of people came and went. Brothers, sisters, cousins, uncles. Some only stayed for a night or two, or some, like Koen, stayed for months. As long as they paid board or contributed in some way, Jon wasn't too worried. If the house was ever too full, Jon would make it obvious people had outstayed their welcome. You never knew who you were going to meet when you stayed with Jon. Sometimes the house was nearly empty, with only the immediate family of six, and sometimes it overflowed with a dozen or more people hanging around. Jon never seemed fazed by any of it.

But Jon hadn't been happy last time Koen had stayed with him. Kicked him out of his house after he'd had yet another run-in with the law and lost his job, told him to come back when he wasn't behaving like such a dickhead. Jon had managed to get Koen a job in his building company, where he could use his carpentry skills. But he'd screwed it up and made Jon look bad as well. And regretted it ever since. He'd liked that job. Liked the self-respect it gave him, liked using his hands to create something meaningful. He was a dickhead back then, he hadn't realized what he had until it was too late. Now he needed to convince Jon he'd changed, was ready to be a man, take on the job and keep it this time.

Yep, he'd camp here for the night and wait till morning to go to Jon's. After all, he'd slept in much worse places. And better places. The image of the hotel room he'd just left came into his mind. Even sleeping on the floor, it would've been more pleasant than out here. At least there were no huge bugs or spiders crawling about in the undergrowth to worry about in a hotel room. Koen drew his feet in closer at the thought. The Top End of the Northern Territory sported an impressive array of large—sometimes deadly—insects and other not-very-nice animals. Cane toads and snakes, just to name a few.

But it wasn't just the idea of a safe, snug room keeping him awake.

It was guilt, plain and simple.

Sometimes he was an idiot. A complete fuck-up.

Sometimes he didn't even understand himself, what drove him to do the stupid things he did. Like steal his uncle's motorbike. And Rose's money.

Would she report him to the police? He wasn't sure, but if he'd read her right, for some reason, she seemed to want to keep a low profile. With any luck, she'd keep the theft to herself.

Why had he stolen it? On the whole, money didn't mean a lot to him. All he needed was enough to live on, no more. He'd never had any aspirations to be rich or famous, just wanted to live a happy, free life.

It'd been a spur-of-the-moment thing. Because he was so bloody angry and riled up and just anti-all-white-people. But now he'd calmed down, and sobered up, he knew without a doubt he'd reached a new low in his life.

The look his mum would give him if she ever found out what he'd done made his toes curl just thinking about it. His mum, Dinah, was a strong woman. The local community nurse in Balgo, she'd been tenacious enough to follow her dreams, go and do a nursing degree in Perth, so she could come home and give back to her community. Help her community thrive. His mum had taught him the value of respecting women. Many of the women he dealt with every day at the Balgo Warlayirti Art Centre also demanded respect. The women artists who bared their souls for their art, who showed the rest of the world, through their compassion and flair, just how talented the Aboriginal people were. Who kept the community strong and viable by selling their art and bringing recognition back to country.

Koen never knew his father, he was killed in a car accident when Koen was only nine months old. Sadly, it was an all-too-common occurrence in the desert, unroadworthy cars being driven on dirt roads in terrible conditions. And more-often-than-not, the occupants weren't wearing seatbelts. But

Koen didn't think he missed having a father's influence, Dinah more than made up for it. She guaranteed he had a proper education, said it was the most important thing in the world. Koen was smart, had completed year twelve at school, an achievement not many of his peers had done. Had become skilled at carpentry at the Kutjungka Centre. Learned a trade to see him through. But he didn't feel all that smart right now.

He'd let his mum down, let them all down. When he got to Jon's place and got himself a job, he was going to turn over a new leaf. He was determined to do something good in this world. Make something better of his life.

* * *

Bleary eyes stared back at Rose from the bathroom mirror. She looked like she hadn't slept a wink last night. Probably because she hadn't. The sound of water running behind her reminded her the shower was on, so she stopped her scrutiny and stepped under the hot water.

A few minutes later, feeling more refreshed and awake, Rose pulled on her jeans thoughtfully. No blinding lightbulb had flashed on in her head last night, no full-proof plan had presented itself to solve her dilemma. She was still stuck in a dingy hotel in the middle of Darwin, with no money and no prospects.

But she was forever the girl who saw the glass as half-full, the optimist, who looked on the bright side. Nothing could keep her down for long. And the price of the hotel room included a free continental breakfast, which was calling to her empty stomach. No good decisions were ever made on an empty stomach, so she headed down the corridor to the room the Pink Kaftan Lady on the front desk had loosely called the restaurant.

There were only two other patrons in the dining area, probably because it was still early, only just past seven am. The choice for breakfast reflected the price they'd paid for the room, certainly not gourmet by any means. Rose slipped two pieces of whole meal bread into the toaster and poured herself a glass of orange juice. Or should she say orange cordial, because this stuff really didn't resemble freshly squeezed orange juice.

Carefully balancing her plate of toast with butter and Vegemite and glass in one hand, she picked up the local newspaper from the sideboard and went to find a table. It was hot in here already. Which meant today was going to be a scorcher. The windows were open, allowing a tepid breeze to flow in. And while Rose was used to the heat of the outback, this humidity plus the heat up here in the tropics was another thing altogether. Rose could see an old air-conditioner up on the wall, but it wasn't turned on. She wondered how hot it would have to get before the hotel staff thought it was time to use it. The two other patrons didn't seem to be bothered by the heat, so perhaps it was just her. She'd have to get used to it. Perhaps swap her tired old jeans for a pair of shorts.

Rose bit into her toast and sighed as the food hit her tongue. Heaven. The trick was lots and lots of butter, with only a scraping of Vegemite. Only an Aussie could truly appreciate the taste. Then she flipped to the back pages of the newspaper to search the jobs column. She needed a job, fast. Any job would do.

Her finger traced the line of ads as she ate her toast with gusto, and suddenly she found herself humming. Even though she was stuck here, without any money, or seemingly any options, she was absurdly happy. Why? Because she was away from the station. She'd achieved her goal, escaped. And now here she was, having breakfast in some run-down hotel, looking for a job so she didn't have to sleep on the streets. But it was what she wanted, to experience life first-hand, and she was most definitely doing that.

If she had to, she would probably even resort to sleeping

on the street, just to stay here a little longer, although the thought terrified her.

A woman in a tired-looking light blue uniform wandered into the dining room and started to tidy the food table, refreshing the bread and milk and scraping a few stray crumbs off the plastic tablecloth. A waitress of sorts, Rose thought. Then the woman ambled over and started clearing dishes from the tables and Rose was struck with an idea.

'Good morning,' she said brightly.

'Morning,' the waitress mumbled back, a surprised look on her face. Perhaps not used to the customers taking much notice of her.

'It's going to be hot today, huh?' Rose thought she'd try for a bit of small talk first.

'What? Oh, yes, it is,' the woman replied.

Rose decided she wasn't much of a conversationalist and so she may as well dive right in and ask what she wanted to know. 'I was wondering if you know if this hotel has any jobs open at the moment? You know waitressing, or cleaning, that kind of thing?'

The woman looked even more startled at Rose's question and backed away, saying, 'I don't know, missus, you should go and talk to Wanda about that.'

'Oh, okay,' Rose said. 'Is Wanda the lady on the front desk?'

The waitress just nodded and then scuttled away with her armful of dirty dishes.

Rose sighed and went to help herself to a strong cup of coffee. She'd need it if she was going to tackle the Pink Kaftan Lady.

Half an hour later, she found herself standing at reception, facing Wanda. Who was now wearing a bright green kaftan.

'What do you want, luv?' The woman's bright, flirty air when she'd been dealing with Koen yesterday was nowhere in sight today. Instead, she glared at Rose coldly, her fake eyelashes and layers of foundation more obvious in the early morning light. Rose drew in a fortifying breath.

'Good morning,' she said boldly, giving the woman her most professional smile. 'I'm a guest here at the hotel. And I was wondering…'

The woman's face turned even more unfriendly as Rose trailed off, perhaps expecting Rose to deliver a complaint.

Rose straightened her spine and continued. 'I was wondering if you had any job openings here? I'm looking for work. I'm very proactive, resourceful and trustworthy.' She cringed inwardly, knowing she sounded like some kind of nerdy advertisement. And those traits she'd just mentioned were probably quite low on the priorities list for a job in this hotel. 'I'm also not afraid of hard work, and getting down and dirty,' she ended with another bold smile that she didn't feel.

'Hmm.' Wanda eyed her up and down speculatively. 'What happened to that cute guy you were with last night?'

'Ah, he had…other business to attend to.' Rose couldn't believe the woman was still stuck on Koen. But perhaps he might be a bargaining chip she could use. 'But he'll be back in a day or two.' Rose crossed her fingers behind her back. It was a silly thing she used to do whenever she lied to her parents.

'Will he now?' Wanda mused. 'And you need a job to tide you over till he gets back then?'

Rose was about to retort that she didn't need any man to look after her, she was an independent, undaunted woman, but bit her tongue just in time. If the woman was prepared to offer her a job on the off chance that Koen might wander back into the place, then who was she to argue.

'Something like that, yeah.'

There was more silence while Wanda continued to appraise

Rose. 'We might have something available. One of our cleaners just up and left. Left us high and dry, and poor Tilly has to do all the rooms by herself now. We could do with another hand to clean the toilets and make the beds. You up for that?'

Rose was surprised. She hadn't really expected anything, certainly not from this woman.

'Yes, yes, definitely, I can clean toilets.'

'It's only a few hours a day at the moment. But it would cover the cost of your accommodation.' Wanda narrowed her eyes at Rose, one of the long fake eyelashes curling up at the ends under her examination. The woman wasn't dumb, Rose had to give her that much. But she could also see Rose was in trouble and was at least offering her a solution. 'Tilly starts at ten, can you start today?'

'Yes, that would be great, thank you. See you then.' Rose raised a hand to wave farewell as she headed back to her room, but Wanda had already turned away and was looking down her nose at the computer on the desk, poking the keys with a long fake nail. Strange woman, but who was Rose to look a gift horse in the mouth? At least she had her accommodation sorted for the next little while. But she'd still need spending money, money to live on and to travel with.

The pub down the road opened at nine. Time to go down and have a chat with the barman before she had to be back here at ten for her first cleaning shift. Her insides trembled at the thought of what she was about to do. But what other choice did she have?

CHAPTER EIGHT

Jenna was desperate to do something. All this waiting and hoping was killing her. It was three days since Rose had left the note and fled Shiralee, but as far as Jenna could tell, they were no closer to finding her daughter.

At least Jenna had the station chores to keep her busy. That never changed. The amount of work needed to keep a large cattle station running was never-ending. Not a lot of work was happening right now, however, as Jenna stood in Chainsaw's stall, talking quietly to the horse. The gorgeous appaloosa had lived a long and happy life, and at the age of twenty-five was getting toward the end of his days. But he was still Jenna's favorite. Her loyal friend and partner ever since she'd started working on the station so long ago. She kept him stabled and well-fed and gave him gentle exercise almost every day.

He lowered his head and lipped gently at her fingers. All the carrots she'd brought down as a treat were well and truly gone, but he was ever hopeful she might have another one hidden in a pocket somewhere.

'I miss her,' she mumbled into the gelding's copper-colored mane. 'If only she'd let us know where she is, that she's okay. If only she'd come home, then we could work something out. Arrange for her to travel if that's what she wants, give her more freedom.' Chainsaw snorted and leaned against her shoulder, lending her some of his calm surety. Jenna had turned these same words over and over in her head for the past few days, wishing them to come true, but knowing deep down that it was too late to change anything now. Rose had taken her destiny into her own hands and there might well be nothing Jenna could do to alter it.

Jello got up and stood next to the stable door, giving a small whine so Jenna knew Dan was on his way. She gave Chainsaw one last sweep with the currycomb and let herself and the dog out of the stable. Chainsaw hung his head over the half-door, ears pricked, and all three of them, horse, human and dog, watched Dan stalk down the center of the stable block.

Jenna still enjoyed watching Dan take his long-legged strides toward her, well-worn jeans hugging his lean hips, broad shoulders filling out his blue chambray shirt. Her husband hadn't changed much since she'd first met him. Still tall and lean, with curly hair bleached blonde at the ends by the unforgiving outback sun.

For the thousandth time, she thanked her lucky stars for sending this man to her. He'd saved her in more ways than one.

'Thought I'd find you here,' he said, slipping his arm around her waist and kissing her gently. 'Hey, old buddy.' One hand snaked out and gave Chainsaw's forehead a rub. 'Don't suppose any of the horses know where she's gone?' he asked, half-hopeful.

'No, I told you that the other night.' She planted a kiss on his cheek and stepped back out of his arms. 'Rose never left a hint of what she was up to. Not to anyone, human or animal. All we know is that Jello watched her sneak the Land Cruiser out very early on the morning she left. Dogs don't work with time the same way we do, but from the image he gave me, it must've been really early in the morning, probably around three a.m.. Late enough for even Lex to be in bed, but early enough that she'd still have a good three or four hours before anyone went to check on her.'

Dan snorted. 'She planned her escape well, then.'

Lex had worked on the station for longer than either Dan or Jenna knew, he was always a little vague about the details. Had been the station manager right up until a few years ago, when he'd given the reins over to Mark O'Brien, another long-serving station hand. Lex was a bit of an insomniac and could often be found prowling around the farm buildings late at night, saying he was just checking to make sure everything was okay. But even he was usually in bed by one or two a.m. at the latest.

'If you're asking me, then you've had no more news either.' Her tone wasn't hopeful. Dan would've said by now if he'd heard anything.

'No. I haven't heard from anyone, not even Damien. Not since yesterday lunchtime. But I do think he's right. He's pretty clued in about these kinds of things. Dealt with quite a few runaways in his time. In his opinion, she's probably headed for Darwin. It's the most likely large city for her to go to.'

Jenna nodded, but was unconvinced. There were so many directions her daughter could have gone. If it were her, she'd probably head for Perth. It was the largest city in Western Australia, and once there it'd be easy to stay hidden. Or she could be heading for the Queensland border, toward Cairns or Townsville, but admittedly, that was a lot further away. Even Broome had a large international airport. If she'd made it to Broome, Rose might already be on a flight out of the state, or even out of the cquntry. Jenna's heart constricted painfully against her ribcage. Please, please don't let her daughter have left the country. She wasn't sure if she could live with that.

'How are Rodney and Tallow?' Dan asked, changing the subject.

Jenna dragged in a deep, ragged breath and tried to turn off the churning emotions. 'They don't seem to be as upset as one would imagine,' she replied. 'They miss Rose, and they want her back, of course. But they've always had such blind faith in her, ever since they came to live with us when they were so little. That she can do anything, that she's invincible.' Jenna sighed with frustration. 'If only I had their conviction.'

'Hmm,' Dan muttered.

'They're down with Cookie and Lex at the moment.' Jenna waved her hand in the direction of the staff quarters. 'Cookie's feeding them a big breakfast after their early morning ride, which is what she does best.' Dan smiled, and Jenna couldn't help but raise a small grin as well. The twins were both the delight and the bane of Dan and Jenna's lives. Always getting up to mischief. They loved Rose like a sister and she loved them back just as fiercely.

Cookie, as her name implied, was the station cook. She'd been here longer than Lex, more than twenty-five years at Jenna's guess.

'It's probably a good thing they're out from under our feet for a while.' Dan took off his Akubra hat and ran his hand through his hair.

'Yes, probably. They keep saying they want to go out and look for Rose. I've had a devil of a time stopping them from riding off into the desert to find her. You know, so young and full of testosterone, they reckon they can locate her when the rest of us can't.' Jenna snorted. 'Boys, so full of self-confidence and bravado. At least they're keeping Rose's horses occupied,' she mused.

'Yes, but I've promised them a stock horse each for their sixteenth birthdays. So their plates are going to be extra full if…' Dan let the unsaid words hang in the air. If Rose didn't return.

Jenna didn't know what to say to fill the silence. She wanted to be angry at Dan for even implying Rose wouldn't come home. But she couldn't seem to raise the energy. Jello stirred at Jenna's feet, raising a plume of fine red dust.

'Jay's coming,' she said, for Dan's benefit.

Sure enough, the man strode around the corner of the stables a few seconds later. 'I've just had word from Paul, the private detective,' he said without preamble.

Jenna straightened at his words. Had Paul found their daughter? They'd rung him as soon as she'd disappeared, hoping against hope he'd be able to find her trail when Damien and the police couldn't.

'He says that Corey Pallan is definitely in Darwin. He's been lying low at a biker clubhouse for a few weeks now.'

Jenna let out a low moan of dread. Was it just a coincidence? Or did he somehow know something about Rose?

'That's not good,' Dan admitted. 'But we shouldn't be jumping to any conclusions, not just yet.'

'Plus, we don't even know if that is where Rose is going. It's so frustrating we can't get any leads.' Jay grimaced, clenching his fists by his side. 'Someone must've picked her up along Padbury's road. She must've hitched, because she certainly didn't walk that far from where we found the Land Cruiser. It's the only thing that makes sense. Someone knows where she is. But they're not letting on.'

The only other possibility was Rose had organized for someone to pick her up. But who and why? As far as they knew, Rose had very few friends, except for the people who worked and lived on Shiralee. Should Jenna be suspicious of any of their station hands? The thought was preposterous, they'd known all their employees for at least the past two years, most of them longer. And they'd all seemed just as shocked by Rose's disappearance as the rest of them.

But if Corey was in Darwin… 'We need to go to Darwin, too,' Jenna declared. 'I need to go and talk to Corey.' This had gone on long enough. This avoiding Corey. Jay and Dan thought he was no longer a threat. They wanted to believe Corey had finally grown up and just forgotten about Alexander's death and everything that'd transpired in Margaret River. Jenna wasn't so sure.

Up until now, they'd thought it better to keep a low-profile, not approach the man. But it was time to stop hiding in the shadows. Dan was right, they had been keeping Rose wrapped in cotton wool. And now Rose had forced their hand. It was time to go on the offensive.

CHAPTER NINE

Koen sat at a table right in the back of the pub. The beer was cold on his tongue, but he hardly noticed it going down. He couldn't believe what he was seeing. Rose was there. She was up on the stage. Singing. And she was good. Damn good.

Her hair was left out of its normal ponytail to flow down over her shoulders. And she was wearing makeup. Not a lot, but enough to highlight her eyes with a dark smoky ring that made them stand out sky-blue against her dark dress. That was another surprise. She was wearing a dress. A little sparkly black and gold number that hugged her hips and showed off her legs. He'd thought she looked good in jeans and a shirt, but this was an altogether different kind of good. Sexy and alluring.

And her voice. It was strong and sweet with a hint of the Aussie country singer Kasey Chambers. She sat on a high-stool, a guitar balanced on her knee, and she was singing like an angel. There was a wobble in her voice, Koen could tell she was nervous, but she was hiding it well. Some of the audience had even stopped their conversation and were listening to her.

Koen's guts churned as he looked at her. Was he the reason she was up there singing? Had he driven her to do the one thing she was terrified to do only a few nights ago? Because he'd stolen her money? It'd be a quick way for her to make some dough. Maybe the only way she knew how.

She looked like she belonged up there. Was this the kick in the butt she'd needed? He thought so, but she might not see it quite that way. He scrunched down lower in his seat. There was no way she'd be able to see him, tucked back here behind the corner of the bar, but he was still dreading their first meeting.

He'd come to give her money back.

It was Wednesday night, two days since he'd last seen her; since he took her money. Watching her sing, he almost couldn't believe it'd been that long, and how much she seemed to have changed. As he waited for her to finish her gig, his mind churned back over the events of the past few days.

The morning after he left Rose, Koen found himself driving the bike up a long, rutted dirt driveway, stopping in front of a large, tumble-down house. It was still early. Would anyone even be up? He looked up to see Jon amble out of the fly-screen door and lean on the veranda railing. This was a typical house found in Australia's Top End, wooden, built up high on stilts to keep it away from the threat of flooding.

'Hey, Cuz,' Koen called out. 'Long time no see, huh?' Jon rubbed the back of his hand over his face, gave a huge yawn and proceeded to scratch his balls. Koen hid a grin. The man hadn't changed.

'Hey, yourself,' Jon replied. He was a big man, in his early thirties, with a thick beard and a broad smile. A tiny cherub face appeared between the wooden rungs of the railing. This must be Nulla, the youngest of Jon's brood. She was only a baby last time Koen had been here. Jon dropped a big hand onto the top of her head, which was a tangle of black curls.

'That looks like Uncle Billy's bike. What you doin' riding that?' Jon came down the wooden steps, eyes glued to the motorbike.

It was a distinctive bike, a red Yamaha WR450. Koen should've known better than to just ride up to Jon's on it. He pushed the kickstand down and hopped off the bike. 'I… borrowed it for a while, that's all.' He did intend to return it. At some stage. He'd needed to get out of Balgo, and it was the only transport available to him at the time. Surely Billy would understand that?

'Oooeee, Uncle's gonna be mad as a cut snake if you stole his bike,' Jon said with glee. 'Careful, or he might even get old man Pinjarra to point the bone at you.' Jon cavorted around like a child in front of Koen. He glared back, unamused, until Jon doubled over with laughter. 'What, you can give it, but you can't take it, hey, Cuz?'

Sure, Koen was normally the larrikin of the bunch, but this wasn't a topic to be taken lightly. There was a slim chance Uncle Billy was mad enough to do just that. Koen really, really hoped he didn't.

'That's bullshit,' Koen muttered. This wasn't going at all how he'd planned. How was he going to convince Jon he'd turned over a new leaf, when he already knew he was arriving on a stolen bike?

'So, what ya doin' on Uncle's bike, then?' All the mirth had left Jon's face, his eyebrows now cocked at a serious angle.

'You know about the funeral?' Koen threw the question at Jon, hoping to put him off balance. Who did Jon think he was, his bloody father or something?

Jon's dark eyebrows lowered. 'Yep, we heard about the Sorry Business. Terrible. The boy was so young.' The big man's eyes clouded over with sympathy.

Jon was careful not to say Mack's name. A lot of his mob still believed it disturbed a spirit to say the name of the deceased. Koen wasn't one for such thinking, but he respected the others for theirs.

'How's Aunty Teal?' Jon asked.

'She's not good. That's one of the reasons I had to leave.' Koen kept his gaze fixed on his boots. He was going to say more, but a sudden, large lump in his throat stopped the words from coming.

'Come on then, bring your bag and get inside.' Jon laid a big hand on Koen's shoulder for a second before motioning him to follow him up the stairs. Koen pulled the duffle from one of the satchels and slung it over his shoulder, releasing a quiet breath through pursed lips. Jon would have questions, plenty of questions, but if he was inviting Koen into his house, it meant he'd been forgiven. For now.

Koen spent the next two days hanging out with the mob at Jon's place, kicking back and taking it easy. Jon finally relented and said he'd see if he could get Koen his job back working with the building company. As long as he promised to stick around this time.

All the while, guilt ate away at Koen's insides.

How was Rose faring? Was she still at the hotel? Or had she left, moved on? She was undoubtedly pissed off at him. Cursing his name and probably cursing every black fella from here to Broome as well. The money sat in his bag, untouched. The idea of it burning a hole in his psyche.

Until finally a light-bulb went off in his head. If he really was turning over a new leaf, as he kept declaring he'd done, then the only fair thing was to give the money back. Prove to himself once and for all he was a different man.

A great weight lifted off his chest as soon as he made the decision. It was the right thing to do. And of course, the chance to see Rose one more time had nothing to do with those feelings of rightness.

So, he'd headed back into town, gone to the Blue Lagoon Hotel on the off chance she might still be there. Wanda was delighted to see him, finally confirming Rose was still staying at the hotel after a fair bit of cajoling and flirting on his part, saying she'd seen Rose heading for the pub an hour or so ago.

Koen snuck in the back way and was amazed to see Rose up there, bold as brass, singing for her supper. And doing a great job of it.

* * *

'What the hell are you doing here?' Rose felt the blood rise in her face as she stared daggers at Koen. 'You've got three seconds to get out of my sight before I call Tod and have him throw you out on your skinny ass.'

How dare he think he could come up to her, smiling like the bloody Cheshire Cat? All happy as Larry to see her, giving her that easy, charming grin. Like that would win her over. She should punch him in the face. She wanted to punch him in the face. How dare he stand there as if nothing had happened, palms up in supplication, looking as innocent as a babe?

And all hot, sexy and dangerous.

She'd only just got offstage, after the most frightening fifteen minutes of her life. Her legs were like jelly, and she desperately needed a drink of water. People were congratulating her as she walked back through the tables toward the back office. They seemed as if they were genuinely happy with her performance. She was almost starting to believe she'd been half-good up there.

And then Koen appeared out of nowhere, and her euphoria morphed into anger. Was quickly turning into a blinding rage.

'I want to talk to you. Apologize, if you'll let me.'

'Apologize, my ass. Get outta my way, you two-faced little thief.'

'Look, Rose, I'm sorry. Can we go and talk about this? Somewhere a little more private.' He cast an anxious glance around the crowded pub, a few people looking in their direction with interest at their raised voices. Good, the more people who knew what he was up to, the better. She wasn't going to let him get away with anything this time.

'Why? Why would I do that with you? So you can steal the last of my money?'

'Keep your voice down, girl, please,' he pleaded. Rose noticed Tod the barman staring at them as if he were about to stalk over and ask what was going on.

'Why should I?' She wasn't about to let this one go. Perhaps she could get Tod to hold Koen, then she could call the cops and get him arrested? But that idea disappeared as soon as it came. The last thing she needed was the cops involved.

'Because I want to give your money back, but only if you calm down, and listen to me.'

What had he just said? Her righteous anger faded slightly. 'I don't believe you,' she replied suspiciously. 'Why would you do that?'

'Because I felt guilty,' he said. 'And because I like you.' That wicked grin was back on his face.

'Don't you even go there,' she demanded, then sighed heavily. 'Alright, I'll give you five minutes to explain yourself. I need to pack up the guitar into the office and say thanks to Tod, then you can walk me back to the hotel. Okay?'

'You were fantastic up there, by the way.'

'Don't,' she growled. 'It's your fault I was up there. I had no money left, what else was I going to do?'

Koen had the grace to look a little shame-faced. But the grin was back a second later. 'Maybe I did you a favor. Because you really looked like you belonged up there.'

'Hmff,' was all she said in reply. She picked up the guitar and took it into the back room. Tod had kindly leant her a guitar that he never used. Said he had dreams of becoming a rock star in his younger years, but it'd never eventuated. Which was why he'd decided to start open-mic-night, give other singers a chance at the limelight. The guitar was a good one, and Rose put it back in its case with care.

Five minutes later, they walked through the front door of the hotel lobby. Wanda nodded at Rose, and then her face brightened at the sight of Koen behind her. Bloody woman, he wasn't that good-looking, for God's sake. Rose hadn't said anything to Koen, just stalked along in front of him down the footpath, trying to calm herself enough so she could speak to him like a decent person.

In the corridor outside her hotel room door, Rose stopped and said, 'You're not coming into my room, so you can say what you need to out here.' Hands on hips, she stared at him beneath the flickering fluorescent light.

'Really. You not gonna invite this lonely black fella into your room?' He tried on the charm, but Rose gave him the cold stare of death. She wasn't going to be taken in, not this time. 'You're looking mighty fine in that dress.' He ran an appreciative glance up and down her body and she felt her nerve-endings come alive.

'You've now got four minutes,' she ground out between clenched teeth. What did he think, that she'd crumble at his first kind words, be affected by his hot gaze?

His grin lost its shine as he saw she was serious. Reaching into his back pocket, he pulled out a very fat looking wallet. Then he handed over the money he'd taken from Rose. Just like that, he gave her back the almost three thousand dollars he'd stolen from her. She didn't need to count it, she could see it was all there.

'Oh,' was all she said as he pressed it into her hand. She'd half-expected this all to be some sort of game Koen was playing.

It was his turn to become serious. 'I'm really sorry, girl. I was wrong to take the money. I was angry at those dickheads from the bar and all their bullshit. I guess I was angry at the whole world, especially ignorant white people. And I took it out on you.' He hung his head, but still managed to watch her askance from beneath the brim of his hat.

Rose stared at him for many long seconds, trying to decide what to say. He leaned back against the wall, long legs crossed at the ankle, blue jeans sitting low on his lean hips. Her gaze ran up his torso, following the line of buttons up his plaid shirt where the top few were left undone, revealing a triangle of dark skin. Sleeves rolled up, he'd crossed his arms over his chest, and she noticed the smooth flex of his muscled of forearms. An image of those arms wrapped around her to keep her warm on their first night in the desert swept through her. A memory of how the spark from his touch had felt against her own skin.

He just leaned and waited for her to speak.

'Thanks, Koen. I'm not really sure what else to say.' Searching for the right words, she used the time it took to put the money back into her own wallet to gather up her thoughts. 'It was completely unexpected, you turning up here again. And I'm glad you finally did the right thing and brought back the money. But I'm not sure I'm ready to forgive you yet.'

'Okay.' To the uninitiated, it might seem Koen was unfazed by her comment, the grin never shifted from his face, but she could see she'd hurt him. It was there in the crinkle of lines around his dark eyes. Perhaps he'd been hoping she'd invite him into her room. Or at the very least, ask if they could remain friends. But she wasn't sure she could trust him. And if she couldn't trust him…Well, it was better if they never saw each other again.

'I guess I'll be off then.' He half-turned in the corridor, but then hesitated and looked back over his shoulder. 'One thing before I go, Rose. You didn't tell the cops, did ya?'

'No, I didn't,' she replied.

'Thanks,' he said, emitting a relieved breath. This time he did turn and started to stride toward the reception area.

'Koen.'

He stopped and looked back.

'I just wanted to say thanks…Well, thanks for everything. For picking me up and giving me a lift. You really saved me.' It was the truth and the least she owed him.

'No problem, girl.' He gave a wave and flashed that gorgeous grin, then kept walking.

Rose started to hum as she put the key in her door. Her life was looking bright again once more. She had her money back. She didn't have to work for snotty old Wanda anymore, cleaning the hotel toilets. And she wouldn't have to sing for her supper anymore at the pub to try and earn some spare cash on the side. Which was a good thing. The less of a spectacle she made of herself, the better.

Rose pushed the door closed and flicked on the light switch. The hair on the back of her neck stood on end as a wave of sensation hit her. Her gift suddenly went into overdrive, warning her someone with evil intentions was nearby.

'Hi, Rosalind.' The deep male voice took Rose completely by surprise, and she spun around with a squeal of shock. A large man stood next to her bed. He was bald, with a long beard and an extremely thick neck. Piggy little eyes stared at her out of a slab-square face, gleaming in the fluorescent lights. Every nerve-ending in her body was screaming at her to get away from this guy. Hate and vengefulness oozed outwards from his aura. But she didn't need her gift to tell her he was bad news. It was more than obvious just looking at him.

'Who the fuck are you? And what are you doing in my

room?' She backed up against the door to get as far away from the stranger as possible. How did he know her name? That's when she noticed the evil switch-blade knife in his hand.

'Don't you recognize me?' the man asked. 'You should.'

Rose's mind raced. Who was this guy?

He stared at her, one corner of his mouth turned in a leer. Then, as if running out of patience, he said loudly, 'Me mates know me as Bull, but my real name's Corey Pallan. Does that ring any bells?'

Oh Jesus, God Almighty. Her knees suddenly felt like they were made of water and she had to grab for the door-handle to hold herself up.

'Nice to finally make your acquaintance. I've waited a long time for this day.' He smiled and his beard moved on his face as if it had a life of its own. 'And nice of you to make this so damn easy for me. You're coming with me, Rosalind Simmonds. This is going to be so much fun.'

Corey Pallan. The very man her parents had warned her about.

They'd been right all along. She opened her mouth to scream. Then he came at her with the knife.

CHAPTER TEN

Koen took a run-up and slammed his shoulder against the door with all his might. It gave with a sickening crack, sending a searing pain through his shoulder as he hurtled into the room, landing on the floor with a thud.

A woman screamed. Rose? Disorientated, he shook his head and looked around to try and get his bearings.

'What the fuck…' A large tattooed bald man stood over him, a knife pointed at his chest. Koen had spent quite a bit of time brawling, fighting, and generally getting into trouble. All that knowledge and experience came back to him in a flash and he feinted with his left hand, punched the guy in the face with his right, then crawled between the big guy's legs before he knew what'd happened. Rose was cowering in the corner near the door, but he only had time to cast her the briefest of glances before he rounded on the man. Crouching, he held his fists up loosely in front of his face.

Who the hell was this guy, and what was he doing in Rose's room? All Koen knew was he'd heard voices and then Rose screamed. Twice. It was enough to send him crashing into the room. For some reason he'd returned, was about to knock on the door and ask Rose to come back out with him for a drink and to talk some more. It hadn't seemed right, how it'd ended. So he was hovering outside her door, like some sad, pathetic loser, when he'd heard it.

'Rose, get out. I got this,' he called out of the corner of his mouth, never taking his eyes off the big man. She didn't move or respond. 'Go, goddamnit. Get out of here while you can.'

'It's Corey,' she said in a small voice. Which made absolutely no sense to him, but the fear in her tone told him all he needed to know. She seemed to be frozen in terror, because she still wasn't moving.

The man shook his head and felt his jaw where Koen had punched him. A feral light came into his eyes. 'You little fuck. You're gonna be sorry you did that.'

The man lunged at Koen with the knife, but he managed to sidestep and land a right hook in the man's guts, shoving him against a chair at the same time. The man was big and strong, but seemed to rely mainly on his brute strength. While Koen was light and nimble, using speed and stealth. Koen knew brute strength would win out in the end, it always did, but if he could keep out of the man's reach long enough for Rose to get out, then that's all that mattered. There was little room to move in here, with the bed taking up most of the space.

'Rose, will you get outta here? Now!' he roared, trying to shake Rose out of her stupor. He had no time to see if Rose obeyed as the guy came at him again, slower and more intent now, knife held low in one hand. Bald Guy pounced, and Koen felt a slash of fire burn across his ribs as he kicked at the man's knee and sidestepped up onto the bed to get out of his reach.

'Ha, got you that time, you little black punk,' the man snarled with glee. Koen was now standing on the bed, and he resisted the impulse to look down at his chest. Instead, he glared at the big guy, waiting for his next move. At least now Koen had the height advantage, but even standing on the bed, the other guy could almost look him squarely in the eye.

And his neck was as thick as a tree-trunk. He could use that bald head of his as a battering-ram if the mood took him.

Over the top of the man's shoulder, Koen caught a glimpse of movement. Thank God, Rose was finally doing as he asked and getting out of the room. Then a lampshade crashed down on Bald Guy's head and he dropped like a lead balloon.

That was all Koen needed. He leaped off the bed and grabbed Rose by the hand. 'Come on, let's get outta here.'

But Rose resisted. 'Oh, Jesus, did I kill him?' Her face was as pale as a ghost and she was shaking all over as she peered down at the man on the floor.

The big man groaned.

'Nope, which is why we need to get out of here,' Koen said again. He leaned down and scooped his hat off the ground, where it'd fallen when he'd first burst through the door. 'My bike's out the back. This way.' He tugged on Rose's hand, and this time she followed him. They ran down the corridor and out a back door which led to the small carpark. Koen's motorbike was right next to the exit, and he jumped on and kick-started it into life. Rose was a bit slower to climb on behind him, the black skin-tight dress hampering her movements. As she hiked the dress up to her hips and settled her backside on the seat, a woman stepped out of the driver's side of an old blue van, parked at the end of the lot.

'Hey, you, stop,' she yelled.

Who was this woman? Rose's hands snaked around his middle and he gunned the bike, spinning it around so it faced the exit. The woman took two steps away from the van and stood with her hands on her hips, directly in his path. She was covered in tattoos, he didn't think he'd ever seen that many tattoos before, not on a woman, anyway. Long scraggly blonde hair hung down over her shoulder and a very short, very tight black leather dress stretched over her tall, lanky frame. But her blue eyes held the same rancor as Bald Guy's from the hotel room.

'I said stop! Where the hell is Bull?'

Koen revved the bike and took off, making the woman jump out of his way as he sped past her.

* * *

Rose held on to Koen for dear life as he raced the motorbike through the back streets of Darwin. Twisting and sliding he took the turns way too fast and Rose was almost as scared he was going to crash the bike as she was that Corey, Bull... whatever his name was, was going to find them. But after five minutes of break-neck riding, Koen finally slowed down, casting many glances back over his shoulder.

'I'm gonna head for a little park I know on the outskirts of town,' he yelled back to her. 'Then you're going to tell me what just happened.'

Yeah, well, that was going to be harder than Koen might realize, because Rose didn't really know herself.

Corey Pallan. Bull. The names rolled around and around in her head. She tried to remember everything her parents had told her about him. Ebony had run away from Alexander twenty years before. Corey had been just a kid of seventeen when Alexander took him to Margaret River to help him kidnap his wife. Things had not ended well for Alexander, he'd fallen into the ocean and drowned. And Corey had been arrested and spent four years in jail for his involvement in the kidnap and terrorizing of Ebony.

Her parents—well, her mother really, she was the paranoid one—had kept tabs on Corey through a private detective, and they knew he'd become deeply involved in a biker gang called The Sinners. For a while, he'd stalked the family, making baseless threats against them, when Rose was still young. But then it seemed Corey lost all interest in Ebony and Jenna, or any kind of retribution on their family, instead intent on building his illegal business with the bikers. But

Jenna had remained suspicious. She said she didn't trust him, and to be fair, she probably had good reason not to, after all she'd been through with Alexander and the rest of his cronies. Her mum told her that Corey had even come to Smokey Creek one day to confront them, which Rose found a little hard to believe. Jenna had shown Rose pictures of Corey, told her to memorize them in case she ever came across him. Little good that had done, Rose hadn't recognized him, even when he was standing right in front of her.

Something gnawed at the edges of her consciousness. Then she remembered. Her mum warned her that Corey had a gift of his own. Hypnotism. Stronger than anyone else. The type of hypnotism that would stop a person in their tracks. So why hadn't he tried to use it on her? Or Koen? Surely if he'd just wanted to subdue her and then take her away as quietly as possible, that would've been the best way to do it?

The rhythm of riding the bike, hanging onto Koen, and the vibration of the engine finally calmed Rose's runaway emotions until her heart rate returned to something akin to normal. The houses became sparser and then a large dark space opened in front of them. The park Koen mentioned. It was hard to see now the streetlights were few and far between. Koen guided the bike into a carpark, then onto a dirt track that Rose would never have seen in the dark, but Koen obviously knew was there. It dove deeper into the bush and once they were out of sight from the carpark, Koen parked the bike and motioned for her to get off.

Even now, her legs were still a little shaky as she shuffled a few steps away and watched Koen push down the kickstand. She tugged at the dress, readjusting it, so it settled back down over her hips. None of the faint glow from the carpark reached back here, and it was dark. A three-quarter moon was on the rise, hanging low on the horizon, shedding just enough light for Rose to see as Koen lifted a leg and dismounted from the bike, then turned to face her. As he got off, he winced and hunched over, holding a hand against his side.

'Oh, Jesus. Are you hurt?' Her hands flew to her mouth as she took in the dark patch on the front of Koen's shirt. Was that blood? In the mad rush, Rose hadn't realized he was injured.

He looked down and pulled at the shirt, trying to see what damage had been done. 'Yeah, he got me. Wasn't quick enough.'

'Let me.' Her fingers fumbled with his buttons. She pulled out her phone and switched on the torch app and held her breath as she opened the shirt. A long red slash ran across the left-hand side of his ribcage. But it'd already stopped bleeding.

'Ah, it's only a scratch,' he said brightly. She pointed the torch at his face. Definitely more than a scratch, but by no means life-threatening. 'I'm too quick for that bastard,' Koen bragged, but she could hear the shake in his voice.

'Come and sit over here.' She gestured to the trunk of a large milkwood tree. 'Have you got any water?' she asked.

'In my satchel.'

Still using the torch, she rummaged around in the bag tied onto the back of the bike and found a bottle of water wedged in the top. She also pulled out a spare t-shirt and went over to where he was sitting amongst the grassy fronds. Wetting the t-shirt, she offered him a drink, and he gulped down some water as she gingerly opened his shirt again. He took off his hat and dropped it into the grass beside him, leaning his head back against the bark of the tree.

'I'm just going to clean it up a little,' she said, dabbing gently at the semi-dried blood. He didn't reply, just grunted whenever she hit a sore spot. It was hard to see his face in the dark. Careful not to let her fingers touch his bare skin—she didn't want that same zing of electricity she always got when she touched him to make her flinch and perhaps hurt him—she leaned in for a closer examination. But even though she didn't touch him, the sight of all that wonderful cocoa skin was doing strange things to her insides. Her eyes followed the row of ridged abs down to where they disappeared beneath his belt buckle. Drawing back, away from the intriguing sight, she said, 'I don't think it needs stitches.'

'Course it don't need stitches, girl. And that's a good thing, because there ain't no way you're getting me near no damned hospital, either.'

Rose leaned back against the tree and took a slurp of water from Koen's bottle. Their shoulders bumped together lightly as she moved, switching off the torch and letting the dark engulf them once more. 'It may not need stitches, but it still needs to be cleaned properly and bandaged.'

'Hmff,' he replied. They sat in silence for over a minute, until Koen finally said, 'That was pretty intense back there. You gonna tell me what all that bullshit was about? Why I had to save your ass?'

What did she tell Koen? If she told him the truth about Corey, or Bull, or whatever he was called, then she'd also have to tell him the truth about her family and the fact she was just some stupid runaway girl who wanted to experience life. And look where that had gotten her so far?

But of course she had to tell him the truth. She needed to get back to her family as soon as possible. To warn them. Tell her mum she'd been right all along. This ruse, these lies she was spinning, had to stop.

But then, would Koen even believe the true story? To the layman it might seem far-fetched and fantastic. Perhaps if she told him an abbreviated version, the one without her family's magical powers in it, that might be enough.

Rose drew in a deep breath. Only one way to find out.

'That man, Bull, he's…' How did she put this, so it didn't sound like some made-up story? 'He's a bad man.'

'Yeah, I got that bit,' Koen said sarcastically, then winced as he shifted position.

'He's kind of an old enemy of my family. Of my grandmother and my mum, really. He's got some long-held grudge against them, and now he wants revenge.'

'What does that have to do with you?'

'I guess he figures if he hurts me, then by default he hurts my family. Perhaps he figures an eye for an eye, something like that.'

'What do you mean, an eye for an eye?'

Rose sighed. 'It's a long story, but my grandmother killed his father. It was self-defense,' she added quickly as Koen turned sharply to face her. 'And my mum also played a part in his demise. Bull was there and saw it all. He was only seventeen at the time, and he sees it as my grandmother and mum murdering his father. But he's got it all twisted around and just plain wrong. Alexander was a narcissistic son-of-a-bitch, who was all about using fear and violence to dominate everyone around him. Including Bull. He brainwashed the poor guy.'

'And this Alexander, I'm also getting the vibe that he's related to your family?'

'Yes, he was my grandmother's husband. My mum's father. Which makes him my grandfather,' she mumbled, not happy with revealing so much about her life.

'So that makes this Bull guy, your what? Your uncle?'

'Half-uncle,' she said defiantly.

'Wow, that's some interesting story. Your family is almost as fucked-up as mine.' He grinned, showing all his white teeth.

She grinned back. It was all a little twisted and even a little funny if you looked at it like that, she had to agree.

'I'm also getting the vibe you weren't some lost tourist stranded out in the desert? Am I correct?'

Here came the moment of truth. The time she admitted she'd been lying to him all along. But then he'd had the gall to steal her money, even if he'd come crawling back to ask forgiveness later. So who was he to throw stones at her little white lies?

'No, I'm not.' She kept her eyes on a blade of grass she'd picked, twirling it in her fingers. 'I live on a cattle station called Shiralee, not too far from where you picked me up.'

'Mmm,' he replied. She looked up, and he speared her with a stare from those chocolate dark eyes.

'I just needed to get away for a while. I was suffocating out there,' she said defensively. 'My mum, well, she was more than a little over-protective. And I felt like a prisoner in my own home sometimes.'

'Families,' he muttered. 'But it does seem like your mum might've had some good reasons to be a bit insecure, hey?'

'Maybe,' she agreed.

'So, what's the plan now?' he asked. 'I can't take you back to my cousins, not looking like this. He'd kick me out straight away,' Koen muttered, almost as if to himself. That didn't sound good, but Rose didn't want to pry into Koen's situation right now, her own was precarious enough.

'I have to call my parents and let them know what's going on,' she said. 'Then I need to get back home. We need some place to hide out for a few hours, so we can get things sorted. I'm not sure how Bull found me, but he must have some pretty good information to have located me that quickly, especially when my parents can't. We probably shouldn't risk staying in Darwin.'

'Lemme think for a second,' Koen grunted, laying his head back against the tree and closing his eyes. Rose studied the surrounding bushland while Koen contemplated their options. Now the moon was higher in the sky and the forest was revealed in shades of black and gray. It was so completely different from the outback she was used to. There were many large trees, some sort of eucalyptus she was unfamiliar with, as well as a few tropical palms scattered throughout. When she'd first arrived in central Darwin, she'd been amazed at all the local parks where the grass was so green it almost hurt the eyes. But on the outskirts, it was still scrubby and dry-looking, with some of that famous Top End red dirt visible through the silvery leaf-litter covering the ground.

'I got it.' Koen suddenly leaned forward. 'I know someone who works in Kakadu. In Jabiru. It's kind of a mining town, but it's good for tourists too. My sister, Bindi. Works at The Crocodile lodge. We can go there.'

Rose's heart rate picked up. Not only had Koen come up with a place to hide out and a chance to gather her thoughts, but he was offering the chance to see Kakadu. It was the one place she'd wanted to go when she first left the farm. 'It sounds good,' she said a little warily. 'Bull won't know where we've gone. But are you sure Bindi will put us up?'

'Yeah, of course.' Koen looked at her as if she'd gone a little crazy. 'She's family.'

'How far away is it?' asked Rose

'Around two-and-a-half hours. And I hate riding at night.' He sighed and picked up his hat, placed it firmly back on his head. 'Come on, let's go.' Getting up, he let out a short bark of pain.

'Shouldn't we tend to your wound first?' Concern rose in her chest. He was in no state to ride a bike for the next two hours. Was he?

'Not much we can do out here,' he said pragmatically. 'Leave it till we get there. Bindi will have something to help.'

Rose watched his shadowy form make its way over to the

bike.

'Isn't it a bit late to be riding all that way?' she asked, not really sure where she was going with this line of questioning. After all, what were their choices? They could stay here for the night, but that wouldn't help them. They really needed to keep moving, so Corey had the least chance of finding them.

'Stop your groaning, girl, and get on the bike,' Koen said.

He was doing it again. He was helping her when he didn't need to. And for what? Because underneath it all, Koen was one of the good ones.

CHATPER ELEVEN

It was after midnight when Koen finally pulled into the gravel driveway of Bindi's house. Well, he hoped it was Bindi's house, it'd been nearly two years since he was last here. The battered old 4WD Land Cruiser sheltering under the lean-to beside the house looked like the car Bindi used to drive. There were no lights on in the house. Everyone was asleep.

Koen sat on the bike and listened to it tick as the engine cooled. He wasn't sure if he could summon the strength to get off. His ribs were on fire. It might only be a superficial scratch, but it sure hurt like hell. The two-hour ride through the dark hadn't helped. Every bump and pothole in the road shot a spear of pain through his chest. But at least they were here, safe. For now.

Rose moved behind him, levering her leg over the back and standing on the red gravel a few feet away. 'Is this the place?' she asked, casting a suspicious glance at the nondescript red-brick house.

'I hope so,' he replied, taking a few more seconds on the bike, readying himself to make the effort to stand up and get off. 'She works as a guide for The Crocodile Hotel. This is where she lived last time I was here.'

'You mean you don't actually know?' she asked.

Koen just shrugged. Rose needed to learn to chill a little. He was used to winging it, playing things as they came, being spontaneous. Things always worked out in the end. Well, usually they did. Dragging in a deep breath, he held it as he stood up, managing to keep the grunt of pain at bay. His head swirled dangerously, and he took a few seconds to let the dizziness leave him.

'Are you okay?' She was at his side, touching his elbow. Obviously, he hadn't hidden his pain as well as he hoped.

'I'll be alright when we get inside,' he grunted.

Rose followed him down the gravel driveway to the front porch. There wasn't much to see in the front garden. It was mainly grass, with a few shrubs planted up against the edge of the house, and a large melaleuca tree for shade right in the middle of the lawn. But at least the grass was green and mowed, well-tended.

He knocked on the door with more conviction than he felt and stood back. It took a few minutes, but he finally heard movement in the house. The porch light came on, and a large burly man opened the door. Koen plastered his best devil-may-care grin on his face.

'Hiya. Is Bindi home?'

'Who the hell are you?' the man growled.

'I'm Koen. Bindi's brother. And this here is, Rose,' he said, dragging her into the light. 'Just let Bindi know I'm here, she'll let me in.' He hoped.

Bindi's face appeared underneath the big man's arm, and Koen released a sigh of relief. 'What the hell, Koen? Do you know what time it is?'

'Yeah, sorry.'

'We're really sorry to wake you up,' Rose echoed from behind him.

She stared at them both for many long seconds, then finally looked up. 'This is Mike,' she said by way of introduction. 'Is that blood on your shirt?' She squinted at Koen in the yellow light of the porch bulb. 'Jesus, Koen. And who is this white chick you got tagging along with you?' She turned around in disgust and walked on bare feet, back down the corridor. 'You may as well let them in, Mike, he ain't gonna go away if we don't,' she called over her shoulder.

Mike grunted, but held the door a little wider.

'I gotta work in the morning,' Bindi yawned and leaned against the doorframe of the kitchen as she watched Koen and Rose walk in. 'You know where the spare room is.' Tipping her jaw up, she indicated the second door on the left.

'Thanks, Bind,' Koen said, and reached in to give her a quick hug.

'Don't you be getting that blood all over me,' she scolded, but it was only half-hearted. 'Do you need a doctor?' she asked, slight concern edging her voice. Koen shook his head, and she muttered, 'Thank God for small mercies. Go and clean yourself up, and I'll talk to you in the morning. Both of you.'

'Thank you for letting us stay. It's so nice to meet you,' Rose said, and Bindi cast a sideways glance at her, as if truly seeing her for the first time.

'Hmm, nice to meet you too, I guess. I'm sure you've both got an interesting story to tell. But it can wait till the morning.' Casting another long look at Rose, she said, 'Wait here.' She went back to her bedroom, Mike trailing behind her. But then Bindi returned with a t-shirt and shorts in her hand. 'You look a little smaller than me, but these will fit you for tonight at least.' Without waiting for an answer, she turned on her heel and shut her bedroom door in their faces.

'Right, well that was…interesting.' Rose's face was lined in confusion.

'Let's just say Bindi is used to my shenanigans,' he said. Another wave of dizziness came over him, and he grabbed the doorframe for support. Rose was by his side in an instant, holding onto his arm.

'I'm just gonna lie down for a second.' He made it to the edge of the bed and sat down. Took off his hat and dropped it onto the floor.

'Let me take your shirt off first,' Rose fussed, pulling at his ripped shirt, trying to get it over his shoulders and off his arms. 'Sorry, girl, don't think I can sleep on the floor tonight,' he mumbled as he lay down, his head hitting the soft pillow. 'Too tired.' The last thing he knew was Rose tugging at his boots, before sleep claimed him.

* * *

What to do now? Rose stared down at Koen, fast asleep on the bed. The only bed in the room. Admittedly, it was a double bed. If she didn't want to sleep on the floor, then she'd have to share it with him.

This was all a little odd. The way Bindi had just let them into her house without a word of explanation. She guessed Koen was right when he said Bindi was used to his shenanigans. Her gaze landed on Koen again, and a small smile crept onto her lips. Innocent. That's how he looked right now. Like a child asleep after a long day, head tilted to one side on the pillow. Long black lashes lay against his dusky cheeks. Locks of black hair curled around his temples. Full lips, soft and relaxed now they weren't pulled back into that ready smile.

Then her gaze traveled down his torso and alighted on the slice across his ribs. She winced at the sight. It was looking red and angry now and had obviously bled more from the ride on the motorbike. It really needed to be cleaned up before it became infected. It might be a blessing he was asleep. Maybe she could do this without him feeling it.

She found the bathroom and quietly combed through the cupboards until she came up with some sterile wipes, a bandage and some wound ointment. On tiptoes, she went back to the bedroom and gently cleaned the wound. It was a long gash, the length of her hand, or perhaps even more, skimming over the curve of his lower ribs. The knife had only just broken the skin, Koen must've twisted out of the way, so it sailed past him, instead of imbedding deep in his torso, like Bull planned.

Koen never even stirred as she dabbed and wiped, then plastered on a thick layer of antiseptic ointment. Poor guy must be totally shattered. After all, he'd fought off a large, bearded man, been wounded in the attempt, escaped with her on the motorbike in a mad dash through the streets of Darwin and then ridden another two hundred and fifty kilometers to Jabiru. All to keep her safe.

Why had he done that?

Koen was an enigma, that much was for sure.

Staring at the wound, Rose was suddenly struck by an idea. What if it'd been worse? What if Bull had killed him? The man had been crazy enough to do it, obviously intent on doing harm, and wasn't going to let anyone get in his way. It brought home to her how much danger they were really in. Her hands began to shake as the truth sunk in. This wasn't a game anymore. It was real. There was a man out there who wanted to hurt her. To hurt her family. And she'd been so blithely unaware she'd almost let it happen.

Were they truly safe? If Bull found them in Darwin, could he find them here, too? And how had he found her, seemingly without much trouble?

It was too late, and her brain was too muddled to find a proper answer to those questions. Deciding she'd done all she could for his wound, she eyed the other side of the bed. She was shattered herself. It'd been a long day. A very long day. She wished she hadn't left all her belongings in the hotel room when they fled. This stupid little dress wasn't much good for anything. Turning her back, in case Koen decided to choose that instant to wake up, she shucked out of the dress and put on the t-shirt and shorts Bindi had offered. Flicking off the bedroom light, she felt her way over to the bed and lay down carefully beside Koen, then let out a quiet sigh. Sleep would be good. She'd be able to see everything much clearer with a little sleep.

* * *

Light streamed in through the window. Damn, she'd forgotten to pull the curtains shut. Opening her eyes, Rose went to move her arm to rub the sleep away and stopped, frozen. There was a warm body right next to her. And to make matters worse, it seemed her head was pillowed on that warm body's shoulder. Oh, no. Koen. She must've snuggled up to him sometime in the night. His arm was draped under her neck and curled protectively around her back.

Inching her head up, she stared into his face. Would it wake him if she moved? He looked wonderfully peaceful, like a child sleeping. And he was still naked from the waist up. It was like her eyes had a mind of their own. Her gaze traveled down his athletic form, resting for a few seconds on each ridge of stomach muscle, before drifting down to the flat planes which disappeared below his waistband. Then roaming back up, her gaze landed on his chest. There were small, tight curls of black hair scattered across his breastbone and over his pecs. What would they feel like beneath her fingers? There wasn't an ounce of fat on him. He was all lean muscle, sculpted, almost like a brown Adonis statue.

The corners of Koen's mouth curled up. Oh shit, he was awake.

'Enjoying the view?'

'I wasn't…' She went to pull away, to sit up, but his hand tightened around her shoulder, keeping her pinned to his side.

'I don't mind if you like what you see.' He opened his eyes and grinned at her.

She knew she was turning red with embarrassment. Damn him.

'And I don't mind the feel of you lying here with me either,' he admitted, eyes sparkling with amusement. And something else as well. What else was it in his eyes? Was it desire? 'You feel good. Right…If you know what I mean.'

She stared up at him, head still pillowed on his shoulder. What was he saying? Did he feel it too? This connection they had. That hit of adrenaline, or whatever it was whenever they touched? She was acutely aware her body was in contact with his all down her right side. Aware of how his hip bone rested next to hers, his long thigh warm against her own leg. Her breasts pushed into his rib-cage.

She couldn't look away from his chocolate eyes, a question hovering there in the depths. Her tongue darted out, and she licked her lips as her body unconsciously reacted to his stare. His eyes were drawn to the movement, and he shifted slightly, turning toward her. Before she knew what'd happened, his other hand came up to cup the side of her cheek, his thumb sliding across her lips.

'You have a beautiful mouth. Has anyone ever told you that?'

She couldn't answer. Didn't know how to answer. No, no one had ever told her that. And no one had ever looked at her quite the way Koen was looking at her now, either. The movement of his thumb over her lips was doing odd things to her insides, making them weak and shaky, like leaves being swirled around in a whirlwind.

His head came up off the pillow and his mouth met hers. The question still there in the gentle way his lips caressed hers. Did she want this, they were asking.

And the answer surprised her. She increased the pressure,

letting her tongue flick in and out as she explored his supple mouth. Heat surged through her body.

This was nothing like any of the men she'd kissed before. Like the *boys* she'd kissed before. This was on another level. It felt like her brain had switched off and she'd become a kind of corporeal being, run only by her body and its demands. Her mouth was on fire, her skin was on fire where his thumb was roaming over her jaw, and the heat was quickly pooling lower, setting the spot between her legs on fire as well.

Her fingers roamed over his naked chest. The curls were soft and springy as they brushed beneath her palm, exactly how she imagined they'd feel. He pulled her against him tighter, rolling up onto one elbow so he could claim her mouth from above.

As he moved, he let out an involuntary grunt, and Rose remembered he was hurt. It was the jolt her conscious mind needed. What in hell was she doing? She needed to stop this reckless thing before it went too far. She broke the kiss and stared, panting, into his brown eyes.

'Nothing better than kissing a good-looking chick first thing in the morning to wake you up,' he said with a characteristic grin.

Rose made a guttural sound and rolled out from underneath him. Trust Koen. Always the joker, he just couldn't help himself. Thankfully, things hadn't gone too far. She needed to get her head back on straight. Just because she was madly, inconceivably, unexplainably attracted to this guy didn't mean squat at the moment. They were on the run from a vengeful madman, and she wasn't sure she could trust Koen, not after he stole her money. Even if he had risked his own life for her.

Huffing, she sat on the edge of the bed. Time to get up and face the music.

* * *

Koen lay back on the bed. He could bloody-well kick himself. Why did he always have to say the most inappropriate things and ruin the moment? Rose had her back to him, sitting on the edge of the bed. There would be no going back to their kissing now, he could see it in the unbending line of her backbone.

Bugger, she'd tasted so sweet. Lips soft and delicious, she'd responded to him with an eagerness that'd surprised him at first. He'd liked the feel of her breasts pushed tightly into his chest. Just the thought of it sent tiny shivers of lust through him.

'I can hear someone up, in the kitchen,' she said. 'We need to talk to Bindi. And then we…' she hesitated, 'I need to make a plan.'

Koen sat up slowly, testing for pain in his ribs. The wound was sore, but not as sore as he might've expected. As he looked down, he could see someone had washed the blood away and smeared some sort of ointment over the wound. Rose had looked after him last night, and he never even felt a thing.

'Thanks,' he grunted.

'What for?' She swiveled around to look at him.

'For fixing me up. It's not too bad today.'

'I'm glad,' she replied, and he could see she really was pleased. But was she glad because she was worried for his welfare, cared about him? Or was she worried in case he slowed her down? Got in the way of her plans?

'I have to go and call my parents.' The look on her face told him everything he needed to know about how tough that call was going to be. He even felt a twinge of compassion for her.

'Yeah, well, I have to explain to Bindi why we're on the run from your idiot Uncle Bull, or whoever he is.' He grimaced at the thought. Would Bindi even believe him? He'd spun her a few stories in his time, and she had reason to distrust him.

She was always tough on him, much tougher than Daisy ever was. But surely she'd see that he and Rose were telling the truth. And the little he'd seen of Mike from last night made him think he might be a reasonable guy. Perhaps Mike would help them convince her.

'Would she let us stay here for a few days, if we need someplace to hide?' Rose asked, worrying at her bottom lip. She was very cute when she did that.

'Probably.' Bindi had never let him down before, not when he'd really needed her help, and he couldn't see why she'd change now. There were a few things he was loath to tell her about, though. The motorbike stolen from Uncle Billy, for one. And the money he stole from Rose, for another. Both of those things wouldn't go down well with Bindi, even if he did have solid reasons for why he'd done them.

'Sure you don't want to snuggle back in here for a few more minutes.' He patted the bed beside him. 'We could go back to some more kissing.' Couldn't hurt to try, could it? Put off the inevitable for a while.

'No,' she said. 'That's definitely not happening again.' To put effect to her words, she stood up and backed away from the bed as far as the cramped room would allow.

'Can I ask why?' A cold lump formed in his stomach.

'Because...Because I'm not sure I can trust you.'

Damn, was he ever going to live down the fact he'd stolen her money? He was suddenly so mad at himself. He'd ruined his chance again by doing something stupid. By letting his anger and that chip on his shoulder his mum was always talking about take him over. So much for turning over a new leaf.

Strangely, it wasn't being a complete idiot that hurt the most. It was the idea he'd never get to taste her lips again that was driving him crazy.

'That's bullshit,' he said, louder than he intended. But he

was angry. At himself, mainly. But also at her. For not trusting him. Hadn't he put himself on the line for her? Fought that big bastard so she could get away? Taken her on his bike to a safe place they could hide?

Getting out of the bed, he hid his grimace of pain by bending down to pick up his ruined shirt.

'Let's get this over with, shall we?' He held the door open and beckoned her through in a parody of a chivalrous knight.

CHAPTER TWELVE

Jenna jumped as the phone rang loudly from the kitchen, fraying her already jangled nerves. It was still early, she'd only just got out of the shower and had been staring moodily out the bedroom window, wrapped in her towel, hair still dripping. Not that she hadn't already been up for hours, pacing about the house in an aborted attempt to get rid of some of this pent-up worry that was driving her crazy.

Ebony and Dan had so far talked her out of the idea of going to Darwin to track down Corey and *have a chat with him*, as she put it. They said it would be stirring up trouble where it wasn't warranted. But Jenna wasn't going to wait much longer without any news from Rose. She'd have to do something soon, or she was going to go stark raving mad.

As the phone kept ringing, she threw on a t-shirt and pair of shorts and was half-way down the corridor, Jello padding in front of her, when she heard Ebony say, 'Hello?' into the phone. Ebony and Jay were still here, staying at Shiralee. Keeping vigil with Jenna and Dan. Jenna had told her to go home, there was nothing they could do until they had some more clues as to where Rose could've gone, but her mother had refused.

Jenna stopped in the doorway, staring at Ebony, hoping against hope.

Ebony let out a gust of air and turned to smile at Jenna as she spoke. 'Rose, oh my God. It's so good to hear from you.'

Jenna's knees went weak, and she had to grab the back of one of the kitchen chairs to steady herself. She wanted to call out to Dan, who was outside on the porch, talking to Jay, but she daren't make a noise in case she missed what Ebony said next.

'I'm glad you're safe,' Ebony said, and beckoned Jenna over, holding the old-fashioned phone a little away from her ear so they could both listen together. They still used a landline out here, it was the only way they could guarantee reception 'Where are you, sweetheart?'

Jenna got to her mother's side in time to hear Rose say, 'I'm...ah, well, that's not really important right now...'

Not important, thought Jenna. It was the whole crux of the matter, wasn't it?

'... and I'm not sure I should tell you, just in case... well...'

What was the matter with her daughter, why was she speaking in half-sentences that didn't make any sense? She opened her mouth to say just that, to berate Rose and tell her to stop playing games, when Ebony held up a hand and frowned, her message clear; let the girl speak first. Jenna bit her tongue.

A sob came through the phone and Rose said, 'Oh God, Grandma, you were right. You and Mum were right after all.' Jenna and Ebony exchanged wary glances, a frisson of fear stalking down her spine. What was she talking about?

'Hi, baby, it's me,' Jenna said into the phone. 'What do you mean? Are you safe? Please tell me you're safe.'

'Yes, yes, we're safe, for now, I think. But, Mum, you were right. About Corey. He found me. In Darwin. He tried to...'

'Slow down,' Jenna demanded. 'Are you saying that Corey Pallan contacted you?' There were hundreds of questions all swirling around in Jenna's mind, like who did Rose mean by *we* are safe, and how did she get to Darwin, and why had she felt the need to run away in the first place? But she concentrated on the important facts for now.

'He more than contacted me. He tried to…I don't know, abduct me, or something. I think he had some woman helping him, too. She tried to stop us from getting away. If it wasn't for Koen, I'm not sure he wouldn't have succeeded. Corey had a knife. And he said he'd been waiting for me for a long time.'

Okay, well at least she had a name to put to who she meant by *we* now. And it sounded like they were safe for the moment.

'Tell me where you are. I'm coming to get you,' Jenna said loudly. She'd had enough of this, it was time to take charge of the situation.

'No, Mum. It's fine, Koen is going to bring me home.'

'He's going to what? Does he know how far it is? Does he know these roads? Who is this guy anyway?' Too many questions, she knew, but she couldn't help herself. Before Rose could even draw breath to answer, Jenna spoke again, 'No, I'm coming to get you, end of story. Once you're back on the station, we can keep you safe—'

Ebony took the handset away from Jenna and put it firmly against her own ear, frowning at Jenna. 'Sorry, sweetheart, your mum's just very worried about you, that's all. As are we all.' She gave Jenna another hard stare as she reached out a hand for the phone and shook her head. 'Not unless you behave yourself,' she mouthed silently.

Jenna stared at her mother, but it was obvious she wasn't backing down. Finally, Jenna let out an exasperated sigh and nodded in resignation. Ebony let her listen at the handset again.

'Okay, if you're sure this Koen can keep you safe, and get you home as soon as possible. But can you at least tell me where you are, so if anything goes wrong—'

'But what if Corey's bugging our phone or something?' said Rose in a frightened voice. 'I mean, how did he find me in the first place?'

Jenna snorted. It would take a lot more finesse than Corey Pallan had to get a trace put onto a phone, she was pretty sure of that. 'I don't how he found you, baby, and I'm going to call Damien as soon as you hang up and see if he can shed some light on the subject. But I'm sure he's not listening to our calls. Tell us where you are.'

'We're in a little town called Jabiru, in Kakadu National Park. We're staying with Koen's sister. But we're going to leave this morning and come straight home. Koen's got a motorbike.'

Jenna's heart sank. The back of a motorbike was no way to be traveling these dangerous outback roads. It was a two-day drive from Kakadu, anything could go wrong. But she caught the look in her mother's eye and sighed.

'Can you at least call us along the way, to let me know you're okay.'

'Sure,' Rose said. 'And, Mum?'

'Yes, baby.'

'What are we going to do about Corey? He calls himself Bull now, it's like his bad biker name or something.' Jenna could hear the shudder in Rose's voice.

'We'll figure something out,' she said. 'For now, we just need you home safe and sound, okay?'

'Okay, Mum, see you in two days.'

'See you, Rose. We love you.'

Jenna was most surprised when Rose replied, 'I love you all too.' And then the phone went dead.

Rose wasn't prone to saying she loved them, had never been big on any show of emotion, and the words struck Jenna right to the core. 'Oh God,' she said quietly, just as Dan rounded the doorway to the kitchen.

'What's happened?' he demanded. Jay followed close on his heels.

Jenna took two steps and was in Dan's arms, needing to feel his strong, beating heart beneath her ear before she could speak.

'That was Rose on the phone. She's safe. But Corey found her.' The words tumbled out of her mouth, and she found she was sobbing against his shirt, unable to form coherent words any more. Surprised at her own release of emotion, she tried to get her crying under control.

Jay strode through the kitchen, his eyes glued to Ebony. 'Is it true?'

'Yes,' she breathed. 'Come and sit with us and we'll explain.' She nodded toward the kitchen table.

Jay's broad shoulders sagged with relief as he followed his wife. He pulled out a chair for her and then gave her a quick but meaningful hug before she sat.

'Oh, thank God,' Dan sighed into the top of Jenna's head. He guided her to another chair where she sat, but he kept hold of her hand. Jello lay under the table at her feet and whined, anxious because his mistress was upset. Jenna laid her hand on top of his head, letting him know everything was alright until he finally settled his nose on his paws with a snort.

'Where is she?' Dan asked.

Jenna and Rose filled the two men in on their short conversation with Rose. By the time they finished their explanations, Jenna had recovered her composure.

'We need to go and meet her half-way,' she said intently. 'I can't just sit around here for two days, waiting for her to arrive.'

'Jenna, I don't think—'

Ebony interrupted Dan. 'You have to cut the apron strings,

darling. Hasn't this little escapade of Rose's taught you anything? Stop hovering over her like a helicopter parent. Let her do what she said she would. You need to start trusting her.'

'But, Mum, Corey Pallan is out there. He's after her. He—'

'I know, Jenna. I'm as sick about it as you are, but you need to listen to me.' Her mother laid a placating hand on her arm. Jenna looked toward Dan for support, but he just gazed at her, not saying a word. Traitor.

'Perhaps our time would be better spent finding out more about this Corey fella,' Jay said quietly. 'If he did threaten Rose, it sounds like he might have grown bold enough to not wait in the shadows anymore. I think we should see him as a serious threat.'

'I always saw him as a serious threat,' Jenna huffed.

'I know, babe,' Dan soothed. 'And I know I'll be eating told-you-so pie for a long time to come now because we didn't take you seriously.' His brown eyes sparkled impudently. 'But perhaps Jay is right. We need to focus on what's important and come up with a plan to handle Corey and whatever he might have up his sleeve. Paul, the private investigator, told us Corey has hooked up with some biker gang. If that's true, and he's not working alone, we might have some big trouble on our doorstep before too long.'

Jenna's mind went back to the time she and Dan defeated Liam. Liam had a gang of thugs under his control, and it'd taken all the crew at Shiralee to win in the end. The last thing they needed was an all-out gun battle with a gang of bikers.

'We need to talk to Damien,' she said succinctly, already ticking a list of things to do off in her head. 'He has to find out more about this biker gang of Corey's and what they might be capable of. Are they actually the mean mothers they pretend to be?'

'I'll get on the phone straight away,' Dan agreed.

CHAPTER THIRTEEN

Rose chewed quietly on a piece of toast while Bindi continued to berate Koen. Loud and long. She'd hardly paused for breath in the past five minutes. Koen sat at the kitchen table, hunched in the corner, picking at the laminate top morosely, not daring to meet Bindi's eyes. Mike leaned against the kitchen counter, saying nothing, watching the drama unfold in his calm manner. Clad in only a pair of shorts, his long legs stretched out and arms crossed over his bare chest, Mike reminded her of a large, friendly bear.

Rose agreed with most of what Bindi was saying. She'd listened as Koen had told his version of their story, from the time he'd left Balgo, to when he'd picked Rose up on the road, right through to arriving in Jabiru last night. Bindi demanded he leave nothing out, and after a shrewd glance at her dark, knowing gaze, he'd revealed everything. It'd been news to Rose that Koen was riding a stolen motorbike. Admittedly stolen from his uncle, who wouldn't report it missing, but still. Bindi, however, didn't seem quite so surprised.

He even told her about stealing Rose's money, which shocked her the most. Although he made sure to add very quickly how he'd decided almost immediately to give it back to her. Bindi scowled at him all the way through his story, waiting for him to finish before she unleashed her torrent at how disappointed she was in him and why couldn't he see his own worth and start acting like an adult and stop being a complete idiot all the time. She also threatened to tell his older sister, Daisy, what he'd been up to, and Koen winced. Rose almost felt sorry for him. Almost.

But only part of her mind was concentrating on Bindi's words. Her thoughts were mainly occupied with the kiss. Specifically, the way Koen had kissed her this morning. As if she mattered. As if he'd opened a door into her mind and could see right into her soul. Their connection had been immediate, fierce and strong, and it'd scared the hell out of her. Because she hadn't wanted it to end.

'So now what have you two got planned?' Bindi said finally, yanking out a chair and sitting down heavily at the table with them, as if her diatribe had exhausted her. Rose dragged her thoughts away from the kiss and back to the small kitchen.

Koen just glared at Bindi, so Rose answered for them both. 'I've talked to my mum on the phone. I need to get home as fast as possible. And Koen has offered to take me.'

'What, on his stolen motorbike?' Bindi scoffed. This woman really was a hard-ass and Rose briefly wondered if she treated the tourists she took on the tours around Kakadu the same way. 'Where do you live?' Bindi asked.

'Shiralee. It's a cattle station down on the edge of the Great Sandy Desert. About five hours south of Halls Creek,' Rose added lamely.

'Hmm,' Bindi mused, pushing a chunk of long, black hair over her shoulder. She cast a glance at Mike, and they had some kind of wordless conversation. 'That's a two-day drive.' Bindi was still dressed in her sleeping attire, her hair a mess of snarls and tangles. Dark circles hovered beneath her eyes. Rose felt a stab of guilt at having woken her last night, as she obviously hadn't slept well afterwards.

'I have to leave just after nine, my first tour starts at ten this morning,' Bindi finally said.

'We'll be gone in half an hour,' Koen said, a little sullenly, obviously still smarting over his dressing down. Rose didn't blame him, she would've been too. 'We'll grab some breakfast and get out of your hair.' It was just after six now, perhaps still early by city standards, but to Rose, who was used to getting up at sunrise most days, it was normal.

Bindi's gaze softened. 'You can stay as long as you need to.' She didn't say the words, but Rose heard the unspoken sentiment; Bindi would do anything for him, he was her younger brother, after all.

'You can have one of Mike's shirts.' Bindi eyeballed Koen's ripped and bloody shirt with a grimace. 'It might be a bit on the large side, but it's better than that rag you're wearing. The cops will take one look at that shirt and stop you for sure.'

'No probs, bro,' Mike said, and ambled out of the kitchen to get the shirt.

'He doesn't say much, does he?' Koen commented at the large man's retreating back.

'That's exactly why I like him,' Bindi snapped back. 'And he's solid as a rock. I can trust him one-hundred percent.' Bindi narrowed her eyes at Koen, and again Rose felt sorry for him. Sorry that Bindi thought so little of him. Rose had only known him for less than a week, but there was a good man inside, struggling to get out. Koen shouldn't be defined only by his bad actions. People needed to see the good he did as well. The good heart he kept hidden behind that jovial smile.

But perhaps Bindi understood and was just showing her frustration at his lack of progress by busting his balls all the time, hoping against hope that some of her words got through that thick skull of his.

Mike came back with a dark blue button-up shirt for Koen. 'It's the smallest one I have, but you're welcome to it.'

'Thanks,' Koen said, taking it with a grin. 'Is it alright if I grab a quick shower?'

'I guess,' she agreed. 'But keep it short, we're on tank water, and we're getting low.'

Rose was used to the idea of ultra-quick showers. Water was at a premium in the outback, not to be squandered or wasted. Even though a lot of the water they used on Shiralee was from bores, the main house still ran on rain water for most of the year, collected in a large tank during the wet season.

'Are you sure that cut is going to be okay?' Bindi glanced at the gap in Koen's shirt.

'Yeah, Rose looked after it for me last night. It's just a scratch, really.'

Bindi gave another of her trade-mark disbelieving snorts, but got up and started to busy herself at the kitchen bench.

'Thanks, Bind.' Koen surprised them all by taking the small, black woman into his arms and holding her there for a long time. 'Don't know what I'd do without you.'

'Go take a shower, you bloody rascal.'

Koen turned and padded down the corridor on silent feet. Bindi turned back to the bench and reached up to a cupboard to take down four mugs for the tea. Rose wasn't sure, but she thought she caught the glint of tears in the other woman's eyes.

* * *

They'd only been on the motorbike for less than twenty minutes when Koen saw the sign for Nourlangie Rock carpark and turned off the asphalt road.

Rose stirred behind him. 'Where are we going?'

'It's just a short detour,' he called back over his shoulder. 'Won't take too long.' He could feel the irritation in the tension coming through Rose's arms, which were locked around his waist. But he ignored her. This was a place he'd wanted to visit for a long time now. The only other time he'd been to Kakadu, when Bindi first moved out here to take up her job as tour guide, he'd had to leave town again in an almighty hurry. And missed out on his chance to come. This time he was determined to see the rock images he'd heard so much about. Mainly from his mother, but also from other family and even Bindi herself.

The road took them right beside a shallow expanse of water, with long green grass waving at the edges and a flotilla of water lily leaves dusting the surface. A large projection of red rock rose up at the back of the billabong, it's striations like that of an orange layer cake. He slowed to get a better look and then stopped the bike right next to a large yellow sign.

Rose read it out loud. 'Danger, Crocodile Safety.' Then she giggled, probably at the depiction of a person being eaten by a crocodile on the sign and the other dire warnings about not entering the water otherwise you would die. 'Well, I certainly won't be going in there. Even though the place looks absolutely divine. How mean of Mother Nature, to create such a wondrous place and then make it absolutely out of bounds for us mere mortals.' She sighed as she stared out over the vista of green and red.

'It is beautiful, isn't it? This is why thousands of tourists come here every year, because of this wild, untamed beauty. Pity it's the dry season. Can you imagine what this place would look like in the wet? With the billabong overflowing, teeming with bird life, everything so lush and green and larger than life.'

'Yes, it is wonderful,' she replied, but there was a question in her voice at his uncharacteristic words. He made a loud grunting sound. What was wrong with waxing lyrical a little?

He could appreciate natural, untamed beauty just as much as the next guy.

'But don't be fooled by that beauty,' he warned. 'That sign ain't there for nothing. There could be a big old Mr Croc hiding in there and you'd never know.'

Rose gave a delicate shudder and took another long look at the billabong. Then she changed the subject. 'Are you going to tell me where we're going?' she asked again.

'To see some paintings,' he answered cryptically.

'Paintings, out here? But—' The rest of her words were lost in the roar of the engine as he took off up the road, grinning quietly to himself. She'd see soon enough.

The road suddenly ended in a large carpark. There were two other cars parked neatly in between the lines, but no buses yet filled the larger spaces set aside for them. It was too early for most people. Which was a good thing, it meant they might enjoy the artwork in peace. He found a spot at the end of the carpark, under a large tree and used his foot to ease the kickstand down and waited until Rose hopped off before he leant the bike on its side. A twinge across his ribs made him wince, which he immediately tried to hide from Rose. If she saw, she might think him incapable of the long ride ahead. Bloody women, always worrying. He was fine.

Rose eyed him as he pulled his trusty Akubra from the top of his bag and placed it back onto his head. Bindi had gone above and beyond again this morning, presenting Rose with a folded pile of clothing as she went to have a shower. She'd given her an old pair of jeans, some even older Blundstone boots and a hat to keep the sun off her face. Bindi said that she couldn't ride all the way into the desert in a silly little black dress, and she was right. Koen's heart expanded as he'd watched the exchange between the two women. He really needed to tell his sisters that he loved them more often.

Rose put on the hat Bindi had given her. It cast a shadow

over her face, her eyes becoming a darker blue beneath the brim. Piercing him with their intensity. On impulse he took her hand and headed toward a bush track with a sign that said, Nourlangie Rock, one-point-five kilometers return.

'Come on, you want to go see some real art? I'm gonna show you paintings made over twenty thousand years ago,' he said, striding out and she followed eagerly. The other good thing about getting here early was the heat of the day wasn't yet blazing down on them. It would be nice to walk in the cool shade of the trees.

'Are we going to see some Aboriginal rock art?' she asked as it finally dawned on her.

He just nodded in reply.

The savannah woodlands opened up in front of them, with piles of sunset-colored sandstone tumbled next to the walking trail. Rose stopped talking, and they both enjoyed the silence of the bush and the crunch of the dry leaves under their boots.

He remembered the feel of her lips when they'd kissed this morning. That's when he'd made the decision to take Rose home. As he kissed her. And not because her mouth was causing his insides to catch fire. But because it was the least he could do. He owed her a debt. It would probably mean the loss of the coveted job at the building company. He was supposed to start work today. Jon was gonna disown him. Again. Probably for good this time. But it was the right thing to do. He'd been the one to take her away from her home—albeit unknowingly—and he needed to be the one to see her back safely in one piece.

The warmth of her hand in his felt nice, so much smaller than his. The further down the trail they got, the more his mood lifted. He was about to see paintings done by his ancestors, paintings of animals and dreamtime figures, created by the Bininj people. He found himself needing to try

127

and explain to Rose what she was about to see, so she might understand some of the significance.

'We're going to the Anbangbang Gallery. That's where the main rock art can be found,' he said, not looking at her, but her fingers squeezed his gently. 'There are lots of different styles of paintings. My people came here and used the site again and again, over many thousands of years. My mum told me about some pictures of the creation being, Namarrgon. She said they were the most awe-inspiring thing she'd seen in a long time. Made her shiver right down to her toes, just looking at him.' Rose made a grunt of interest, and he turned around to grin at her. 'Namarrgon, that means lightning man, by the way. There are also depictions of some European sailing ships. Drawn right back when my people first made contact with the whites.'

'Wow,' Rose breathed, sounding as intrigued as he was.

'And then there are the typical ones you see in all the tourist brochures. You know the ones of the x-ray art of animals and fish?'

She nodded in agreement.

'We're lucky, we got here early enough to miss the rangers. They give tours of the place, but they're also a bit like policemen. They don't like you getting too close to the artwork.'

'I can understand why they want to protect it,' Rose said.

'Yeah, but this is my traditional country, I have a right to be here.'

It didn't take them long to work their way around a small overhanging bluff, and there in front of them was the gallery. A sandstone rock wall towered above, overhanging in some places, as if the rocks were suspended in mid-air. A wooden platform with a railing to keep them from touching the rock reared up in front, but Koen ignored it. He needed to get closer, to see the drawings for himself. So, he stepped over the railing onto the red earth beside the wall.

'Koen,' Rose hissed, but he ignored her.

At first the artwork was hard to see, almost a jumble of lines easily missed on the rock face. But then they began to morph and become clear as his eyes grew accustomed to what he was seeing. Most of the paintings were either in white or a deep red ochre. Some had faded, so he had to squint to see them as they blended with the natural color of the rock.

All kinds of figures vaulted across his vision, some so bright and realistic he could almost imagine them coming alive. Bindi had told him that to the ancient painters, the act of painting was generally more important than the painting itself, so many older paintings were covered by more recent works. Resulting in a jumble of pictures which were hard to decode.

There were humanoid figures, of course, some of them taller than him, reaching all the way to the rock-wall roof. Kangaroos and turtles and birds, as well as other strange-looking creatures that Koen couldn't decipher. Depictions of spirits and ceremonies. There were powerful stories being told here. Even Koen wasn't entitled to know them all, only the most senior respected elders were entrusted to carry the knowledge. And then he saw Namarrgon, the lightning man. He was responsible for the spectacular lightning storms and rain that brought Kakadu back to life every wet season.

His ancestors would've used this spot for shelter. Stood here in the cool shade of the rock, gazing out over the escarpment, perhaps even watching Namarrgon at work, as monsoonal rains poured down over Arnhem Land.

'They're amazing.' Koen had almost forgotten Rose was there, and he jumped at the sound of her soft voice.

'Come on, there's more up here. Come and look.' He vaulted the railing again and took Rose's hand, leading her around the side of main wall and off toward another jumble of rocks.

'But the sign says not to leave the path,' Rose said.

'Do you always stick to the rules like a good girl?' he asked, laughing. 'Besides, remember, this is my—'

'Your country, I know,' she said with a smile. 'I'm glad I came here with you. It's a bit scary. A bit sacred and powerful.' She shivered slightly, even though the heat of the day was setting in. They were lucky to have the place completely to themselves. The people from the two cars in the carpark had probably chosen to walk around the billabong first and would head up to the gallery later. His mum had told him about more paintings further around the escarpment that he should go and see.

He had to let go of Rose's hand, as they scrambled up a steep incline, then a narrow ledge appeared and he followed it around the edge, making sure it was safe for Rose, until the land became a flat area with piles of jumbled sandstone rocks rearing into the sky. Every flat surface of every rock was covered in paintings here too.

Taking Rose's hand in his again, they went up close to one wall and stood together, peering at the paintings. He enjoyed the feel of her hand in his. A physical connection running between them. As always, when they touched, there was that instant buzz spreading through him. He remembered her words and was glad he'd brought her here. She seemed to understand the significance this place held for him. His mum used to say that the art was an expression of cultural identity and connection to country for the artists. He'd never truly understood what she meant until he saw it for himself.

They wandered around the site for another half-an-hour or so, until Koen's internal clock began to tick. It was time to move on. He could've stayed here for hours, but they had a long ride ahead of them. Rose's hand was still warm in his as he led her back around the escapement and onto the path toward the carpark.

There was no need to speak as they walked down the trail, their silence said more about their awe of the place than words ever could, and he was again thankful it was Rose he'd brought with him to view these spiritual paintings. The path was running flat and wide now, as they got closer to the carpark. A large jumble of boulders appeared at the side of the trail, as if thrown there by a careless giant's hand.

'Oh, look at that beautiful lizard.' Rose stopped to peer intently at the rocky surface.

'It's a little rainbow skink,' he said, amused by her delight in the small reptile.

They stood and studied the skink as it blinked at them, but it was in no hurry to scurry away. Acting on impulse, Koen drew Rose in to his side and wrapped an arm around her waist. She fitted beneath his shoulder perfectly, molding to his side. His heartbeat ratcheted up a few notches at the feel of her. Hip bumping gently into the top of his thigh, her breast pressed against the side of his chest through the fabric of his shirt. The air stilled around them as he became aware of every breath she took in, and then out again. A rock pigeon flew into a nearby tree and cooed at them as if annoyed at their presence. Koen pretended to be looking at the bird, but really, he was trying to get the raging fire in his veins under control.

The urge to kiss her grew with every passing second. He'd wanted to kiss her up at the Gallery, but that would've been improper. Not in a sacred site. But now? What would she do if he bent his head and gently tasted her lips?

CHAPTER FOURTEEN

Rose stilled as Koen pulled her in close. Up till now, he'd been holding her hand. And she was able to cope with that level of touching. Just. She could almost ignore the friction of his palm against hers as they walked. But now, the whole left-hand side of her was jammed against him. A trembling started low in her belly at the idea of him. At the memory of running her hands over the hardened muscles of his chest. Was it only this morning she'd done that?

She'd been surprised when Koen had come out of the shower this morning, looking clean and scrubbed. The dark shirt Mike lent him made him look more capable somehow, a little dark and sinister. And sexy. With the long sleeves rolled up to reveal his cocoa-colored forearms, the shirt fit him better than she expected. And then, walking through the woodlands today, her vision had been filled with his strong broad shoulders, tapering down to a lean waist where the jeans rode low on his hips. She'd devoured the sight of him, enjoying watching him stride ahead of her. His air of eagerness and the feeling of self-assurance—that he knew what he was doing, and no one was stopping him—was extremely appealing.

Her hat was suddenly lifted off her head and landed at her feet in the dust. Then his hat did the same. She drew in a deep breath. And tilted her head up.

Brown eyes, the color of dark, luscious chocolate, stared back at her. The tremble in her belly increased. Koen brought his hand up and laid his palm along her cheek, his thumb rested, feather-light on the spot where her pulse pounded in her throat. Could he feel how much her heart was thundering? He bent his head slightly, a slight smile on his lips. A question, really. There was no sign of the larrikin Koen now. Instead, he stared at her with serious eyes. A hint of obvious desire, a bone-deep hunger in their intensity. Her own bones seemed to dissolve at the recognition of how deep his hunger went. Because she wanted him just as badly as he wanted her.

With a mind of their own, her lips parted, and she stretched her neck so she could meet his mouth as it came down on hers.

He tasted the corner of her mouth, then his lips were gone, doing an exploration of her jawbone and down her neck. Koen hadn't shaved in a few days, and the dark stubble on his cheeks rasped over her skin, sending shudders through her body. The feeling was carnal and uncivilized. Tilting her head back, she closed her eyes and allowed the sensation of him kissing her neck to overtake her.

Lower still went his lips, down over her collarbone, until they met the top button of her shirt. Nimble fingers came up to undo the first few buttons and the blouse she'd borrowed from Bindi fell open. His mouth trailed down even further, over the lacy cup of her bra. She groaned quietly. Her breasts began to ache with need. As if he could read her mind, Koen's tongue drew lazy circles over the top of the lace, right above her nipple. His tongue was hot and moist as he suckled her through the fabric of her bra, and every nerve ending in her chest felt like it'd suddenly come alive.

Skin. She needed to feel his skin. With her eyes still closed, she tugged at the back of his shirt until it came free of his jeans. Then she let her fingers explore the breadth of his back, run up and down the ridges of his spine. He sucked even harder on her nipple, and she dug her fingernails into the muscles beneath his shoulder blades.

His mouth came back to hers, and he kissed her fiercely, demanding. Both hands went beneath her buttocks, and he picked her up and backed her against the rock wall. She felt the cool rasp of the stone through her shirt. Legs wrapped around his waist, she heard the hoarse sound of his breathing. Or was it hers? Strong arms supported her weight easily, his thighs were driven up against her legs, holding her in place.

She was losing her mind. Everything was Koen. Nothing else mattered. Not the fact they were outside in the open, where anyone might see them. Not the fact he had her pushed up against a rock wall. Not the fact that she never intended to do this with Koen. She'd never intended to get close to anyone, not while all she wanted was her freedom. Her freedom now seemed inconsequential to the feeling of Koen. Of him kissing her. Of his hands all over her body.

The faint sound of voices broke through her sense-addled brain. But it wasn't her who stopped the mad touching, fondling, needing. Koen ended their kiss with a grunt of frustration. Then he laid his forehead against hers and stared into her eyes.

'Bloody tourists,' he muttered.

He moved back a fraction to allow her legs to drop to the ground, but didn't let go until he was sure she was steady on her feet. When she looked down, she quickly rearranged her blouse, which was hitched half-way up her chest and did up her buttons. But her breathing was still ragged and uneven, and try as she might, it was much harder to get that under control. She noticed with some small satisfaction that Koen was struggling equally with his breathing.

He caught her eye and held it for long, drawn out seconds. 'It was probably a good thing they came, hey?'

'Why is that?' she asked.

'Because when we do have sex, I want it to be somewhere we can take our time. Enjoy each other…' His eyes still burned with the promise of what he wanted to do to her, and her mouth went dry at the thought.

* * *

The tourists looked up, surprise in their eyes as Koen and Rose shouldered past them on the trail. Koen grunted a greeting and kept going. He wasn't going to stop and hold a conversation with this young couple. They were the reason he'd stopped kissing Rose. And boy, had he been enjoying himself. So lost in the feel of her that he'd almost been prepared to take her there, up against the rock.

Maybe he owed these two people a debt of thanks after all. For stopping him just in time. Not that he had anything against sex outdoors. In fact, he thoroughly enjoyed it most of the time. But with Rose, he wanted it to be…special. Even he wasn't sure why, he just had a gut feeling he should take his time with her. Was he assuming too much? That there would be another time, a better time, where he could make love to her? Had she been as caught up in the moment as him? And when it came down to the crunch, would she refuse him?

Koen grunted and glanced back, watching Rose pick her way across the uneven pathway, her feet small and delicate in her borrowed boots, her hips swaying elegantly. Perhaps she wasn't meant for him. He quickened his step. It was time they got going. They had a long way to go today. The less time Bull had to track them down, the better.

They were almost back at the carpark when the sound of low, growling engines made him hesitate.

'What is it?' Rose asked, nearly running in to his back as he stopped to listen.

'Sounds like motorbikes. A couple of them.'

She cocked her head. 'Yep, you're probably right. So?'

'Didn't you say that Bull was part of a biker gang?'

'Yes,' she replied, but her eyebrows lifted as she suddenly understood what he was getting at.

'Well, those bikes sound a lot like Harleys.'

'Jesus, he couldn't have found us, could he?'

'I don't know, but I think we might take a peek before we barrel on into that carpark.' He took hold of her arm and guided her off the path. Both of them hunkered down low and crept at an angle through the scrubby woodland toward the edge of the carpark. He made sure he kept behind the larger trees and thicker bushes. The sound of motorbikes got louder, and then suddenly the engines cut off at the same time. Koen crept forward a few more feet until he could see glimpses of the carpark through the fluttering foliage. Rose stopped next to him, eyes wide as she too tried to make out what was going on.

'Fuck,' Koen swore softly. It was Bull. And at least two other biker mates. They'd arrayed their bikes across the entrance to the carpark, most likely to stop him and Rose from making a dash for it on their own bike. One of the black leather-clad gang members stood next to the Harleys, legs akimbo and bulging arms crossed over his chest. He was short and stocky and bald as a badger, with tattoos covering most of his bald pate. Bull and the woman who'd been in the van at the hotel, plus another mean-looking dude, were walking toward where he'd parked his bike under the shade of the big eucalyptus tree.

Koen took in the three of them, judging how he might overcome one or all of them. Now he could see him in broad daylight, Bull looked even bigger and nastier than when Koen had fought him in the hotel room. He had a thick neck, like a bull, set on shoulders wider than most doors. Perhaps that's where his name came from? The guy obviously kept in shape, muscles bulged out beneath his black t-shirt and there was no evidence of fat, not like the guy walking at his shoulder. He was also big and burly, but with a large beer-gut hanging over the top of his black leather pants. All three men wore sleeveless leather jerkins, with their patch on the back, proclaiming they were indeed from The Sinners gang.

'What are we going to do?' Rose whispered with a squeak beside him. He risked a quick glance at her. She looked terrified, like a little girl who'd just seen the bogeyman. Which was true, this was a man from her nightmares. Her parents had tried to scare her with their stories of him, but she hadn't believed them. Until now, when the apparition she'd thought mere fantasy had morphed into a terrible reality right in front of her eyes. He put a comforting arm around her shoulder and drew her in. Small tremors ran through her shoulders, but she kept her bright gaze trained on the approaching trio, narrowing her eyes as she weighed them all up. She was scared, yes. But she wasn't going to let that stop her from doing what needed to be done.

How to get around these men who stood in the way of their freedom? There was always a way out. A way to circumvent a situation. He knew this from years of practice. Koen needed time to work out a plan, that was all, and one was already starting to form. The stocky man was still in the middle of the road, guarding the only exit out of the carpark. And Bull and his girlfriend, or whatever she was, and the other bloke was now standing next to his bike, staring at it. Confirming it was the one they were looking for, probably. He needed a distraction.

'Can you ride a motorbike?' he whispered.

'Yes.' She nodded.

Good. One part of his plan slotted into place. Bull looked

up, toward the spot where the walking path disappeared into the bush and pointed. Then all three of them moved toward the pathway, arranging themselves around the opening, leaving his motorbike unattended. Bull obviously thought they'd get the jump on them as they walked unawares back out into the carpark.

'I'm going to create a distraction,' he whispered low into her ear. 'Then I want you to—'

'What,' she squawked, and he almost put a hand up to cover her mouth.

Checking to make sure the three people waiting by the path hadn't heard, he glared at her. 'Like I said, I'm going to create a distraction. Lead these guys away. And you're going to jump on the bike and take off.' She shook her head angrily, but he bulldozed over her arguments, ignoring the way she narrowed her eyes dangerously at him. 'But you're not going to ride on the road.' He pointed to the stocky guy blocking the exit. 'You're going to ride cross-country, off that way, around the billabong. Hopefully, no one will follow you. Harleys aren't great for riding through the bush. I'm hoping they won't risk damaging their precious machines.'

'And what are you going to do while I'm getting away?' she asked softly, her voice deceptively calm.

'I'm going to take off into the bush that way. They'll follow me and leave you alone.'

'Great. Just great. What an amazing plan, Koen.' Her voice was no longer calm. Instead, she was snarling like a cornered cat. 'You're going to get caught, so I can get away. Is that correct?'

'Slow down there, girl. I don't plan on getting caught. Those big blokes there, they won't be able to catch me when I'm running through the bush. I know my way around. They're just big city blokes who haven't got a clue.' He was hoping what he was saying was true. He was light and nimble and quick on his feet. Knew his way around the Kakadu scrublands. They were slow and fat and wouldn't stand a chance. 'Besides, it's you he's after, not me. As soon as he figures out it's me he's chasing, they'll leave me alone. I'll meet you back at Bindi's place. Do you remember how to get there?'

'I can probably find my way,' she admitted. 'But how—'

He didn't let her finish. 'Don't worry about me. I'm good at this kind of thing. It's what I do.' More is the shame. Who would've believed his skills at running and hiding would come in handy? He bent his head and planted a fierce kiss on her mouth. 'You ready, girl? You can do this. I'll meet you back at Bindi's place.'

She nodded, but she didn't look happy. Not one little bit. He dug in his jeans pocket and pushed the keys to his bike into her hand. This was going to work. It had to.

'I'm going to creep around in the bush and come out over there.' He pointed to a spot on the opposite side of the car park. 'I'm going to walk out as if I didn't know they were there, spot them, and then turn around and run back into the bush as fast as my little legs will carry me. You need to wait ten or so seconds, until they start to follow me, then jump on the bike and you ride like hell.' He grabbed her hand, holding it tight. 'Don't stop for nothing. Keep off the walking trails, head for the thickest scrub you can, it'll put them off your trail and hopefully they won't be up to following you. It's a good dirt bike, strong, it can handle the rough stuff.'

Rose was no longer looking at him, her shrewd gaze directed at the men in the car park, but her fingers were slippery with sweat in his grasp.

'If you follow the billabong all the way around, you'll eventually come out on the main road back to Jabiru. But remember, don't get too close to the water. Watch out for them big crocodiles. Then you hightail it back there. Don't you stop for nothing,' he repeated.

'Koen, this is crazy.' She stared at him, her blue eyes the same color as the sky. He wanted to kiss her again, but instead pushed her away. Took a step backward.

'I'll see you soon.'

'Koen, wait…'

Without looking back, he made his way on stealthy feet through the scrub until he was near the spot he'd pointed out to Rose. Bull and his other mates hadn't moved. Good. Taking a deep breath, he pushed his hat more firmly onto his head. Time to do this thing. Hopefully Rose did what she was told, then all of this might have a happy ending.

He started walking, making as much noise as possible, crashing through the bush and careening out into the car park. Then he stopped, as if seeing the group for the first time. Checked that they'd all seen him, and turned and ran back into the bush.

* * *

Rose watched as Koen appeared between two trees, making as much noise as a bull in a china shop. Then he made a pantomime of stopping and staring, eyes wide, before turning around and running back into the bush. There was no way his plan was going to work. Bull wasn't stupid enough to fall for this. But to her utmost surprise, the woman with Bull turned around and yelled at the sight of Koen. Then she and the other two men took off after Koen's disappearing back.

Flashes of dark blue showed Koen's progress through the scrubland until finally Rose could no longer see him. He was gone. With the other three hot on his tail. The guy guarding the exit was still there, but he'd turned in the direction the rest of them had gone. Rose mentally shook herself. Time for her to play her part. Please let Koen's sacrifice not be for nothing.

As quietly as possible, she crept up to the bike, crouching down low behind it, slotting the keys into position. She was surprised to see her fingers were as steady as a rock. When she first spotted Bull, she'd started to shake like a leaf. But now she had a plan to follow, something to focus on, her body was back under control. Carefully taking her hat off, she scrunched it into the front of her waistband. Took a deep breath. Stood up and was on the bike and had it started before the short guy even knew what was happening. The wheels spun in the dry leaf litter as she pulled the accelerator lever and took off into the bush in the opposite direction Koen had taken.

There were shouts behind her, but the noise quickly faded as she got further into the woodland. The billabong was on her right, she could see flashes of silvery blue through the trees as she flew by. Then she heard the sound she'd been dreading as one of the Harleys started up. Turning, she chanced a quick look behind and saw the short guy nudging his big black bike into the bush after her. But he would be no match for her. Koen's motorbike had cross-country tires on it, meant for riding in terrain such as this. It had heavy shock absorbers, and the chassis was high off the ground. It was a dirt bike, designed to take plenty of hard knocks and just keep going. The Harley, on the other hand, was sleek and shiny and low-slung, only meant to travel on smooth wide-open roads.

A line of scrubby bushes appeared in front of her. She pulled the brake lever hard, leaned the bike on its side and slewed around the edge, spitting out a trail of dust and debris behind her. Now she was heading straight for the billabong. She hit the accelerator and gunned it toward the water. At the last second, she slammed on the brakes and swung left around the trunk of a large tree. Adrenaline was coursing through her veins. Fizzing like bubbles, and it made her feel alive. And free. The wind tugged at her ponytail, leaving strands of hair to fly around her face. Another large tree appeared in front of her and this time she swung the bike sideways around the left of the tree, then kept going.

Instinct took over, years of riding motorbikes on the farm helping her ride the bike almost on autopilot. After a few more minutes of ducking beneath low-hanging branches, wheeling around trees and piles of sandstone, she was deep into the bush. Keeping the billabong to her right-hand side, she kept going, following Koen's orders, knowing that as long as she did so, she'd eventually come to the main road again. Then it hit her, the sound of the Harley had died away. The guy following her had either given up on the chase or got completely lost. Either way, she was on her own. How was Koen faring? Had he got away too? There was only one way to find out. She didn't have time to think about the repercussions of what might happen if Bull did catch Koen. The only thing on her mind now was to make it to Bindi's in one piece.

CHAPTER FIFTEEN

Rose slowed the bike once she was sure she wasn't being followed. She didn't want to kill herself, after all. It took her another fifteen minutes to circumnavigate the billabong. She had to backtrack a few times when the ground became too boggy to ride through. But eventually the trees began to thin, and she could see a sliver of asphalt ahead. Was this the road to Jabiru? She wasn't one-hundred percent sure. Koen had taken a few turns on the way here, and she hadn't been paying attention.

Where were Bull and his gang? Were they still blundering around in the bush, chasing Koen? Or had they given up in disgust and left the area? The only sound was that of her motorbike as it idled beneath her, as if waiting for her command. The savannah woodland stretched away from her on all sides, flat and unforgiving. And unhelpful. An eerie silence seemed to hang in the heat haze that shimmered above the road. She was completely alone. Reaching around, she pulled her phone out of her back pocket. Shit. No signal. She needed to call her mother and let her know what was going on. To warn her. She wished her mother were here right now. Which was strange. For most of her life she'd wished her mother far away, or at least far enough away to give her some breathing space. Now, when she was scared out of her mind, she realized she wanted her mother's solid presence to keep her safe. Nothing ever seemed to faze Jenna. Rose had never appreciated her mother's quiet dignity and strength before. It was a revelation to find out she missed it.

Rose was scared. Scared to go forward. Scared to go back. But she couldn't leave Koen. And she couldn't sit here forever. Forward it was going to have to be. Releasing the handbrake, she kicked the bike into gear and took off down the road, not sure what she might find ahead.

Nearly forty-five minutes later, Rose breathed a sigh of relief as she saw the sign welcoming her back to Jabiru. She'd made it with no hint of Bull or any black Harleys. Slowing down to the town speed limit, Rose sat back on the bike and tried to remember the best way to get to Bindi's house. The road was flat and wide in front of her, the dry bushland still marching on either side. Low houses huddled in the distance, the start of suburbia.

Would Koen be waiting for her at Bindi's? She had no idea how he was going to get there. It was too far to walk. But like he said, he was a resourceful guy. Perhaps he'd hitch a ride with a tourist. God, she hoped he wasn't stupid enough to try and steal one of the Harleys. That would be the last straw. If he was irreverent enough to steal a bike from under Bull's nose, who knew what the man might do. No, she'd probably have to wait for Koen. It might be hours before he found his way back to town. Perhaps she could ask Bindi to go back and get him. Would Bindi still be at home, or would she have already left for work?

A shadowy figure stepped in to the road in front of her. Rose's heart leapt in her chest, started beating double-time. Then the figure became clearer as she throttled the bike down through the gears and it separated into two shapes. One of them Bull. The other one, Koen. Now her heart stopped beating altogether and her breath froze in her throat. Bull was holding a knife to Koen's throat and had his left arm pulled up behind his back. Rose could see the grimace on Koen's face. Whether it was from pain or fear, she didn't know. Rose glanced wildly around, looking for someone or something to help her. But the road was empty of cars, not a soul in sight. An evil grin spread across Bull's bearded face.

She had no choice. She pulled the bike to a stop in front of him. One of his gang members sidled out from behind a large tree next to the road.

'You can give the bike to Snake, over there.' Bull snarled. 'Then you can come along like a good little girl and do what you're told. Otherwise…' Bull didn't need to finish the sentence, his meaning was crystal clear.

'I'm sorry, Rose,' Koen rasped.

'Shut up, you black punk.' Bull yanked on Koen's arm and he gave a yell of pain. He was covered in dust, shirt ripped, a dark bruise forming on his cheek. Blood trickled from a split in his lip. It looked like he'd put up a fight. But Bull had triumphed in the end. A wave of nausea washed over Rose, and she felt as if a great weight had landed on her chest. Bone-numbing lethargy took over as she passed the bike to Snake. He pushed it further into the bush and hid it behind a thicket of thorny shrubs. She watched dully, a small part of her registering the tattoo of a snake winding up the man's neck, its evil forked tongue resting just below the guy's left ear. This was it. It was over.

'Just do what you're told and you won't be forced to watch your hero here die.'

A small groan escaped her lips. She knew she'd do whatever it took to keep Koen safe.

* * *

The room was dim, even though the bright midday sun was still shining outside. They must have taped sheets of black plastic over the window, Koen thought vaguely. He lay on the floor, trussed up better than a chicken at a Christmas feast. These bastards had tied him up so tight his arms were already going numb. Koen didn't know exactly where they were, but it was most likely the biker's clubhouse. They were back in Darwin, on the outskirts somewhere. That much Koen had seen from the back of the bike as they'd rumbled into town.

He'd been forced to sit behind the gang member called Snake, with his hands tied around his middle so there was no way he could jump off. The same had been done to Rose. She'd sat behind another guy with a flat featureless face, called Mongrel. Bull hadn't blindfolded them, probably because he didn't want to attract any undue attention. So Koen was able to see where they were going. But it hadn't helped him, as they'd ended up in an industrial area of Darwin he'd never visited before.

He turned on his side, as much as the ropes would allow. 'Rose,' he called softly. There was no answer, but he heard a shuffling sound as if she was moving around. 'Rose,' he called again. 'Are you okay?' They hadn't been allowed to speak to each other as they'd been frog-marched into the building surrounded by high metal walls. And no one had spoken to them as they'd been shoved into the darkened room and then tied up like pigs on a spit and left on the floor like garbage. Rose hadn't seemed physically harmed, but she had a look about her, as if she was in a trance. She was lying on the far side of the room, also tied at the ankles and wrists. There was no furniture in the room, not even a chair or a bed. What was this room used for? The few ideas that came to mind made him shudder. They needed to get out of here. 'Rose,' he called for the third time, anxious now.

'What?' she asked flatly.

'Are you okay?'

'Yes, I'm fine.' Her voice was low, her tone almost

uncaring.

'I'm so sorry.' He wanted to say more, but wasn't sure where to start. It was all his fault they'd been caught. He was stupid and arrogant. Thought he'd be able to easily outrun them. Thought that Bull was too city-boy to keep up with him. After all, he was in his element, out there in the bush. He'd been on his way back to steal one of the Harleys after leading them a merry chase through the scrub, but hadn't figured on Bull doubling back and lying in wait for him. He would've been okay, could've beat Bull if it was only one-on-one. But then the one with the flat face, expressionless eyes, and a fist as hard as a hammer had caught up to them and it was all over. The guy had crash-tackled him to the ground, then started pounding into him while Bull looked on and laughed.

'It's not your fault,' she said. 'You did everything you could. And it isn't even your fight. I dragged you into this. It's my fault. And I'm the one who should be sorry.' She sounded like she'd given up. Which wasn't good. None of this blame-game stuff was going to help them. They needed to start focusing on the future. How to get out of here. Alive.

He needed something to pick her up, to get her centered and thinking again. 'You sure kicked some butt out there today, girl. I saw you. It was like you were riding in a motor-cross race, or something. Where did you learn to ride a bike like that?' He'd seen flashes of her when he scrambled on top of a boulder. Followed the sound of the motorbike and saw her racing through the scrubland, leaving the other guy on the Harley for dead in her dust. It was true, she was amazing. Not many other girls he knew would've been capable of such a feat.

'Not really. No need to flatter me, Koen,' she answered. But there was a hint of lightness back in her voice. 'I learnt to ride on the farm.'

'Yeah, well, you certainly got more balls than most guys I know.'

'How about you? Are you okay? Did they hurt you much?' Her voice had a hint of concern now, which was good. She seemed to be coming back to life again.

'Nah, a few scratches that's all.' And mostly that was the truth. She didn't need to know about the searing pain in his shoulder where Bull had pulled his arm too far up behind his back and nearly dislocated it, or the chipped tooth from where Mongrel had smashed him in the face. Or that he may even have a broken rib or two.

She laughed. 'That seems to be the story of your life. You're always getting *just a few scratches*.'

'Yeah, maybe.' He didn't like to admit it, but there was a pattern emerging.

'How about the gash from before, where Bull sliced you with the knife?'

He'd almost forgotten about that, with all his new injuries. 'It's fine,' he replied. 'But we need to think about how we're gonna get outta here.'

'I don't think we are.' Her voice was small.

'Of course we are—'

The door crashed open and Bull stalked into the room carrying a chair, followed by his girlfriend. The woman with so many tattoos he could scarcely see an inch of bare skin.

'How are you guys enjoying the hospitality? Hope the boys made you feel at home,' Bull said with a sneer. Putting the chair down, he straddled it so he could rest his arms on the back and look down on them. The tattooed woman took up a spot in the corner, leaning against the wall, looking for all the world as if she was about to watch some sort of interesting sport. Koen ignored the woman and focused completely on Bull.

'We're all good, mate. Be better if you took these ropes off us, though. How about it?' He didn't really expect an answer, but would do anything to keep the mood light.

'Perhaps if you behave yourself, I might just do that,' Bull said, to his surprise. 'But for now, you can just shut up and listen while I have a chat with your girlfriend.'

Rose muttered something unintelligible from the other side of the room. Koen had swiveled around to look at Bull, and now he could only see Rose out of the corner of his eye. But he could feel the rage emanating from her. She was pissed off. Good. Anger was better than giving in.

'What are you going to do with us?' she demanded.

Bull just laughed. 'Well now, I'm not too sure of the details, but let me assure you, I do mean to see you die, eventually.'

Rose gasped. Even Koen was shocked to hear him utter the words so blatantly. This really was one fucked up dude they were dealing with.

'Once I have your mother and your grandmother, then we can all play happy families together. And you can all die together,' he added with a snigger.

'You bastard,' Rose ground out between her teeth. 'Why? Why would you want to do that? We've done nothing to you to deserve that. We—'

'Shut up, you little bitch. You know exactly what you've done to me and why you deserve to die. Or hasn't your wonderful mother told you the story? I wouldn't be surprised if she kept the truth from you. After all, no parent wants their child to know that they're a killer.'

'Yeah, you ruined his life. You did. It's time you bitches all paid for what you did.' Koen was surprised to hear the girlfriend speak. Her voice was almost as venomous as Bull's.

'I don't need your help,' Bull snarled. 'If you can't shut up, then leave.' The woman glowered at Bull, but said nothing more.

'How can you think any of what happened in Margaret

River is my grandmother's fault? She was just defending herself against Alexander. He was brutal, a violent narcissist who was trying to abduct her,' Rose said quietly.

'Ah, so you have heard her version of the story, then? Interesting.' Bull tapped a blunt finger against the side of his cheek. 'But that's not how I saw it. I saw her push him over the edge of the cliff. She killed him. She killed my father, took away my life, and sent me to jail for four long years. She needs to pay for that. You all need to pay for that.'

Wow, this guy really was as crazy as Rose said. Keeping a grudge for twenty years, letting it fester and grow inside him until it completely consumed him. Koen almost felt sorry for him. It was no way to live, with revenge driving everything he did.

Rose sputtered, as if she couldn't find the right words to argue against his insanity, but he didn't let her speak.

'There's nothing you can say that will change my mind so you may as well save your breath.'

'You won't get away with this. How on earth do you plan to get away with this? You can't just kill somebody and not expect any repercussions. The cops will be all over you.' Rose's voice was low and incredulous, and Koen had to agree with her. He'd met some bad dudes in his time, but was this guy really serious about murdering them?

Bull chuckled. 'I have my methods. Let's just say that me and some very well-fed crocodiles have an understanding.'

Koen shuddered. He hated crocodiles. Such ancient, cold-blooded, predatory creatures. Capable of ripping a body to pieces in no time at all.

'There's a swamp over at the edge of the park where no one else goes. Your bodies would never be found. If there was anything left of them, that is.' Bull gave another evil laugh.

Koen cast a quick glance in Rose's direction, trying to gauge her reaction. But she was completely silent. It sounded like this wasn't the first time Bull had done this. Grudging respect for the man's evilness bloomed in Koen's chest. He'd underestimated him before. He wouldn't do it again. Now they really needed to get out of here.

'We'll just wait here till your parents ride in to rescue you. They're so stupid and so desperate, it'll be like shooting fish in a tank.' Bull's eyes glazed over, and a small smile spread across his face as he seemed to be imagining capturing Rose's family.

'They won't be stupid enough to fall for your tricks,' Rose shouted.

'Ah, but that's where you're wrong, they'll come, just you wait and see.'

'That's bullshit. How do you know that? You can't possibly know that,' Koen yelled, agreeing with Rose.

Bull tapped the side of his nose. 'I have my eyes and ears, my little spies. A friend here and there in the wonderful police constabulary. Everyone has a price. Or a weakness. And any fool can listen in to a police radio. As long as you have the right equipment, it's not hard.'

Koen's mind was racing. Rose mentioned her parents had a friend in the police force in the town of Karratha. If her parents had been talking to this friend and there was a corrupt cop in the office passing on information, then Bull might've indeed known their every move. It could explain a lot.

'Is that how you found us in Jabiru?' Koen asked.

'That was me.' The girlfriend spoke up from behind Koen. 'I got your number plate when you sped out of the car park that night,' she said with obvious glee. 'And then I told Bull to report the motorbike stolen. So, when the police got a report the bike was seen in Jabiru, we took it from there.'

'Yeah, yeah, whatever, Alesha.' The woman flinched as Bull spoke, probably expecting him to send her out of the room.

But he only flipped a quick glance in her direction, then continued in a thoughtful tone. 'I think that's enough for today.' Bull got up and, taking his chair, opened the door, ushering Alesha in front of him. But instead of slamming it shut, Bull dropped the chair and returned into the room, holding something that jangled in his hands. He knelt down in front of Koen, who flinched back as a knife appeared in Bull's hand. Fuck, was he going to murder them now? Had he changed his mind? Instead, Koen felt the ropes around his wrists being cut. Before he could react, Bull had snapped a set of handcuffs around his wrists. Then he cut the ropes at Koen's ankles.

'What's going on? What are you doing to him?' Rose shouted from across the room.

Bull ignored her. 'Get over here,' he commanded, practically dragging Koen across the floor, then pulling his arms up until he was sitting against the wall. Then a chain clanked above his head, and the next thing Koen knew, he'd been handcuffed to a bolt in the wall. Obviously put there for this exact purpose. He stretched out his legs, moaning as they burned with pins and needles from the tight ropes.

'It's okay, Rose, he's not hurting me. He's not going to hurt you, either,' he called as Bull strode over to the corner where Rose lay.

She screamed as she caught sight of the knife, but then regained her composure and glowered at him, saying nothing, while he cut the ropes.

If escape had been hard to contemplate before, now any hope of getting away was gone. These were police-issue hardened steel handcuffs—Koen knew from past experience —and there was no way they were breaking out of these. They were in all kinds of deep shit now.

CHAPTER SIXTEEN

God, she was uncomfortable. Rose squirmed her hips around, trying to ease the ache in her lower back. But her discomfort didn't matter. Because she was almost free.

'Koen,' Rose called quietly. She waited, but when he didn't answer, she called a little louder. 'Koen.'

'What?' His head snapped up from his chest.

Had he fallen a sleep? How could he fall asleep here? When they were in such a dire predicament. And in such a posture, slumped against the wall, with his hands tied above his head. But then she remembered he'd been through a lot in the past few days. They both had, but he'd been through more. They'd both only had half a night's sleep last night, after he'd ridden through the night to get them to Jabiru. Injured, with a slash across the ribs. And now he'd been beaten again. God knew what other injuries he might have sustained that he wouldn't tell her about.

Her initial reaction faded, replaced by a feeling of gratitude and the sense of a debt that she owed him. And a sudden fierce need to protect him rose up as she stared at him.

'I think I might...' She stopped, suddenly unsure if she should say the words out loud. What if someone was listening at the door? Or they had a bugging device in the room? She'd scanned the room for an obvious camera earlier but hadn't found one. 'How long do you think they'll keep us here,' she asked instead. But while she listened for Koen's answer, she kept working at the handcuffs. They were loose around her wrists. Very loose.

At first, when Bull had snapped them on, she'd felt only utter defeat and let her arms hang, the handcuffs biting painfully in her skin. No one could get out of handcuffs. Police used them on hardened criminals. They weren't supposed to be broken out of. Ever.

But when the pain had become too great, she moved her arms, trying to ease the ache. That's when she discovered how loose they were. She was a small woman, had often bemoaned the fact that she was never tall enough to reach anything on the top shelf in the kitchen. And she also had very small hands. Petite hands. But were they small enough to be able to slip through the handcuffs?

Slowly and carefully, in case anyone came in, she'd worked her hands around in the cuffs, trying different angles, contorting her fingers into all kinds of strange positions. With a bit of grease or Vaseline, she'd probably be able to slip them off. But she had none of that in here. Suddenly an idea formed, and she pulled herself up and spat on her hands. She did it a few times, and she was almost sure she was going to be able to get free.

She didn't know exactly what time it was, but many hours had passed since Bull had issued his dire threats, then locked them into the handcuffs. No one had been back in to the room since then. Not even to bring them any water or food. And Rose was busting to go to the toilet. She was scared if she waited much longer, she might just end up wetting herself. It'd been around noon when they'd first been brought into the…well, whatever this place was. A biker clubhouse, probably. The high walls topped with barbed wire she'd seen as they'd been brought in on the back of the Harleys was some indication. At a guess, it was probably just after sundown, although it was hard to tell with the plastic covering the windows.

There was a constant nagging fear eating away at the edges of her conscience. A need to call her mother. To warn her. To keep her grandmother safe. To stop them from doing something stupid and coming to help her. But Bull had taken both their phones and their wallets. If she wanted to keep her family safe, she needed to convince them to stay on the farm. Her mum would be starting to worry by now. Rose was supposed to check in with them on the way back down to the station. At the very least, she was supposed to ring them when they stopped for the night. She could see her mother's face, the faint lines around her blue eyes creased with worry. Her faithful dog sitting at her feet, like an extension of her mistress. Jello was almost like a confidant for Jenna. But neither her dog nor her father would be able to stop her if she got an idea in her head. It would be just like her mum to jump into the car and drive to Darwin if she didn't hear from Rose. Which was exactly what Bull wanted, and exactly what Rose had to stop.

Did Bull plan to leave them here all night? With no food and no water? She wouldn't put it past him. But his mistreatment might just aid in their escape. If no one came into the room, then no one could see what she was up to.

She wanted to tell Koen the good news about her handcuffs, but was terrified someone would overhear her. But she needed to know what to do if she did get free. Because Koen would still be handcuffed to the wall. How was she going to help him?

'I don't know,' he replied sleepily. 'But I think we might be a little bit fucked. Unless you can come up with something. I've plain run out of ideas.'

As he spoke, Rose continued to tug and wind her hands

through the cuffs, until all of a sudden, with one big pull, her left hand slipped free. She scraped the skin off the edge of her thumb and one of her knuckles, but her hand was free.

'Koen,' she breathed. 'Look over here.' She put her finger to her lips in a sign to be quiet as he turned to stare at her. Quickly, she held her hand aloft, waved her fingers in the air to show she was free, then just as quickly pulled her hand back down so it looked like she was still in handcuffs if anyone happened to walk in.

Koen's eyes widened, and he let out a low whistle. He said nothing, but his eyebrows rose in admiration as he started to contemplate options, run through scenarios. Hope was back in his face. Rose started to work on her other hand, using more spit to lubricate it. This one was tighter, and she was probably going to scrape off more skin getting her hand out. It took another five minutes of twisting and pulling, but then her right hand came free. It hurt. She almost had to dislocate her thumb in the process. But the pain was overwritten with the pure elation that surged through her. She was free. But what now? Nervously, she kept her hands next to the handcuffs as she planned her next move.

'Psst,' Koen called to her. 'Are you free?'

She nodded in reply, a large grin splitting her face. The urge to shout and jump with joy shook her, but she managed to stay seated on the ground, grinning like a maniac at him. Then her mood plummeted. Koen was still bound and trapped. And there was no way she was going to leave him here.

As if reading her mind, he said, 'Great. Well done, girl. Now you gotta get out of here, as fast as you can.'

'I'm not leaving without you.'

'Don't be stupid, Rose, you're free. I'm not about to just slip out of my handcuffs, not with these big hands. And aside from getting the key, that's about the only other way to get out of here.'

'I'm not going,' she replied stubbornly. 'I'm going to get you out of here, too.'

'Look, if you get out now, you can go and find help. Bring the cavalry back to save me, you know. You can be my knight in shining armor.' He gave her that devil-may-care grin as if he was describing an adventure, not giving her permission to leave him here to the mercies of a crazed killer.

'No,' she replied. 'I'm not arguing with you, I'm not leaving without you.' Still sitting on the floor, pretending her hands were in the cuffs, in case someone came in, she shifted her weight, getting ready to stand up.

'Shit, girl.' His grin morphed into an angry frown. 'Has anyone told you how stubborn you can be?'

'Once or twice.' She grinned back at him. Getting to her feet, she rubbed at her raw wrists while she walked over to him. She caught the glimmer of his eyes in the dim light as he watched her approach. And in those eyes, she could see a kernel of an idea forming.

'If you can find something long and thin, I might be able to pick the locks on these handcuffs,' he said.

Rose didn't ask, but she got the impression he might have done something similar in his past. 'Like what,' she asked.

'Like a hairpin or a paperclip, preferably made of metal if you can.'

'Right.' Where the hell was she going to get something like that? There was nothing in this room. Kept clean for just this reason so a prisoner couldn't escape. She did a quick circuit of the room anyway, just to make sure. Coming up empty-handed, she said jokingly, 'I'm going to go find something. Don't go anywhere.'

He looked at her with concern showing in ridges around his mouth, but nodded and said, 'Be careful.'

She planned to be that and more. If she got caught now,

there'd never be a second chance at escape. Taking a few deep breaths, she laid her fingertips on the door handle and twisted it slowly. The door opened a crack, and she put her eye to the slot. There was a long corridor outside. It was deserted. She could hear the faint sounds of what might have been a television coming from the door at the end of the corridor. Taking a deep breath, she opened the door wider. A loud laugh came from behind the same door and Rose drew back in fright. But after a few seconds, when no one appeared, she decided it was now or never.

There were three or four other doors leading off the main corridor. She may as well start with the one right opposite. Slipping through the door, she closed it quietly behind her.

* * *

Time seemed to have slowed down. The seconds ticked away like drops of treacle from a can. Where was Rose? Why was she taking so long? Had she been caught? He hadn't heard any kind of kerfuffle. He should never have let her go. But then, there was no way he could've stopped her. Bloody stubborn woman.

The door suddenly opened quietly, stealthily, and he tensed, shifting his feet, ready to attack if it came to it. Rose's face appeared in the crack and he almost sighed out loud with relief.

'I've got something. It's a hairpin, I think it must belong to Alesha. I found it on the floor in their bedroom.'

'You went into their bedroom?' he gasped in horror.

She nodded impatiently. 'I think they're all down the corridor, watching Telly.'

'Well done,' he said quickly. She'd gone out to find something, and she'd done it. That was all that mattered. She held it up where he could reach it with his handcuffed hands. Pulling himself up, so his face was level with his hands, he started working on the hairpin. First, he nipped at the rubber tip with his teeth until it came off. Then he bent one arm of the pin at a forty-five-degree angle with his fingers. Finally, he took the tip in his teeth again and bent the end to ninety degrees. Now he had a pseudo-key with which to pick the lock. He put the pin about halfway into the lock and tried to maneuver it, so it put rotational pressure on the internal lock bars. He'd been shown how to do this by a mate one day when they were mucking around. But he'd never thought he'd use the half-learned skill for real. He'd never asked his mate how he learnt to do it. Or where he got the handcuffs from.

'This might take a little time,' he muttered, tongue between his teeth.

'I'll go and watch at the door,' she said helpfully. Although what she was going to do if someone came along the corridor, Koen didn't know.

It was tricky doing it with both his hands constricted as they were, but after only a couple of minutes he felt something give in the left-hand cuff. The one bolted to the wall. It took a few seconds for him to realize. He was now free, with the cuffs still dangling from his right wrist. He stood up quickly and made his way over to Rose. She looked around in shock, which turned to delight when she saw him up and walking.

'Oh, thank God,' she breathed. Then surprised him by throwing her arms around his neck and burying her face in his chest. He could feel the light tremble running through her body. She was scared. A mixture of fear and anticipation showed on her fine features as she pulled back to stare at him. A stupid urge to kiss her stopped him in his tracks. Her mouth was just there, and she was looking at him with wonder and relief. Blue eyes wide and sensual.

Not the time, Koen. They'd achieved the first part of the plan, but now came the hard part. Getting out of here. Alive.

This place was probably like Fort Knox. But hopefully it was meant to stop people coming in, more than people trying to get out.

'I think the exit is to the right,' she whispered. 'There's a door at the end which looks like it might lead to some kind of storeroom, then out to the courtyard. I had a peek when I came out of their bedroom.'

He nodded. 'That sounds good,' he agreed.

But then what? How did they get out of the fortified compound? It was more than likely alarmed, possibly with security cameras. He tried to think. When they'd come in, someone had opened the large gates to let all the bikes through, but he thought he remembered seeing a smaller door set off to the side of the gate. It was a large courtyard, with room enough to park twenty or more motorbikes easily. Buildings formed the other three sides of the compound, all made from blank metal, painted dark gray, probably to make it look even more intimidating than it already did. He and Rose had been led straight into the right-hand building, and from what Rose told him, Koen thought this wing might be a section for the commanders of the club. And their *guests*. The other wings might be for the lower members of the gang. Koen had seen two gang members come out of the left wing just as they were led away, which strengthened his conviction. From the little Koen knew about biker gangs, they all wore patches on their jackets, proclaiming their affiliation, as well as any rank. Bull had mentioned in all his bluster and bragging after he caught them that he was high up in the hierarchy of the club, which meant he was possibly the vice-president, or even the president of this little chapter.

Perhaps there was a back way out of this place. But did they really want to go bumbling around in the dark and perhaps alert whatever bikers inhabited this compound to their presence? No guards had been placed on their door, which told Koen they never expected a break out. No one had ever escaped before. There was a first for everything, however, and Koen planned on this first escape from The Sinner's compound to be a success. They stood just inside the doorway, hopefully hidden from any guard who might be patrolling the courtyard as they contemplated their next move. The faint sound of music drifted to him from the left-hand building. Definitely people in there, too.

'Could we steal one of the Harleys?' Rose whispered thoughtfully.

'No, that wouldn't work. The sound would alert them too quickly.' He chewed at his lip while he stared out into the dark courtyard. 'And we don't know how to get the gate open.' As his eyes adjusted, he let his gaze roam over the fortified walls, assessing them, documenting their strengths and looking for weaknesses. A lone street light cast a dull glow from behind the gate, showing the metal structure in eerie back-lit shadows, adding to the sinister feel of the place. A bare lightbulb hung above a doorway in the section Koen thought of as the members' quarters. It, too, caused flickering shadows to hover around the edges of its glow. A roll of heavy barbed wire ran along the top of the tall metal gate. They wouldn't be scaling that wall easily. He located the small door to the side of the gate. They were too far away to see in clear detail, but it looked like a heavy padlock kept that door locked. He could possibly pick the padlock with his little pseudo-key, but that might take some time. Time they didn't have, but he kept it at the back of his mind as an option. Then he saw it. Over in the corner on the other side of the large gate where the barbed wire met a brick wall. More barbed wire ran along the top of the bricks, but in the corner, there was a small gap. But how to get up there? In the time they'd been standing here, he hadn't seen any movement. No sign of a guard. But that didn't mean there wasn't one. There were too many dark shadows someone could hide in and not be seen. They'd have to go slowly and carefully. Take their chances.

'Follow me,' he whispered. She groped for his hand in the dark and he wound his fingers through hers, then pulled her behind him, keeping the dangling pair of handcuffs tight in his other hand, to stop any clanking noise they might make.

Bending at the knees, he crept along, keeping to the recesses and deep shadows cast by the overhanging roof. In some ways, the courtyard was arranged in a pattern that was almost a godsend in disguise. The motorbikes were all lined up against the back building and they made great hiding places as Koen and Rose slipped, wraithlike, in and out of the machines, avoiding the glow from the light as best they could. A stack of large oil drums piled into the far corner also made a great place to hide as they worked their way around the enclosure. Koen stopped and cast another shrewd glance around. So far, so good. It didn't look like they had posted a guard after all. Perhaps not expecting any trouble. Or perhaps it was just arrogance in the extreme. Which sounded like Bull.

Now they had to get past that naked light overhanging the door. There was a window on either side of the door. Anyone looking out of a window would see them as they ran past. Curtains were drawn in both windows and one room was black, no one in there. But there was light and noise coming from behind the curtains of the second room. It sounded like the gang members might be having dinner. There was the clatter of plates and the clang of cutlery mixed with the voices of men. This was where the music was coming from, a heavy metal band. But all this noise might be a good thing, as it would cover any sound he and Rose made. As long as no one saw them.

'We're going to crawl underneath the windows,' he said quietly into Rose's ear. And just hope and pray no one walked out the door at the wrong moment. He kept that thought to himself. She nodded her understanding, and they crept to the edge of the building, then got down onto their hands and knees in the dust. Rose kept so close to him, her forehead kept bumping against the back of his thigh. She must be terrified, but she was doing a good job at keeping a lid on her emotions. His respect for her grew. She was tougher than she thought. Even the way she stood up on that stage and sung for her supper proved she had courage in spades. It took a lot to bare your soul like that. But now, she was proving her bravery tenfold. Most girls he knew, would be a blubbering mess by now. But not Rose. She just kept on going. Getting the job done.

They inched their way along, keeping their heads low beneath the sill of the window. Koen was hampered by the handcuffs still attached to his wrist, so he went slowly, to make sure they didn't clank against the ground and give them away. They passed the window with no lights. Koen found he was holding his breath as they came to the doorway. Exhaling quietly through his lips, he glanced quickly behind him at Rose. When she nodded, he surged forward, feeling the gravel scuff up his palms and dig into his knees, even through the fabric of his jeans. He kept going, not daring to stop beneath the next window where all the men were eating, hoping Rose kept up with him. Then he was in the far corner of the enclosure, where the building met the wall.

They'd done it. He stood up, keeping to the deep shadow in the corner. He felt Rose stand up behind him. Now they just needed to get onto the roof and then over the wall. Feeling around blindly, Koen's fingers met something hard and plastic. A garbage bin perhaps? Half afraid of what he might find, he gingerly felt around the object. Yes, definitely a large bin of some kind, with a flat lid closed down on top of it. Hopefully, it was strong enough to meet their needs.

'Come over here,' he said in a hoarse whisper. 'Help me with this.' It was too dark in this corner to see anything more than shapes moving against darker shapes. Her hands felt along his back, and then ran down his arms to come to rest against his own fingertips. 'We need to move this over a bit, so it's directly under the eaves,' he said.

Being as quiet as possible, they moved the heavy bin between them, until it was directly under the guttering of the roof above. Despite their best efforts, they still made a few loud creaks and bangs as they shifted the plastic object. Every time they made a noise, they stilled and listened, afraid they'd been heard. Thank God for that music playing in the building next door.

'Right,' Koen said as soon as the garbage bin was in place. 'I'm going to help you up on top of this, and then I want you to climb up onto the roof. Can you do that?'

She just snorted in derision. Of course, how could he ever have doubted her? He gave a wide smile, knowing she wouldn't see it in the dark. He helped her clamber up on the plastic container, which was mid-chest height on him, placing one hand under her bum, the other under her elbow to steady her. Her bum was soft and round, small enough that he could nearly span one cheek in the palm of his hand. It brought back immediate memories of kissing her against the rocks this morning. The weight of her on his thighs as he held her up. He'd like to be able to explore the plump roundness of her backside some more, but she was already standing up on the lid and he let go of her bum so he could hold on to her legs instead. She wobbled slightly, and he could now see her silhouette against the skyline, a grey form against the pinpricks of light. Then her legs lifted and disappeared as she hauled herself up onto the roof. Try as she might, she couldn't quite muffle the few grunts of exertion as she used her arms to hold her weight, then lever her legs over the side.

164

He lost sight of her then and assumed she remained prostrate along the edge of the roof. Clever girl, it would minimize her being spotted from below as well as curtail any noise she might make. Luckily, the roof was made of clay tiles. As long as they didn't slip or dislodge a tile, they'd be able to keep the noise to a minimum as they crossed over the ridge-line and then down to the other side.

Now it was his turn. Normally he'd make easy work of climbing up and over the guttering, but tonight he was hampered by his injuries and he had to stifle more than one gasp of pain before he finally made it onto the roof. The small gap in the barbed wire beckoned to them, and they made their way carefully up and over the roof and down to the other side, where it butted up against the high brick wall. The wall rose another five feet or so above the roof-line, a bit of a clamber, but nothing he couldn't manage.

'I'll go first, then I'll pull you up,' he said in a stage-whisper. This was a bit trickier. There wasn't a lot of room up on top of the wall, and the gap between the two rolls of barbed wire was only about ten inches. Enough for them to squeeze through, but they'd have to be bloody careful, or they'd end up with more than a few scratches by the time they made it out.

It was harder than he thought, levering himself up onto the wall, with the handcuffs still obstructing him and trying not to get snagged by the sharp teeth of the barbed wire. Glancing out over the wall, he checked the street, just to make sure. It was deserted, not many people had any need to be in this part of an industrial area after dark. He positioned himself in the gap in the wire and then reached down a hand to help Rose up. When they were both up on the wall, teetering precariously, he edged his way through the gap. Sharp teeth snagged on his shirt and a few sliced through, leaving scratches on his back and chest. He pulled free, and then he was through. Bugger. It was a long drop on the other side in to the street. At least twelve feet. Onto a hard pavement. But he should be able to do it, he'd jumped from things this high before. He'd have to take care of Rose, however.

'It's a long way down on the other side,' he said. 'Turn around and lower yourself down on your hands till you're hanging off the wall. The drop shouldn't be too far from there. I'll catch you.'

'Okay,' she replied, and he could hear the trust in her voice. Again, respect for her blossomed. And showed just how wide the gap was in their lives. He'd done this kind of thing before, enough times that he'd almost become blasé about the whole thing. Well, he'd never run from a vicious biker gang before, but he'd had his fair share of run-ins with the law, got into— and out of—more than one scrape while he was a kid. But she'd never done anything like this in her life. Ever. She was good and pure and decent. He hoped her trust in him was warranted.

Turning around, he put his back to the street and lowered himself down the wall, hanging on to the top with his fingertips until he was stretched out full and there was just air beneath his feet. Then he let go and prayed, bracing his knees, then hitting and rolling to absorb the impact. The hit on the ground caused pain to sear through his rib-cage, where Mongrel had beaten him. If the rib wasn't cracked, it was pretty bruised. Ignoring the pain, he stood up and turned around, watching as Rose gave a quick, nervous glance down, before grasping the lip of the wall and lowering herself.

'It's okay, girl. Jump, I'll catch you,' he called out.

Then lights blazed into the sky from inside the biker compound, and loud voices echoed through the night.

'Shit, they're onto us.'

CHAPTER SEVENTEEN

'Isn't it amazing?' Rose sighed. 'It kind of helps put things back into perspective, don't you think?' She kicked her legs like a child as she swung gently. They were in a kiddie playground on the edge of the ocean. A wide, sandy beach stretched out before them, the tide low, exposing shallow sand banks almost as far out as the eye could see. To their right, the sun was rising in a spectacular show of pinks and oranges and purples, painting the rippling water with its colors. Rose loved to watch the sunrise, the start of a new day, full of potential and surprise. Today, the sunrise heralded a day where she was still free from Bull, and that part alone was amazing in itself.

'If you think so,' Koen agreed half-heartedly. He was sitting on the other swing, gently pushing it forward and back with the toe of his boot. His height made him look utterly ridiculous, crammed into the child-size swing. They'd been walking all night, and both of them were exhausted. It was showing on Koen's face. The bruises from where Bull's men had beaten him were turning a nasty dark purple, lip split in two places, eyes sunken and hollow, shirt almost in tatters. He was looking worse for wear. She probably didn't look much better herself. Hair all in a tangle, blouse filthy and ripped from where it'd snagged on branches from her wild ride through the bush.

But they were alive, and for the moment Bull's henchmen were nowhere in sight. Which was a major achievement after last night. She still wasn't sure how they escaped. Just as they'd jumped down from the wall, all hell had broken loose on the other side of the barbed wire. Bull must've discovered they were missing and raised the alarm. Bright lights flashed and loud male voices boomed. Koen had taken her by the hand and they'd sprinted down the darkened street. Dragging her behind him, he'd taken the first turn to the left and an immediate turn to the right, zigzagging them through the maze of industrial streets. Then they'd dived down a dark alley just as two motorbikes roared past, bright headlamps turning night into day. The next few hours had been a real-life game of cat and mouse, as they evaded the biker gang searching for them. Koen finally recognized where they were when he saw a large airplane taking off.

'We're round the back of the international airport,' he'd said grimly. 'We need to head north, into the suburbs, to get away from this bastard.'

After that, they'd trudged through the empty streets, constantly checking over their shoulders, listening for the telltale sound of the unmistakable motorbikes. Koen wanted to steal a car, to make a swift getaway, but she persuaded him not to. After Bull's tale of how he found them in Jabiru, getting a dirty cop to track down the motorbike number plate, she was certain he'd be able to find them in a stolen car just as easily. She'd tried to hide her shock at the casual way he suggested the car theft. As if it was an easy answer to their problems, as if breaking the law was a simple thing to do, a trifling thing of no importance. But it'd obviously shown on her face, because then he said, 'Don't worry, I'd make sure they got the car back. We'd only be borrowing it, really.' She believed he meant what he said, but she thought the reality might be a little different.

Koen had spent ten minutes working on the handcuffs with his little hair pin key when they'd first sat down on the swings, and now he was completely free of the dratted things. Had thrown them into the nearest bin.

'Do you know where we are?' she asked, tearing her eyes away from the spectacle of the sunrise.

'A spot called Lee Point,' he answered. 'It's the northern-most tip of Darwin. We're close to where my cousin lives. We'll head there after we've rested.' The grimace on Koen's face suggested he wasn't all that happy with the idea. Perhaps Jon might not appreciate them turning up looking like they did.

'Shall we get going then?' The streets were empty behind the little park, not many people around yet this early in the morning. But she was still nervous and jumped at the distant sound of a car engine purring along one of the back streets. 'How far away is it?' she asked, standing up and stretching her arms above her head. Needing another drink, she headed toward the nearby water fountain, where she had to bend over nearly double to reach the child-height nozzle. The water was cool against her cracked lips, and she slurped the fresh liquid thirstily.

'Not too far now.' He joined her for a drink, then took her hand and they paced along the pathway, side by side. Koen had held her hand for most of the night. It felt natural and easy now, kept them connected, conveying without words what needed to be said. The warmth of his palm against hers made her feel safe. He'd been her beacon of light, leading her through the dark night. She never would've escaped Bull if it hadn't been for Koen. And now he was helping her again by taking her to his cousin's place and perhaps placing his cousin in danger as well.

They walked in silence, one ear still open for the sound of

motorbikes. After fifteen minutes or so, Koen turned up a steep dirt driveway with an old wooden house on stilts perched at the top of the hill. The place was quiet, everyone probably still asleep.

'Stay here,' he said, pulling her into the darkened area below the veranda. The house towered above them on its high stilts. 'I'm not sure how Jon's going to take this, it's better if you wait here. I'll come and get you soon,' he said. She stared up into his face. It was the first time she'd really looked at him since they escaped. There was something different about Koen's face now, a hardness that hadn't been there before, a determination. But as he stared back at her, his expression softened, his dark eyes mellowing, a smile tilting the corners of his mouth. His hand came up to touch her cheek, the briefest of gestures, but the hint of tenderness wasn't lost on her.

Rose wasn't sure she wanted to stay down here in the damp amongst the tall weeds, but she trusted Koen now. She had no other choice, so she nodded her head in agreement. Then watched his tall form disappear around one of the towering pylons and listened as his booted feet tapped out a quiet tattoo on the wooden steps up onto the veranda. It took a few minutes for someone to answer the door, and then she heard hushed, muffled voices. Jon's voice was deeper than Koen's, and even from this distance she could hear his displeasure. Soon Koen's boots came back down the stairs, followed by the soft thud of another pair of bare feet.

Straightening her shoulders, she turned around to meet the two Aboriginal men coming toward her. Jon was taller than Koen, but also thickset and of a heavier build. At least ten years Koen's senior, he had a long dark beard, with lips set into a thin line. She didn't need her Empath gift to tell how annoyed this man was. And how afraid. But the aura around him left her in no doubt he wasn't a man to be messed with.

Rose would need to tread carefully around him, she wasn't his favorite person right now.

'So, you're the one causing all the problems,' Jon said. No introduction or pleasant greetings.

Rose wasn't sure how to answer, but in the end, she didn't have to, Koen jumped in instead. 'None of this is her fault,' he denied hotly. 'Some dickhead is out to kill her and hurt her family.'

'Yeah, well, your family's been hurt, too. I got a call from Bindi yesterday. She was the most upset I've ever heard her. Seems like your *friends* paid her a visit just after you left her place yesterday morning. They threatened to break Michael's leg if she didn't tell them where you went.'

Rose's heart plummeted, and she grabbed hold of a pillar to keep herself upright.

'Oh Jesus,' Koen breathed. 'Is she okay? Did he hurt them?' Koen asked the questions hovering on her own tongue.

'Exactly, Cuz. Now you're starting to see how serious this shit is. No, they didn't hurt them, just scared the absolute shit out of them. Bindi is so pissed off with you right now. You'll be lucky if she ever talks to you again. But she's also scared for you. Worried sick about what might've happened. And so am I. We didn't know whether you'd been caught by this guy, or got away, or what. She was just about to go to the police. What the hell have you gotten involved in this time?'

It was true. Rose could feel how worried Jon was for Koen. It sat like a gray, all-consuming cloud just above his shoulders.

Koen hung his head, then took his hat off and threw it to the ground. 'Fuck. This is so much bullshit.' The words were quiet, berating himself, not directed at Jon. 'I didn't mean—'

'Of course you didn't, Cuz, you never do. And that's the problem.'

'Oh God, I'm so sorry,' said Rose, cutting in. 'Poor Bindi.

Poor Michael. That's all my fault, they were targeted because of me.' Rose's stomach tied in knots. She hadn't known. Hadn't dreamed Bull would go that far. It was one thing to endanger her own family, but to hurt other people?

She had to leave. She couldn't keep doing this to Koen and his family. Turning to Koen, she said, 'I'm going. You've done more than enough for me already. It isn't fair, what I asked you to do.'

Koen's emotions were blocked to her, and she didn't bother to stop and examine his face, but she felt the surprise radiate from Jon as she turned to go back down the hill. She'd only taken two strides when Koen caught hold of her elbow and swung her around.

'What are you doing? Don't be stupid, Rose. You'll never survive out there on your own. I won't let you go.'

She glared up at him. She didn't want to fight, she just wanted to leave and get this over with. Where would she go? Her mind was already playing different scenarios through her head. Bull had taken her wallet and phone, so she didn't have any money but—

'I hate to say it, but for once, Koen is right,' Jon interrupted. She hadn't even noticed he'd come to stand beside her. 'After what Bindi told me about those biker dudes. They seemed like they meant business. I believe Koen when he says they're going to kill you.' He flicked a quick glance at Rose and then focused back on Koen. 'The other thing Bindi told me was I needed to look after you, to help you. She'd never forgive herself if something happened to you.' Jon speared Koen with his gaze. 'And if we need to protect her,' he flicked a quick glance in Rose's direction, 'to protect you, then you know we'll do it without any hesitation. Family is all that matters. Your blood and my blood are the same. And if you want her, then we'll help however we can.'

Koen let go of Rose's elbow and turned to look his cousin square in the face. He didn't speak for many seconds, but his expression said all. He was devastated at what he was putting his family through and at the same time terribly proud of the way they stood up for him. But there was also confusion. It was in the lift of his shoulders. Rose wondered if he was as confused as she was by his cousin's use of the word *want*. Koen didn't *want* her, he was stuck with her, that was all. It wasn't like he'd chosen her or anything like that. What was Jon implying? She'd need to touch him if she wanted to find out the true depth of his emotions, but she wasn't prepared to do that.

'I'm assuming that going to the cops is out of the question?' Jon asked. They couldn't take the risk, not when Bull had boasted about the tame cops in his pocket. When Rose shook her head, Jon continued, 'Yeah, I figured as much. I might have a solution to your problem.' Jon took a step back and released Koen from his arrow-like gaze. A large hand came up and rubbed at his beard thoughtfully as he considered his next words. 'At least it would get you out of sight for a few days. I have a hut, down in Kakadu, by a little billabong near Nourlangie Creek. Not many people know it's there. And even fewer people use it. I go there if I want to get away from the missus for a few days.' A hint of a smile played around Jon's lips. 'Which happens less than you think. But it does happen. Anyway, there's good fishing in the billabong and it's got a small stash of food. What do you think?'

Koen pursed his lips and then ambled over and picked up his hat, which was still on the ground where he'd thrown it. Rose watched, as unsure as Koen how to take Jon's offer. Placing his hat with great care on his head, he walked back over. But instead of answering Jon, he surprised her by taking her hand in his. His fingers were surprisingly cool against her own sweaty palms. But the contact brought her focus back to him.

'What do you think? It's probably not a bad idea. It would get us out of harm's way for a while. Throw Bull off our scent.' He lowered his gaze. 'I'm not sure I can come up with anything better. It would give us a chance to regroup.' He still wouldn't quite look her in the eye, and Rose was suddenly struck by the idea he was uncomfortable. Was it because he didn't like having to hide from the enemy rather than confront them? Or was it because he couldn't come up with a better idea himself? Had to rely on Jon to save them? If only her gift worked on him, then she'd get a better read on what he was feeling. But she had to go with her gut instinct, and it told her that while Koen didn't like the thought of placing his family in any more danger, this was possibly the best option.

She also had other people's safety to consider. Rose knew about her father's friend the cop, Damien. Dan had talked about Damien's help when her mother had been attacked. And Damian had visited them more than once on the station. Was it possible he might be able to help? Perhaps come and arrest Bull and stop all this madness. She'd have to talk to her parents first, to be sure.

'I think you're right. It's a good solution for now. But I need to phone my mother.' Her reply caused a ripple of relief to cross his face, and she gave a weak smile in response. She hated to do this. Jon had already helped them so much, but Bull had taken her and Koen's phones. Turning toward Jon, she asked, 'Do you have a phone I could borrow? We lost ours back at the biker clubhouse. I have to tell my family what's going on. Tell them to stay put, where it's safe. They'll be worried sick about me.'

'Sure, I've got a mobile upstairs, I'll go bring it down.' Jon cast her a quick, appraising look. 'I think it's better if you don't come up. That my family doesn't meet you. I've got young kids. The less they know. I hope you understand…'

'Of course, completely.' This man was taking a huge risk to help her and Koen. She wanted to tell him not to worry about it. Forget about her and keep his own family safe. But she was in way too deep for that now. The debt weighed on her like a heavy, suffocating cloak. How many more people would she owe her life to before this was over?

* * *

Koen only just fitted into the front seat. The little red Suzuki hatchback was a small car by anyone's standards, not meant for tall guys like him. This was Jon's old car, parked in the backyard, hidden by tall weeds and long grasses, not driven for many years. But they managed to get it going. Jon had filled it with gas from an old tank beneath the house and they topped up the oil and water in the engine, put some air into the tires. The floor was almost rusted through in places, a small hole visible at Rose's feet. The driver's door didn't close properly, and the window only came halfway down. But it'd started on the third try and hopefully would get them to their destination in one piece.

It wasn't the sad state of the car, however, that was making Koen miserable. It was the fact that even though he let Jon down again—Jon told him the building company had rung and berated him when Koen hadn't turned up for his job yesterday, told him his own job was on the line if something like this ever happened again—his cousin was prepared to help him, protect him, because he was family. And that's what you did for family.

This was all his fault. He was such a screwup. He thought he could turn his life around, but instead he was making everything worse. God, how he wanted to cut and run, leave Rose here and just disappear. Then no one else could get hurt. The guilt was eating him up inside. When he'd heard Jon say that Bull threatened Bindi, he almost threw up. For a while after that, all he'd seen was a red haze floating in front of his vision as blood pounded in his veins. He wanted to hurt Bull so bad. That bastard, how dare he! But then realization came crashing down. He led Bull to Bindi. He should've thought about it and gone somewhere else. Not blindly followed old habits, running to the people he knew would always help him, because they always had, putting them in harm's way as he went. And now Jon was involved. Jon had a wife and kids. Nausea rumbled through his guts at the idea of Bull ever finding out. If he could refuse Jon's offer, he would.

But there was Rose to think about. He couldn't leave her to the mercies of Bull. Not after what he knew the man was capable of. He'd see this through one way or the other. Make sure Rose was safe. And then he was going to leave. Get as far away from here as possible. Take his worthless ass to Melbourne. Or maybe even Tasmania. He'd heard it was beautiful down there. At least over there, he wouldn't be a disappointment anymore. His mum would probably miss him, but no one else would really care. They'd be glad the thorn had gone from their sides.

None of these thoughts were allowed to show on his face, however. He kept his hat pulled down low over his brow and a grimace of determination on his face.

'You right to go?' he asked, without looking directly at Rose, pretending to be checking the windscreen wipers worked. Which they didn't. She was squeezed into the tiny car next to him, her hat resting in her lap, eyes fixed forward like his own. She was just as miserable about this whole thing as he was, he could tell. But they both knew they had no choice. It was either take his car or steal one. Use Jon's hideaway hut, or blindly walk the streets of Darwin until they were spotted by Bull or one of his gang, or the cops. None of them good scenarios.

'Right as I'll ever be,' she replied. They had nothing to take with them. His stuff was still on his motorbike, parked behind a bush on the outskirts of Jabiru and Rose's bags had been abandoned back in the hotel room—how many days ago was that now? It'd been Wednesday night and today was Friday morning, less than two days ago. Jon gave them a plastic bag full of food, as well as two spare t-shirts he'd thrown at Koen just before he handed them the keys to the car.

The funny thing was, if things hadn't been so dire, and Koen hadn't felt so shit about the whole situation, they could almost have been heading off on an adventure, a trip into the unknown. It would be fun, surviving off their wits and the bounty of nature. If only. Koen wasn't sure he'd ever feel lighthearted enough to enjoy a fun trip away again.

'You got the map?' he asked.

Rose waved the piece of paper on which Jon had scribbled directions.

'Thanks, Cuz,' he said out of half-open window. If only he could say everything he was feeling to Jon. But his cousin would understand.

'No probs,' Jon replied. Then he flicked a glance up at the veranda. Sally was standing there, staring down at them with a thoughtful gaze, a steaming mug of hot tea in one hand and Nulla hanging onto her leg. 'Bindi will come and let you know when it's safe, okay? You better get going,' Jon said, the warning note clearly evident in his voice. Koen wondered how Jon was going to explain this latest escapade to his wife. He was glad it wasn't him having to face Sally.

'Good luck.' Koen waved out the window as the car lurched down the drive, knowing Jon would need it. Sally wasn't a woman to be easily misled or messed with. The little car coughed a few times as they hit the asphalt, then settled into a low rumble, almost as if it were happy to be out on the road again. He wished he could feel half as carefree as the car seemed to be.

CHAPTER EIGHTEEN

Jenna sat in the passenger seat of the Land Cruiser, admiring the gorgeous sunrise paint the outback sky rose pink and ochre orange. They'd been driving all night, and Dan must be exhausted. They'd crossed the border into the Northern Territory a few hours ago now. Glancing over at her husband, she gave him an affectionate smile and laid a hand on his knee.

'Hey,' he said, then rubbed a hand over his eyes.

'Hey, yourself,' she replied. 'I'll take over soon. When we hit Timber Creek. Okay?'

'That'd be good.' He nodded, and they lapsed into silence once more.

Jenna had waited and waited and waited for Rose to call all day yesterday. She hadn't sat by the phone. Well, not exactly. But hadn't dared leave the house, either. Rose promised she'd call to let them know how they were going, where they were on their trip south. Rose was lots of things. Being forgetful when it suited her was definitely one of her traits. Willful, stubborn, determined, self-centered, neglectful, those were all words Jenna had used to describe her daughter in the past few days. But Rose also knew how serious Jenna was that she call her parents. This was now more than just a young adult trying to find her way in the world. This had turned deadly serious. And Rose knew it. She would never let her family get hurt. So, when they hadn't heard from Rose by just after dark last night, Jenna couldn't wait any longer. Something had to be done, and she was going to do it.

Dan hadn't taken much persuading, he was nearly as jumpy as her after Rose's revelation that Corey was after her. He was a man of action and it was chafing on him just as much as it was on her that they were sitting still while their daughter was in trouble. Even Ebony, the pillar of calm, the one who always had an everything-will-be-fine-if-you-just-give-it-time attitude, agreed they should go. Ebony and Jay would stay at Shiralee just in case Rose, by some miracle, made it home. They'd also take care of Rodney and Tallow. Dan wasn't happy about leaving the older couple alone on the farm, but Jenna argued they were surrounded by ten station hands who'd been briefed on the situation and were prepared to act accordingly to protect the family, as well as Cookie and Lex. Once the decision had been made, Dan and Jay had gone off for a quiet conference down in the horse stables. Getting all of their ducks in a row making sure all avenues were covered, checking gun and ammunition stores as well as making sure the CCTV and other security was all in good working order, just in case Corey, or Bull, or whatever Rose said he was calling himself nowadays, showed up.

They'd driven all night, something not advised on these back-country roads, with so many kangaroos and other native animals roaming around in the cool of the nocturnal hours. Jenna assured Dan she and Jello would keep the road free from wayward animals. Of course, Jello was with them, she never went anywhere without him. All sorts of images and feelings filtered through to Jenna from Jello as he hung his head out the window, letting the smells of the outback flash by.

Timber Creek was only ten minutes away now. There was

still no sign of habitation, the desert stretched away flat and featureless on either side of the road. Timber Creek was only small, it was one of those towns, if you blinked as you passed through, you'd miss it. She could see a huddle of trees, green against the brown and a scattering of dark shapes on the horizon which heralded the coming town. From Timber Creek it would be another seven hours drive to Darwin. Jenna was determined to get there before dark tonight.

The square shapes got bigger until they morphed in a spread of low, dusty buildings. As Dan pulled into the only gas station in town, Jenna took out her mobile and checked for reception. Yes, there was a connection here, and the phone lit up with two messages from her mother, Ebony. Jenna's heart leapt into her mouth. Was it good or bad news? She showed the phone to Dan, and his brown eyes filled with concern.

Without bothering to listen to the messages, she dialed the house phone at Shiralee. It was still very early, but that didn't matter, Ebony would be awake. Dan sat in the driver's seat, listening to her conversation.

'Hi, Mum, it's me, what's wrong?'

'Thank the stars you called. I just heard from Rose about fifteen minutes ago. It's not good.' Her mother's voice broke a little on the last word, and Jenna's hand flew to her mouth. 'They never made it out of Jabiru. Corey found them somehow and captured them.'

'Oh no,' Jenna heard someone say in a sobbing voice. Was that her? It sounded like someone far away had spoken.

She didn't even acknowledge Dan's hand on her thigh. 'What,' he said. 'Tell me what's happening.'

But she shook her head and held up a hand, trying to listen to the rest of what her mother was telling her. 'He took them back to his biker clubhouse. But it's okay, they managed to escape last night. Rose called me from Koen's cousin's place this morning.'

'Oh Jesus. Thank God.' Jenna took hold of Dan's hand and squeezed it, giving him a quick smile of reassurance. 'Did he hurt them? Are they okay?'

'I'm not sure,' Ebony replied. 'I didn't have long to talk to her. But they're safe now. Koen's cousin has a place where they can hide, somewhere in the bush where no one will find them. They're borrowing his car and going there now. The only problem is, they have no phone reception. We've no way of getting in touch with them.'

'That's good,' Jenna breathed, loosening her grip on Dan's hand when she realized she must be hurting him with her deathlike grasp. 'They're doing the right thing. The best thing to keep them safe.' For now, she wanted to add. 'But this just shows how serious Corey is. He's got to be stopped. We're still going to Darwin, and we're still going to meet Damien, like we arranged.'

If anyone could help them solve the problem of Corey, it was Damien. He was also on his way from Karratha, with two cops he trusted implicitly, coming to meet them. Damien already knew there was a problem at the local Darwin cop shop. There'd been rumors about corrupt cops in league with one of the biker gangs for months now. So, he was bringing some of his own men to do the job. Dan could call and update him as soon as she finished with Ebony. Damian's phone reception might be patchy as well, but they could leave him a detailed message.

'One last thing,' Ebony said. 'I'll text you this cousin's phone number. His name is Jon and you can keep in contact with him for any updates on Rose and Koen, or if the cops need to talk to him for more information. He can take you out to the hut where Rose and Koen are hiding.'

'That's great, thanks, Mum.' At least it wasn't all bad news, and perhaps it was even good news. They had some solid evidence on Corey now, hopefully enough to put him back behind bars. As long as they could catch him first. 'I'll ring you when we get to Darwin. Love you.'

'Love you too, sweetheart.' Her mum rang off the phone, and Jenna heaved a sigh of relief.

'Tell me,' Dan demanded. 'What in hell is going on?'

'It's not as bad as it sounded,' she said. 'Come on, let's fill the car with gas and I'll tell you what happened. Then you need to phone Damo before we leave town.' Jenna got out of the car and stretched, enjoying the feeling of unfolding her cramped legs and walking around on the dusty pavement. It was only just after six a.m. but thankfully this little gas station was already open, catering for country people's needs. She told Dan what Ebony had said while she watched him fill the car. His big shoulders sagged with relief when she told him Rose was safe. Then she let Jello out for a run and waited as he nosed happily through the weeds at the edge of the pavement. This was all going to turn out okay.

If she kept telling herself that, it *would* come true.

* * *

The car was quiet for most of the drive into Kakadu. Neither of them had much to say, both lost in their own thoughts. But after they'd been driving along the Arnhem Highway for nearly half an hour, Koen asked her to look at the map and tell him when the turnoff was coming up. She studied the hand-drawn map, turning it around three or four times in her hands until she could properly orient herself. So busy was she looking at the map that she nearly missed the turnoff, and Koen had to come to a screeching halt to do a U-turn.

Then they were bumping down a fairly well-used, dusty road, the open woodland fanning out in front, a plume of red dust following behind. The little car rattled alarmingly, and Rose could see the dirt flashing past beneath her feet through the hole in the floor. It was hot now, near mid-morning, the blazing sun beating down from an endless blue sky above. Rose swiped a hand across her forehead. The car had no air-conditioning, and even with the windows wide open the heat was oppressive, turning the car into a human-sized oven. A long way ahead of them, Rose could see patches of green and then further still the green feathered out along the fingers of the winding river-beds, morphing together until the floodplains were one big sea of emerald as far as the eye could see. Here and there, clumps of dark green hovered around the edges of larger permanent waterholes, and she could make out the path of the Nourlangie River by the viridescent line of trees following it. Jon had said the secret billabong was just off this Nourlangie River, so they should be able to see it soon.

'There's another turn coming up,' she said to Koen, studying the map. 'Jon has drawn a big boab tree at the intersection. At least I think that's what it is.' His artwork wasn't the best, and she hoped she was deciphering it properly. Koen just grunted in reply, concentrating on easing the little car down the bumpy road. 'There it is,' she said with relief as a big, wide boab tree, towering over everything else in the woodland, came into view. This time when they made the turn, the road became much narrower and wandered through the trees, almost without direction. But it did seem they were slowly heading toward the line of green and the river. Branches brushed the side of the car and Koen had to slow for large potholes left by the rain from the last wet season. Taller trees bent in over the top of the car, blocking her view of the sky.

'Turn right here, I think,' she said as another, smaller trail appeared through the underbrush. Koen slowed the car to a crawl. The trail looked like it might've been made by an animal, not meant for a car, and Rose became worried.

Koen glanced over at her. 'This is right,' he assured her.

They keep it overgrown like this to deter any tourists from finding it. Now they were running parallel with the river and she could see glints off the water as they drove. After another ten minutes, the branches getting so low Rose felt like ducking down inside the car as they brushed over the rooftop, a small wooden hut appeared. Koen stopped the car under a large melaleuca tree, and they sat and took in the view.

'This is beautiful,' she said, not hiding the awe in her voice. And it was. Perhaps not as classically beautiful as the Anbangbang Billabong where they'd seen the rock paintings, but this was still so typically Kakadu and all the more special because it was just the two of them here to see it.

Koen smiled for the first time that morning. 'Yeah, it is,' he agreed. The hut was nestled under two large eucalypts, and overlooked a flat, grassy plain that ran down a small incline, toward the edge of the billabong, which was edged in a black, oozing mud. The billabong itself was small, only a hundred feet or so across, but it was drenched in hundreds of lily pads, and fringed with pink and white lily flowers. The waterhole was surrounded by a line of gate-keepers, tall trees and smaller shrubs that stood around the edges, enjoying the luxury of a year-round water supply. It gave the billabong a feeling of being hidden, kept secret by the trees.

'Come on, let's go and see what this bloody hut is like inside,' Koen said. A flock of small birds took off from the edge of the water as they got out and slammed the car doors, their wings flashing in the sunlight as they swooped low over the trees.

Koen grabbed the food and shirts and walked toward the hut. It was made up of a mishmash of materials. Once, it'd probably been a slab-hut, constructed of large wooden slabs of rough-hewed wood with a tin roof, but now there were pieces of corrugated iron tacked haphazardly on the walls and a pile of rocks held up one corner of the rickety veranda. There was no glass in the windows, and the dark square openings stared at her blankly. Koen took one giant step up onto the verandah, and then turned and held out his hand to her. The small gesture lit a flame of happiness in her chest. He pushed the door open.

'They don't lock it?' she asked in surprise.

'Nah, don't need to out here. Come on.' He beckoned her into the dim room. It was a little cooler in here, but not by much. It was obvious no one had been here in quite a while. Leaves and debris rustled on the floor as they walked, and a layer of dust caked everything in sight. There was even a pile of bird droppings in one corner, and she could see a tiny nest up in the rafters of the ceiling. Thankfully, it was unoccupied.

'Needs a bit of a clean.'

Rose just glanced at Koen. That was an understatement if she'd ever heard one. But there was a bed, of sorts, a wooden frame with a stained mattress. And an old Formica table and some chairs, all mismatched but serviceable. A sink and a gas burner stove with open cabinets full of blackened pots and pans was obviously the kitchen. This was definitely basic. Rose almost laughed at Jon's description. But it would have to do.

'Where's the toilet,' she asked, but she thought she already knew the answer. It was confirmed when Koen lifted a finger and pointed out the window toward the woodland.

'There should be clean sheets and blankets over here.' Koen beckoned her toward a large metal chest huddled in one corner. 'The mice and bugs can't get in here,' he said, motioning toward the tin lid.

Thank the Lord for small mercies. Rose was no prima-donna, by any means. She was used to roughing it in the outback, camping in the dust for days, with only a campfire for a cookstove, and a hole in the ground for a bush-dunny.

But there was one thing she couldn't stand, and that was creepy-crawlies in her bedclothes.

'Let's get to it then.' She picked up a scruffy broom, leaning in one corner and handed it to Koen, then dug into the metal box for the sheets and blankets and went over to see what could be done to rescue the not-so-clean mattress.

Half an hour later, Rose wiped the perspiration out of her eyes. Her shirt stuck to her back, and she could see dark circles of sweat on Koen's shirt as well. They were hot, sweaty, dusty, and tired. But the hut was now clean and livable. She even found an old mosquito net, and they hung it above the bed. They were going to need it tonight with no covering on windows.

Koen took a chair out onto the veranda and plonked down into it with a grunt. His hat was hanging on the peg behind the door next to hers, and his black curls were plastered to the side of his face. Rose handed him one of the bottles of water they brought with them and he took it gratefully, pushing his damp hair off his forehead and tipping his head back as he took large swallows. Rose watched his Adam's apple as it bobbed up and down while he drank. His throat glistened with sweat as it ran down over his collarbone, beneath the buttons of his shirt. He looked at her and smiled, catching her watching him, almost as if he knew she liked what she saw.

She'd made an effort to check out Koen's injuries before they left Jon's place, to determine for herself they really were just *scratches* as he kept declaring. There was lots of bruising, and perhaps a fractured rib, but none of it was life-threatening, thank God.

'We both need a wash,' she said, bringing her own chair out and sitting next to Koen.

'Well, don't be swimming in the billabong,' he replied. 'Old Man Crocodile lives in there. And he'd think you were quite a tasty morsel indeed.'

'Really.' Rose shouldn't have been shocked, but still, this lagoon looked so peaceful and calm. How could there possibly be a hungry prehistoric creature lurking beneath that lovely water?

'Yes, really.' He turned to stare at her, face serious now. 'And don't be going too close to the edge either, keep at least ten feet back.'

'Okay.' Rose returned his serious tone.

'Jon lost a pet dog out here a few years ago. It got too close to the water and...' He grimaced. 'Jon doesn't bring his animals out here anymore.'

'Oh God,' Rose said quietly. Then another thought occurred to her. 'What about water? What are we going to drink, how we going to wash?'

'There's an old rain tank out the back. I'll go and check it in a minute. But you'll have to boil the water before you drink it.' She just nodded, used to sterilizing water to make it drinkable. 'I'll throw a line in later on, catch us some dinner. What do ya reckon?'

Fresh fish sounded good. Being vegetarian, or perhaps pescatarian might be a better description, she sometimes allowed herself the luxury of fish. She couldn't pass up the opportunity to taste a wild-caught fish straight out of the billabong. 'What's in there?' She asked, staring out at the tranquil water.

'I'm hoping for some black bream. There might be some left, even though it's the middle of the dry season. They taste the best.'

Rose knew that during the dry season, many fish populations become isolated in the permanent billabongs and waterholes.

'There will definitely be Saratoga, but you white fellas don't seem to like the taste of that.' He grinned. 'White fellas only catch that one for sport. But they just don't know how to cook it properly.'

'What about Barramundi?' She'd heard many people talk about the famous Barramundi caught up here in the Top End.

'Nah, they prefer running water and deeper streams. We won't get any of those today. Come back in the wet season and I'll catch you a couple of them buggers. They taste good too.' He licked his lips. 'Baked over the coals of a fire, wrapped in paperbark from the melaleuca tree. Mmm hmm, you can't beat that, so sweet and juicy.' Koen put his fingers to his lips and made a smacking sound, and Rose found herself wishing he could conjure up some Barramundi right here and now.

Her stomach gave a loud rumble. They hadn't eaten anything since yesterday morning; she remembered with a small shock. All day yesterday had been spent tied up in Bull's clubhouse, and last night with nothing to eat and only the water they'd found in the kid's playground. It was time to check out what Jon had given them by way of food in that plastic bag.

She went inside and came back with the bag, rummaging through it as she asked, 'Are you hungry?'

'Bloody oath.' He turned ravenous eyes on her, waiting to see what delicacies she pulled out of the bag.

A packet of sweet biscuits, some apples, two packets of crisps, two tins of baked beans, and a packet of crackers. Rose pulled each item out of the bag and looked at their little hoard in dismay. Not a lot to work with here. But she was too hungry to care. She ripped open the packet of sweet biscuits and crammed a few in her mouth before handing it to Koen. Washing them down with a swig of water, she grabbed an apple and bit into it, watching Koen do the same. They sat back and contemplated the billabong while they chewed their late morning breakfast.

'It's a bit surreal,' she said after a while. 'We're just sitting here as if we're on some sort of fishing trip. A day out. If I let myself, it's almost easy to forget what Bull did to us yesterday, how we spent last night. It's so peaceful and calm out here. As if nothing happened. Like the billabong doesn't care who we are, or what we've done.' She glanced at him, almost apologetic, but then she could see an understanding gleam in his eye.

'I know what you mean.' He twirled the bottle of water around in his hand. The sweat had dried from his forehead, leaving his curls to spring to life once more. That twinkle— from before they were captured by Bull—was back in his eyes. Koen the larrikin was making another show. 'I was thinking the exact same thing. If it wasn't for the fact that I keep waiting for Bindi or Jon to drive up and give us some news, I could almost relax and enjoy myself. Perhaps that's what we should do. It's kind of out of our control, after all. We don't have much choice but to sit here and wait, so we may as well enjoy it.'

What he said made a strange kind of sense. The plan was when they had news, either from Rose's parents, or about Bull's whereabouts, then Jon, or more likely Bindi, would bring them word. There was absolutely no phone reception out here, so they were relying on good old-fashioned people-power to bring in word as to whether it was safe to come back to town. Or the opposite, that they needed to run like hell. Either way, there was nothing they could do to influence the outcome.

'Shouldn't we be worried? What if Bull turns up?' Goosebumps raised up on the back of Rose's neck at the thought of all Bull's Harley rumbling in and surrounding the hut. What would they do? They'd be caught here, neater than a rat in a trap.

'There's no way he'll find us out here. He doesn't know about Jon or this hut, and Bindi's going to go to the police if he so much as sniffs around her again,' replied Koen, in his off-hand way.

Rose nodded her head, but couldn't quite stop the chill running down her spine.

CHAPTER NINETEEN

Koen sat in an old chair, well back from water, whistling a tune. Rose was next to him in another vinyl chair they'd dragged down from the hut. They were sitting in a dry dusty area running all the way to the water's edge. Jon must've cleared it so he could launch a boat. The hot sphere of sun that'd blared down on them all afternoon was now an orange bauble on the horizon. The heat of the day was finally dissipating, leaving behind a balmy evening, ripe with the buzz of insects. The fishing line twitched in his fingers. Something out there was interested in the bait. A small shiver of happiness rose through his chest. This was the most peaceful he'd felt in a long while. He and Rose sat close together, not speaking, just enjoying the vista.

Koen had concealed the tiny red car in a straggle of thorny bushes behind the hut, it was better to keep their presence as hidden as possible. Then they'd lazed away the stifling hot afternoon by dozing, her on the bed, him on the veranda, with nothing else to do but wait. Once the sun had got low on the horizon, Koen had shaken himself and gone to find the fishing gear stored in the dusty cupboard in the corner. Then he'd taken Rose and shown her how to dig up the shiny wriggling insects to use as bait. She'd squealed at first when it squirmed against her fingers, but hadn't backed away, eager to learn how to find some Bush Tucker.

A slight ripple in the grass at the edge of the water attracted his attention. He focused his gaze and after a while he saw a tiny head and two small eyes appear just above the surface. 'Look,' he whispered, pointing, and he almost giggled with glee. 'It's a snake neck turtle.'

Rose turned heavy-lidded eyes to see where he was pointing and nodded with fascination. She must've been just about asleep in the chair beside him.

'You don't get too many of them out here in the dry season. They're good to eat, but I'm not going anywhere near the water without a boat. Not with Old Man Crocodile in there somewhere,' he added.

Her sleepy eyes widened, almost as if she'd forgotten about the crocodile.

Then they both settled back in their chairs and watched as the icon of Kakadu bird life, a Jabiru, with bright pink legs and long black neck poked around in the shallows with its beak. A couple of whistling ducks floated about on the water, bobbing serenely. He listened to the melodic bird calls and watched as more birds floated about in the air above the billabong.

The peaceful serenity was violently broken when a crocodile sprang up from the water, took one of the ducks in its jaws, then the water churned and frothed for a second before it became eerily quiet again. All the birds went silent, and the billabong was completely still, as if holding its breath.

Rose jumped up with a scream. 'What the hell…?'

He laughed at her, as much to release his tension as at how funny her face looked. She'd gone very pale, her eyes wide and staring like a caricature of her normal self.

'Told you, girl.' He laughed. 'Didn't you believe me?'

She edged back onto her chair, but sat up straight, hands clenched on the sides, all traces of sleep gone now. 'Jesus, I don't think I will ever get rid of that image,' she said. 'It was so primeval, so brutal, so...I don't even have words to describe it.'

'Just thank your lucky stars it wasn't you,' he said, fingers still resting easily on the fishing line. Damn, all the fish were probably scared away. He'd have to wait for things to settle again. In a way, he was glad Rose had seen that. She needed to see it. A few minutes later, the birds began hesitantly calling again.

'Tell me more about your family,' Koen drawled, relaxing further down in his chair. 'You said something about having Indigenous step-brothers.' His interest had been piqued when she'd mentioned them in passing, but it gave him some answers as to why she seemed to accept him completely for who he was, something a lot of white people found hard to do.

'Rodney and Tallow,' she said with a grin. 'They're twins, just about to turn sixteen. And both of them bloody pains in the backside. Thinking they know better than everyone else. Always up to trouble. If I was home right now, they'd probably be planning some kind of prank. You know, like loosening my girth on the saddle, so I slide right off when I go to mount up or putting salt in my tea instead of sugar. That kind of childish thing seems to delight them to no end.'

'Yeah, I bet.' Koen chuckled. He'd been known to pull those kinds of stunts, too. When he was younger, of course.

'They came to us when they were only three years old.' Rose got a dreamy look on her face as she reminisced. 'They're actually cousins of one of our station hands, Moon. He brought them back with him after a visit to his mob up in the Purnululu area, you know The Bungle Bungles?'

He nodded.

'One of his aunties wasn't coping with the twins. She's pretty sick, has diabetes and was struggling to care for them.

They were running wild, not getting fed properly, that kind of thing…Well you're probably more familiar with the stories than I am,' she amended.

Again, he just nodded his head. He'd seen it all in Balgo, the health issues, fractured communities and families that struggled to manage.

'So, Moon thought it was time he brought them back to the station with him. Said it was his duty to look after them. We all love Moon to bits, so of course Rodney and Tallow were welcome. We did everything together, being of similar age. I was only six when they first arrived. They became like the brothers I never had. We even did school of the air together, we rode horses together every day…' Her voice trailed off as her thoughts turned inwards.

Koen looked up from the fishing line and saw her eyes fixed somewhere in the middle distance, her face in profile caught in the setting sun's rays. He was struck by just how beautiful she was. That little ski-jump nose, eyes the color of the sky, high cheekbones and her small heart-shaped face.

'But of course, they didn't come without problems, cultural differences that at first were hard to resolve,' she continued. 'That's when my grandmother and her partner began to get more involved. They live on the adjoining property.' She glanced at him to make sure he was following her story. 'And they'd been talking about creating some kind of center for disaffected youth. My grandmother has quite a special…ah, healing talent, shall we say. She has a knack for helping people with both physical and mental problems. They wanted to offer the community something different, a way of reconnecting with themselves and their country. When Rodney and Tallow joined us, it was the motivation they needed to focus on vulnerable Indigenous youth.'

Something twigged at the back of Koen's mind when she mentioned the name. Something his mother had said a few months back when he'd been home in Balgo. 'I think I might've heard about your grandparents. They've got a good name in our community.'

'That's good.' Rose smiled, and Koen could see how proud she was of them. 'They're not doing anything spectacular in the big scheme of things, but what they do is to make every individual feel like they matter. And their culture matters. They do lots of hands-on basic stuff, like teaching kids to ride horses, carpentry skills, even how to read and write. But through the teaching of these skills, they interweave the importance of mental stability.'

Koen reflected on how his mum was making an impact on his people, by becoming the local nurse in the community, proving that by commitment and caring you could do anything you wanted. The Aboriginal artists at the gallery in Balgo were also making a difference, showing how a love for country combined with an engagement with community could bring respect and pride back. He'd so love to be able to honor his own people, too. His mum often said he was too intelligent for his own good, and if he'd only turn that intelligence toward honorable pastimes instead of frittering his time away, there were so many untold ways he might be able to do some good.

'Maybe I could come out and give your grandparents a hand one day.' The words were out before he could stop them, and he immediately regretted them. What was he thinking? He wasn't hanging around after this, he was leaving for the other side of the country.

'They'd love that,' Rose enthused. 'Didn't you say you were good at carpentry? They could do with someone to help them in that field. Especially someone who has—'

'We'll see what happens,' he cut in a little too sharply. Who was Rose kidding? He had no happy ending to give, he was a bad influence, so what would be the point? It was all just bullshit.

A sharp tug on his fishing line distracted him from any more self-destructive thoughts. He yanked on the line to snare the fish securely onto the hook, then stood up and began to slowly wind it in.

'Have you caught something?' Rose asked, standing up as well.

'Might be a little black bream by the feel of it,' he said. 'We'll be eating fish tonight, after all.'

'Great. I'll go and open the tin of baked beans. It'll be a meal fit for kings,' she said happily, almost skipping up the dusty path toward the hut. He watched her pert backside in those tight little jeans as she walked away from him. Telling himself it was no good letting gloomy thoughts invade the happy mood he'd been in all afternoon, he pushed aside the negative thoughts and concentrated on pulling in the fish.

Fifteen minutes later he'd caught two more bream, both bigger than the first, enough for a good meal for the two of them. He cleaned and gutted them and returned to the hut. It was ridiculous, really, but he couldn't shake the feeling of a hunter arriving with his catch. Rose heated the baked beans in a saucepan while she fried the fish over a griddle pan on the gas stove. The smell of cooking made his mouth water. Neither of them had eaten properly for days. They took their dinner out onto the veranda and sat with their tin plates on their knees as they watched the light begin to fade away from the landscape. The silence between them as they ate the delectable fish was becoming familiar and comfortable.

'I've put a big pot of water on the stove to heat so I can have a wash after dinner,' Rose said, once most of the fish was gone from her plate. 'I'll do another pot for you, too.' It was the only way they could wash out here, there was no shower or bathtub. But there was an old forty-four-gallon drum cut in half out the back they could use as a makeshift bath. It was only big enough to stand up in, but it would do.

'Yep, I stink nearly as much as you do.'

'Hey,' she said, and he flashed her a cheeky smile.

It would be nice to feel clean again, and he could put on the new shirt Jon had given him. He was still wearing the filthy old dark blue one Mike had loaned him, ripped and bloodied as it was from where Bull's men had beaten him.

'I'll clean up, if you like,' he offered. 'While you take your wash.'

They finished the meal and carried their plates inside. Rose tested the water. It was almost boiling. Koen helped her carry it out the back, and they tipped it into the drum, topping it up with almost the same amount of cold water.

'I'll leave you to your bathing, my lady,' he said with a mocking bow. Then went to go back inside.

'No peeking,' she admonished.

'The thought never crossed my mind.' And before then it hadn't. But as he made his way inside to the small sink to begin washing the plates, he caught a glimpse out of one of the windows. He could just see the tall tree standing behind the hut and tin drum beneath it, waiting for Rose to step in. She was nowhere in sight, perhaps hidden by the corner of the hut. He imagined her taking her clothes off and laying them in a neat pile on top of the wood heap. The thought sent a sudden pulse of heat through him. No, it wouldn't be right to watch her like some disgusting voyeur. But still...how many times had he imagined what she'd look like naked? More times than you could count on both hands, that's for sure.

Shaking his head, he forced himself to walk over to the sink and start scrubbing the plates. But the idea of her drew him, almost like a physical force, like a magnet pulling him back until he could no longer stand still. Slowly, step-by-step, he inched his way back toward the window. And looked out.

A flash of pale skin caught his eye. It was dusk now; the light disappearing quickly, making way for the night. But there was still enough light for him to see Rose's outline against the backdrop of the tree-trunk as she stood in the drum.

His cock stirred at the sight. She was beautiful, like some kind of water nymph come to life. She had her back to him, blonde hair let loose to fall over her shoulders. A perfectly round butt, molded into a trim waist and well-shaped legs—probably from all that horse-riding. Then she lifted a tin of water and tipped it over her head, rivulets running down over the curves and smooth surfaces of her body.

Koen licked his lips. The front of his jeans grew uncomfortably tight as he watched. She tipped another tin of water over her head and then soaped her hair until it was frothy and tangled. He continued to watch, fascinated, as she washed the soap out of her hair, bending and filling the tin, then leaning back and letting the water run over her face and head. She turned slightly, readjusting her footing in the drum, and now he could see the curve of her breast, the hint of a pink nipple.

Jesus, she was bloody perfect. And he wanted her. He'd wanted her for days, but under the circumstances...But tonight it was just the two of them. Who knew what fate held for them tomorrow? This might be the last time he saw her. What would she do if he walked up to her right now? Would she reject him?

Rose turned again. Now she was facing him and opened her eyes. Caught him staring at her. She stood still as a statue, eyes unreadable.

* * *

Koen stalked toward her through the growing dusk, lithe and muscular as a cat. And she stood there and let him come, not bothering to cover her nakedness. Trapped by the look in his eyes, a mixture of hunger and reverence. She let him look his fill.

Be still, her foolish heart. But she couldn't calm the wild fluttering as her chest vibrated with the pounding of her blood.

'Rose.' Her name was a whisper falling from his lips. A question. She didn't answer, just kept watching him. 'You're beautiful.' Then he was standing in front of her, and she found herself trembling. Thoughts of Bull and his mad band of bikers flickered at the back of her mind, but they were no match for Koen standing there, desire in his dark eyes. She would think about Bull later.

Had she subconsciously wanted this when she'd stripped naked and stood in the tub? She could've moved the tub out of the line of sight. Or she could've made Koen put up a screen. But she'd done neither, knowing he might well glance out the window and see her. The warm water had felt so good against her skin, cleansing the dirt and sweat away, washing away the fear of the past few days. Standing out here, under the spreading branches of the tree, the open sky above, the balmy evening air caressing her skin, she'd felt suddenly freer than she ever had before.

Koen's gaze roved over her uncovered body, burning a brand on her skin where ever it touched. Heat pooled in her stomach, then flowed lower. Her knees suddenly felt weak. The bruise around his eye was almost invisible in this light. Her gaze zeroed in on his lips, seeing the half-healed split in the corner of his mouth. His poor, battered face. But she didn't have more time to contemplate his wounds, as his hand came up and cupped her cheek and he moved in closer. Her trembling increased as his lips landed on hers. Soft, gentle, tender, seeking the answer she hadn't yet given him. But she didn't want soft or gentle. She wanted his fire and spirit. She wanted him to stamp his passion on her.

Suddenly, Koen withdrew his hand and his mouth and she

almost whimpered. What was he doing? Pulling his shirt over his head, not bothering to undo the buttons, Koen dropped it in the dirt and then unbuckled his jeans at the same time as he kicked off his boots and dropped them all in the dust. Now he stood in front of her, completely naked, just like her.

He was as exquisite as she'd dreamed he would be. All defined muscle, lean hips and long lines. His dark skin highlighted every curve and sinew lurking beneath, he could almost have been cast in bronze.

Koen stepped into the drum with her, taking her in his arms. There wasn't really room for two people, but if they clung to each other, then they wouldn't topple over, as the water lapped against their knees.

'Wash me,' Koen said, voice husky.

'Turn around then,' she commanded, and he shuffled around awkwardly until his back was to her. Holding onto his hip with one hand, she bent down and filled the small tin with water, then poured it slowly over his back. She still had the soap in her other hand, and she used it to draw slippery circles over his shoulders. She reveled in the feel of the ropey muscles of his neck and down the length of his spine under her palm. It was hard to see in the dim light, and against the dark color of his skin, but she knew the were bruises there, along the side of his rib-cage where Mongrel had kicked him. She tried to be gentle as she ran the soap down across his lower back and then lower still. Down over his tight buttocks, which clenched at her touch.

'Okay, face me now,' she commanded again, feeling intoxicated as he did what he was told. There was no mistaking his desire for her when he turned, his cock pressed against her stomach, hard and insistent. But she needed to finish the ritual.

This time she tipped the water over his collar-bone, and it ran in rivers over his pecs and down the runnels of his six-pack stomach. The tight black curls on his chest flattened and softened under her wet fingertips as she soaped them. She could feel a slight thrum running through his body, echoing the same tremble running through hers. He watched her, eyes dark and mysterious, as she sluiced the soap away with another container of water. Then her hands wandered down, over the lower part of his stomach, to where his manhood stood to attention. She ran the soap over its velvety firmness, and Koen groaned loudly. The sound sent a thrill through her.

She tipped the rest of the water in the tin over him to clean away the soap and was in the act of bending down for some more when Koen said, 'Enough. You're driving me completely insane, girl.' With that, he stepped out of the drum onto the dry earth and picked her up in his arms as if she weighed nothing at all, holding her tight against his chest. The feel of his bare chest pushed against her breasts sent tingling sensations all down her body. He carried her into the hut and set her on her feet next to the bed.

A small gas lamp burned in the corner of the kitchen bench, where Koen had been washing the dishes, lending a soft light to the room as the night descended outside. Rose pulled aside one edge of the mosquito net, which hung from a hook in the ceiling above the bed, covering it like a gauzy tent. Ignoring the fact she was still dripping wet, she climbed onto the bed and beckoned Koen to follow her, then lay down and watched him come in, closing the net behind him. Thank God she'd made up the bed with the clean sheets earlier on. From her position, she could see through the door they'd left open, out across the darkness where she knew the billabong lay, to the edge of the horizon where the last faint strip of orange light glowed.

Koen lay down beside her, leaning up on his elbow so he could look down at her. His fingers landed softly on her shoulder, traced down her collarbone, and stopped to linger over the black stone of her pendant.

'Interesting necklace,' he murmured, picking it up and rubbing it between his fingers.

'My mum gave it to me,' she replied. Now wasn't the time to tell him about the supposed special properties of her stone. She wanted his hands elsewhere on her body. As if reading her mind, he let the pendant nestle back on her collarbone and traced slowly around her breasts, fingers cool from the water still clinging to her body. Even though the night was warm, goosebumps raised up on her skin wherever his fingers touched. Looking down, she saw the darkness of his hand, cuticles a lighter color than the rest, echoed by the paleness of her skin. His long, dark legs held against her creamy complexion. She loved the dusky hue of him. It was part of him, part of why he was the person he was. The one she'd come to admire so much after only a short time together. But it was more than *admiration*, more than *like*, these feelings she had for Koen. He touched something way down, deep in her soul. Something no one else had ever come close to.

'I need to tell you something first.' His deep voice startled her out of her contemplation. 'I don't have any protection.' Black eyes sought hers, filled with regret, but also a certain hope. Rose was buoyed by his consideration for her, prepared not to go through with this if she told him no. 'I never thought…'

She reached up and placed a hand on his cheek, stroking the rough beginnings of a four-day growth. The scruff suited him, made him look older, more mature. What should she do? So many emotions swirled around behind those dark irises. But he was completely unguarded tonight, he let her see right through to the true Koen. There was undisguised lust, of course. Nervousness, whether that was because he thought she might reject him, or because he hoped she wouldn't, she couldn't tell. And a tenderness that ran far deeper than mere affection. Was he perhaps feeling more than plain old *like* for her, as she was for him?

'Have you got any diseases I should know about?' Would he tell her the truth if he did? He was obviously a bit of a playboy where women were concerned. Women loved him, he was a good-looking guy. A bit of a joker, with an easy smile. He'd told her he didn't have a girlfriend, but she hadn't even asked him how many women there'd been before, or how long ago since his last one.

'Nope, I'm clean,' he replied carefully, as if he was scared she wouldn't believe him. 'I get checked by the doc regularly.' This time he looked a little sheepish, but she respected him for doing the right thing. 'It's something my mum hammered home to me.'

Her answer was to pull his mouth down until it met hers. 'I'm on the pill,' she told him, breaking their kiss just long enough to speak. 'It's something my mother hammered into me,' she said, echoing his words. At least having an overprotective mother was good for some things. Jenna had marched her into the doctor's office just after Rose turned sixteen and told her it was better to be open and direct about things than to sneak around and have an unwanted pregnancy. Not that Jenna was condoning Rose having a boyfriend. On the contrary, she was totally against it. But she knew what teenagers were like, and she wasn't taking any chances. 'And I get checked regularly, too. Just in case you were going to ask.'

'Good to know.' Koen gave a long, slow smile that sent a spreading heat throughout her body. The hand that'd been exploring her collarbone now dropped lower, his finger swirling around her navel, and she shivered. She wanted him to go lower still, to the spot between her thighs that was pulsing with need. As if reading her mind, his fingers left the soft mound of her belly and feathered down the tops of her thighs. She gave a small groan, then captured his mouth with hers, telling him what she wanted by plunging her tongue in between his lips.

And he did so, pushing his fingers gently into her, where she was wet and waiting for him. She groaned again and arched her back to meet him. God, it felt so good. But she wanted more of him. She could feel his erection throbbing against her leg. He wanted her as much as she wanted him.

'Koen,' she pleaded, closing her eyes and he raised himself up in one easy movement and lowered himself down over her body.

'Look at me, Rose. Look at me,' he commanded. She opened her eyes and stared up at him. His face, so strong and masculine, his naked need for her glowing in his eyes. Then he slid inside her and her world became purely physical, saturated by her need for him. A need for release. They moved together, sweat slicking their bodies. It only took a few strokes, but Rose could already feel herself heading for the precipice. She was going to come, and quickly. But Koen was right there with her, she could see it, and so she let herself go, calling out his name as his body went rigid above her and she became unhinged.

For many long minutes afterwards, they lay entwined on the bed, sweat cooling on their bodies. She didn't ever want to leave here; she wanted this moment to go on forever.

'I think we might need another wash,' Koen drawled as he lifted his head and looked into her eyes.

'I won't argue with that,' she agreed, laughing. If it ended up with the same result, she'd be more than happy.

Koen rolled off her and lay on his back, head on the pillow, one arm tucked beneath her neck. She snuggled into his shoulder.

'That was amazing, even if I do say so myself,' he said. 'I

was pretty good, huh?' He gave her a cheeky wink. The joker was back. But she'd seen past that armor, into the depths of his soul. And she liked what she saw.

CHAPTER TWENTY

Jenna rubbed her eyes. The gray light of early morning filtered through the gauzy curtains of the caravan. She let her hand flop down the side of the bed and gave the top of Jello's head a reassuring pat. What time was it? She hadn't slept well, and now she was eager to get up and moving again. The local caravan park in Darwin was the only place that would let them stay with a dog, but she and Dan didn't mind. It was just another place to sleep.

Dan gave a quiet snore beside her and rolled over. But she couldn't go back to sleep, her mind was whirling with the events from last night.

They'd arrived in Darwin just before four o'clock in the afternoon, tired and dusty, needing a shower and a hot meal. But instead they'd driven to a small rundown hotel on the edge of town to meet with Damien, who'd arrived a few hours before them on a chartered flight from Karratha. It would've been over two-and-a-half days of hard driving for him, so he'd *appropriated* a local pilot and his plane for the trip instead. He'd also brought two of his most trusted officers with him as backup.

Dan and Damien hugged, slapping each other on the back like men do when greeting a long-lost friend, while Jenna stood back and smiled. It was good to see him again, and she studied his familiar face. It was a hard face, all sharp angles and slabbed cheekbones, the fierceness formed probably from seeing the undesirable side of humanity for so long. It'd been nearly two years since he'd last visited them on the station. He'd brought his family with him, his wife and two young girls, and they loved their time in the outback. So much so, one of the girls had refused to go home, saying she didn't want to leave the horses. Jenna smiled at the memory. Then Damien engulfed her in his strong arms and whispered in her ear, 'Don't worry, we'll get her back safe and sound.' And Jenna felt a welcome relief flood through her veins, knowing he was here.

They were meeting at the hotel because Damien didn't want to draw any more attention than was absolutely necessary to their presence. He hadn't confirmed anything, but Jenna got the feeling he was keeping out of sight of the rumored corrupt cops. Jenna didn't want to pry in police business, so she'd left it alone. Damien had gone against protocol, not letting the head of the Darwin office know that he was here. Telling Dan and Jenna it was an *unofficial* visit at the moment.

Damien ushered them into a grungy hotel room. 'All I can offer you is instant coffee, sorry,' he apologized, directing them to take a chair each in the corner of the room. 'This is Detective Stan Wolcock,' Damien said, pointing to a tall, thin, sandy-haired man sitting at a cramped desk typing on a laptop.

Dan shook his hand, and Jenna nodded to him.

'And this is Sergeant William Leeman.'

A stocky man with short, dark hair and a square jaw stepped toward them. He shook Dan's hand, a serious look on his face, then shook Jenna's with equal gravity.

'Sorry it's a little pokey in here, but it'll do as a makeshift HQ for a while,' Damien continued.

'Thanks for doing this, Damo.' Jenna took the mug of proffered coffee from his hand, but caught his wrist as he turned away. 'You don't know what this means to us.' This wasn't the only time Damien had gone out of his way to help them, and Jenna knew how much they owed him already.

'I think I do know,' he replied softly. 'Don't forget I have a family of my own.' He turned back to continue making coffee, leaving her with the unsaid sentiment hovering in the air, that he knew what it was like to be a parent. To want to protect your child, no matter what. She hoped he wasn't breaking too many rules to help them.

'So, tell me everything you know, right from the start.' Damien sat on the edge of the bed facing them, his own cup of coffee steaming in his hands. Even though he'd heard it before, Damien listened intently as Dan told the story right from when they discovered Rose missing early last Sunday morning, up until the call from Ebony telling them what she knew about Koen and Rose's flight from the biker gang, The Sinners. Jenna added her bits to the story if she thought Dan left out something important. Stan and William listened intently as well, neither of them saying a word.

'Wow, this Bull has some balls,' Damien finally said when they both ground to a halt. 'Abducting people in broad daylight. He's either completely insane or believes he's untouchable.'

'We've been hearing some things about his biker gang,' William interceded. 'They've been on our radar for a while. Well, on the Darwin office's radar,' he amended. 'We know that Corey, or Bull as he's better known, is the vice-president. But it's quite a small chapter, only twenty or so members. Their main chapter is in Melbourne, and they have other small groups in Kalgoorlie and Albury as well. We think most of their money comes from selling methamphetamines, but of course we can't prove it, which is why they're being watched carefully. We're assembling as much data on them as we can, so we can strike when we have enough to put them in jail.'

'We've also heard a few rumors, about cops being paid off to stay quiet here in Darwin.' Damien took over the conversation again. 'I believe there might be some sort of internal investigation going on, but that's as much as I can say, and even telling you that might put my job on the line. But the internal investigation isn't going to help us at the moment. What it does mean is we can't trust anyone in the Darwin office. We have to do as much of this on our own as possible. Don't get me wrong, though. We will probably need to inform the Darwin office sooner or later.'

'Do you know anything about this cousin, Jon?' William asked.

'No, we've never met him. I spoke to him on the phone for the first time today. He seems like a man of few words,' Jenna replied.

'We need to go over and have a chat with him. I'd like to get the whole story from the source, face to face, if you know what I mean. The three of us can do that in a minute, while Stan and William keep digging up information. There's a lot that still needs to be done. Favors called in, paperwork to be written, leads to be followed, that kind of thing.'

'What kind of favors, what information?' Dan asked.

'We need to know as much as we can about this Sinners gang. I'd like to be able to just go and raid the clubhouse, put them all in jail where they can't hurt Rose or you or anyone else. But it's not that easy. We'd need a warrant for that and I'm not sure we have enough evidence. Yet.'

'But they abducted Rose and her friend and kept her tied up in the clubhouse for hours, beat them, threatened to kill them. Surely that's enough?' Jenna was more than a little surprised.

'Yes, but that's all her word against theirs at the moment.

Circumstantial evidence. We need hard evidence. Which we might find if we're allowed to search the clubhouse, but we need a warrant. And to do that we need to convince a judge of our case. And they'd want to know why we weren't collaborating with the Darwin office. Then we'd be really setting the cat amongst the pigeons, with allegations of corrupt cops. We have to have our story straight first. And we also don't want to tip this Bull off to what we're up to if we can help it. He might do a runner.'

'So, we're in a bit of a predicament,' said Dan slowly.

'Nothing we can't solve, given a little time,' Damien replied. 'Which is why we need to double-check Rose and her friend are safe. Once I know they're out of harm's way, then I can set the ball rolling. But I also need to know you guys are safe, as well as Ebony and Jay. Tick some boxes.'

'Alright let's get moving, I want to meet this Jon myself,' Jenna declared, standing up. She was itching to do something constructive. Needed to hear it from Jon's mouth that Rose was indeed safe. She understood Damo's situation, he was constrained by the rules of the law. But she wasn't. And if it came down to it, she'd do anything to protect her daughter.

They'd gone to see Jon last night, and he'd filled them in on all the missing details Rose hadn't been able to convey in her short phone call. He assured them Rose and Koen should be safe in the well-hidden hut and gave them a hand-drawn map as to how to find it. Damien spent another hour huddled at a small table and chairs in the backyard, talking to Jon, while Jenna and Dan waited by the car. He'd come back looking rather pleased with himself, saying Jon had given him some interesting information they might be able to use. But he wouldn't elaborate, and then he'd sent them off to get some rest, saying William would watch over them for the night. Dan had protested that they didn't need protection, that Jello would warn them if anyone came near, but Damian ignored him.

Rolling over, Jenna lifted the edge of the curtain and peered out into the early morning light. The shadow of the unmarked Holden Commodore could just be seen parked under the trees nearby. It was too dark to see if William was still awake in there. It was time they got up and moving. She needed to talk to Damien again, to see if he'd come up with anything else to help nail Corey overnight.

The need to be able to take Rose into her arms, to make sure she was really alive, really okay, to comfort her, was almost overwhelming. She desperately wanted to see her daughter, and she wasn't sure if she could wait much longer.

* * *

Rose rolled over in bed, watching the early morning light trickling through the window, playing over the translucent mosquito net. Koen's arm was draped over her shoulder, the weight heavy and comforting. She gave a secret smile. Her body was still tingling gently from what they'd done together. Koen was a tender, passionate lover, and she couldn't get enough of him.

She also couldn't believe how fast things had happened between them. But it'd felt so right. Their attraction had been almost instantaneous, she noticed it the first time she got on the back of his motorbike. Had that only been a week ago? It was there when he kept her warm the first night they slept beside Lake Argyle. The first time they kissed. Even after he stole her money, she found she could never really hate him. And the night he gave her cash back, the connection was still as strong as ever. She might be falling in love with him. The idea flickered through her mind. Wait, what? She couldn't possibly be falling in love with Koen. He was a rogue, he even admitted himself that he was a bit of a rat-bag. The word commitment wasn't in his vocabulary. What could they possibly have in common? She was going back to her parent's station when this was all over. Where would he fit into her life?

If only she knew he felt the same way. But her Empath gift didn't work on him, and it was hard for her to trust in her plain old instincts. She mulled the question over in her mind. Perhaps there was a reason her gift didn't work on him. What kind of impact would such strong emotions have on her? Maybe she might become so overwhelmed by the sensations, she wouldn't know what to think or how to feel. Perhaps this lack of impressions from him was allowing her to form her own feelings without influence or prejudice? Then again, perhaps she'd never really know. It would be nice to talk to her mother, or even her grandmother, they might be able to help her understand what was going on. Maybe they had instances where their gifts hadn't worked on certain people, too.

Rose shifted restlessly, wondering what her parents were up to. Had they made it to Darwin already? This not knowing was killing her. If what Ebony had told her on the phone was true, then they should've been in town last night. It was a comforting thought that they were closer to her now.

A part of her wanted to stay here all day with Koen in the little hut, hidden away from the rest of the world. But that wasn't going to happen, not with Bull still out there. Koen grunted behind her, and she rolled over to see his eyes open.

'Morning, sleepyhead.' She grinned.

'Mmff,' he mumbled. But a slow, wicked smile spread over his face.

'How did you sleep?' she enquired, her voice still husky, letting her fingers drift down the length of his arm.

'Great, once I finally got to sleep.'

'I'm sorry, did I keep you up past your bedtime?' she crooned, snuggling in closer so her bare breasts were touching his chest.

'Oh, you kept me up alright. At least three times if my math is correct.'

She giggled at his innuendo. His hand drew lazy circles on her back as he gazed at her. She studied his face in the early morning light. The injuries she'd been able to ignore last night were revealed in all their glory today. His poor face. There was a small cut above his left eye and a large bruise forming on his left temple that would soon engulf his whole eye. His bottom lip was slightly swollen from the cut just starting to heal in the corner. Tentatively, she reached out and traced around his mouth.

'I'm so sorry I got you involved in all of this,' she whispered the words so softly she wasn't sure he'd hear her.

'I'm not. I'm glad I was there. What would've happened if Bull had captured you that night at the hotel? You'd quite possibly be dead by now.' He winced, as if the words hurt to even speak them out loud. 'I couldn't bear to think of that bastard, with his hands on you. If he ever hurts you again, I'm gonna kill him.' He meant it too, Rose could feel the tightly leashed tension running through his arm. 'You mean a lot to me, Rose. I care about you, and I want to see you safe.'

She drew in a sharp breath. 'I care about you, too, Koen.'

He stared at her as if he was about to say more. Did she want him to say more? Did she want to know how he truly felt about her?

Then he grinned, and the spell was broken. 'Really? If that's the case, I think you should show me exactly how much you care.' He rolled onto his back and pulled her on top of him.

The feeling of him stretched out beneath her, skin on skin, body on body, was exhilarating. Even after last night, her body reacted to his touch instantly, wanting more of him. Ever so gently, she placed her lips on his, not wanting to hurt his battered mouth.

'You can do better than that,' he growled, and crushed his lips against hers, funneling all his need and passion into her. She forgot about his injuries, forgot about Bull, forgot everything except for Koen. His tongue, his biceps, his long legs twined around hers and the evidence of his growing desire.

* * *

Rose's hand was small inside his as they walked around the far side of the billabong, looking back toward the hut. He liked the way it felt, her palm nestled against his, her petite fingers entwined through his own. Rose had wanted to watch the sunset from the other side of the billabong tonight. To get a different perspective.

The vista of the red sun sinking slowly below the horizon, with the woodland as a backdrop, was just as spectacular as last night. There wasn't a cloud in the sky—which wasn't unusual for the dry season—and the endless swathes of open blue turning to darker indigo almost stole the breath from his lungs with its beauty. The sound of hundreds of frogs calling softly filled the silence between them. He was glad he'd had this time out in Kakadu. Something had opened up inside him here, allowed him to deepen his connection with country. Almost as if fate had brought him here.

'What makes all those marks at the edge of the water? Where all the mud is churned up?' Rose asked, breaking the comfortable silence.

'Wild buffalo. They're a bit of a problem in the park. You need to watch out for them, they can be dangerous,' he warned. 'We've been lucky none have come around the hut so far.'

'Okay,' she replied vaguely, as if her mind were elsewhere. 'At least we haven't seen Old Man Crocodile today.' He felt a tiny shudder run through her arm and up into his. Seeing the croc grab the bird yesterday had really unsettled her.

They'd spent most of the morning in bed. Making love. He wanted to think of it as having sex, but that's what he did with all the other girls he'd been with. With Rose, it was different. It was more than just a physical sensation, although the physical stuff was amazing. The phrase *making love* applied with her. He cared about her. Cared about her needs, wanted to please her. Which scared the hell out of him.

Rose suggested a walk before dinner, to explore the area and stretch her legs. He'd caught more fish this afternoon, dinner was going to be a repetition of last night. She didn't want to go too far, just in case Bindi or Jon suddenly arrived. He also wanted to check on the hidden car, so had readily agreed.

'If we don't hear something by tomorrow morning, I'm going back to Darwin,' she said.

He was about to open his mouth to argue with her, tell her Jon had ordered them to stay put. And he trusted Jon. Knew he wouldn't put them in any undue danger. But he was just as restless as Rose at the lack of information. Even though his time out here with Rose had been two of the best days of his life, they couldn't keep waiting like this.

'Okay.'

'Really, you agree with me?' She looked up at him, surprise in the lines around her mouth.

'Yep, but we're not going to drive straight into Darwin and announce our presence. We'll sneak into Jabiru and find a public phone box. Call Bindi to see if she knows anything first. Okay?'

'Yes,' she said with a frown, which made him think she wasn't completely happy with his plan, but would go along with it. For now. 'That's good.'

He could tell she felt better now she had something to look forward to, a solid plan that would mean they weren't just waiting here biding their time, like sitting ducks. But he was still worried about what they might find. They knew her parents should be in Darwin by now. But what that meant, neither of them really knew. The one thing he didn't tell her was at the first hint of danger he was getting her out of there. Kicking and screaming if he had to. It didn't matter to him if her parents had been captured, or tortured, or even killed by Bull. Rose was the only thing he cared about keeping safe now.

'Let's go back and cook dinner, I'm starving.' She tugged on his hand, and his stomach rumbled in response at the thought of a meal.

'Mmm, me too. But I'm not just hungry for food.' He cocked an eyebrow suggestively as she turned to look at him.

'We'll just have to see about that, Mr Babroda.' Her eyebrows waggled in response, then she stood on tiptoe and kissed him, hard and passionate, leaving him in no doubt she would be happy to oblige his wants.

'Show me the way home, girl.'

Something kept niggling at the back of his mind, even as he watched her hips sway seductively in front of him. He wanted to go back to the hut and make love to Rose again. Lose himself in her body. And in her soul. But just because he wanted to do that more than anything, didn't mean he had a right to. He was starting to lose himself in her. Perhaps even fall in love with her. Which was the absolute last thing he should be doing. He planned to leave this part of Australia and never come back. He'd hurt too many people, and if he stayed would go on doing so, because he just couldn't seem to get anything right, no matter how hard he tried. He was a misfit. He shouldn't have slept with her, it would only make it harder. And he shouldn't sleep with her tonight, either. But God help him, how could he refuse her. One more night, that's all he'd allow himself.

Rose deserved a proper man. A good man. One who would

settle, be strong and committed, give her a family one day. All the things he couldn't give her because he was cursed. Or at least that's the way it felt.

It would hurt to leave her, if he spent even one more night in her arms, but in the end, he'd be doing them both a favor.

'I'll go and light the stove and the lamp,' Rose said, and Koen was shocked to see they were almost back at the hut. Dusk had stolen in around them as they walked. 'Will you go and clean the fish?'

He'd left the fish in a bucket of water around the back of the hut to keep them fresh. 'Sure, I'll bring them in a minute.'

She was already up on the veranda, but she pulled him back by the hand and looked him directly in the face. This was interesting. Standing on the verandah, she was almost as tall as him. His cock roused at the idea this conjured in his mind, especially when she leaned in and kissed him resoundingly. They stayed locked in their embrace for many minutes, until Koen was about to abandon the idea of fish for dinner and drag her inside to the bed, when he heard the unmistakable sound of a car engine. It was very faint, but sound travelled a long way in the stillness out here.

They pulled apart and stared into the coming darkness, both on high alert. It was definitely a car, not the dreaded sound of a Harley motorbike, which reassured him a little. But Bull could just as easily be driving a car. They couldn't be too careful.

'Quick, go and hide where I told you,' he commanded. They had a plan in place for this exact occurrence. She nodded, gave him a quick, fearful glance and took off like a rabbit into the scrub beside the hut. He took off in the opposite direction, cross-country to a spot where he could intercept the car as it came down the winding track.

He was in place within two minutes, the blood pounding through his veins after his run through the trees. The sound of the car got louder, and now he could see the glow of headlights bouncing crazily through the trees. Bloody hell, the lights in his eyes were making it hard to see what kind of car was coming. It was white, that much he could tell. And the shape looked right. Bindi drove a white 4WD Land Cruiser. His heart-rate refused to slow, however. He needed to make absolutely certain it was her.

The car drew closer. He'd be able to see better if he got nearer to the track, but he couldn't move, not now, it'd give him away, and he still couldn't quite make out the driver. The car was almost level with him now, and he finally caught a glimpse of Bindi through the driver's side window. His breath came out in a whoosh of relief. There was no one else in the car, just her. Thank God they'd finally have some answers.

Hesitating for a second, he resisted the urge to run out in front of the car and wave. Instead, he ran back the way he'd come, toward the hut, to let Rose know it was safe. She would be terrified waiting there in the dark, not knowing what was going on.

Skidding to a stop, he yelled to Rose, 'It's okay, it's Bindi, you can come out.'

A few seconds later, her pale face emerged hesitantly from the side of the hut. He stood and waited for her to come to him, then put his arm around her waist and pulled her in for a relieved hug as they waited for the car to maneuver through the last few twists and turns of the track.

The car stopped a few feet in front of them, the engine still running and the headlights still on. Strange. Then Bindi stepped out of the driver's side.

'I'm so sorry, Koen.' Tears were streaming down Bindi's face. Jesus, what'd happened. He took a step forward, to go to her, comfort her, ask her what was wrong, when another form exited the back seat, right behind Bindi.

'Nice to see you again. I wasn't sure if this bitch was telling me the truth. Lucky for her she was.'

Koen's blood froze in his veins. Rose gasped loudly next to him.

It was Bull, holding a gun to Bindi's temple.

CHAPTER TWENTY-ONE

Jenna paced back and forth inside the tiny caravan. She couldn't sit still, she needed to know what was going on. Glancing out the window, she could see the spectacle of the setting sun coloring the sky, giving one last hurrah before it sank below the horizon. But tonight Jenna didn't care about the sunset. She glanced again at the mobile phone lying on the small kitchen table. It remained stubbornly silent.

'Damn, when is he going to call?' The words erupted louder than she intended, her pent-up frustration needing to be released somehow.

'It's only been an hour and a half, Jenna, sit down, you're making me giddy with all that pacing.' Dan lay stretched out on the bed at one end of the caravan, head propped on the pillows.

'How can you just lie there, and be so blasé about it all? Don't you care what's happening?' she nearly yelled. But then was immediately repentant. 'Sorry, that was unfair. I know you care, it's just that…oooh, I'm so…'

'I know what you meant, babe,' he replied, his eyes softening as he looked up at her. Of course, he was just as worried as she was, he was better at containing his agitation, he always had been. Able to stay cool and calm in the face of uncertainty. It was one of the many, many things she loved about him.

She sat down at the tiny table and began to gnaw on her bottom lip. Damien and his men were right this moment raiding The Sinners clubhouse.

When Jenna and Dan had arrived at the dingy hotel room this morning, Damien was looking more than pleased with himself. He told them Jon had passed along some very helpful information last night. It seemed Koen's sister, Bindi and her partner, had been held captive in a town called Jabiru and threatened by Bull and some of his gang. Terrorized until she finally revealed where Koen and Rose were going the morning after they'd stayed with her. Which was how Bull had tracked them down at the famous rock art tourist spot. Bindi hadn't yet reported the incident to the police, for many reasons, the biggest one being she had an ingrained distrust of cops. But she also didn't want to get Koen into any trouble, and so had been biding her time to see what happened. Damien and William were about to interview the sister and her partner over the phone that morning.

Bindi and Michael had gone on to corroborate the story and said they would be prepared to say the same in court. It'd been enough for Damien to finally get the warrants he needed, and Dan and Jenna had been jubilant. But Damien warned her this was where they'd need to involve the local police, they couldn't possibly pull this off with just him and his two officers. Dan and Jenna listened to Damien on the phone as he approached the Officer in Charge, Senior Sargent Kirk Balldachi, finally managing to convince him that a raid needed to be conducted tonight, before the gang had time to get word and flee. They would be specifically looking for the three men who took Bindi captive, as that was the brief in the warrant, to arrest those three men. But of course, if they found anything else in the process, such as evidence that Rose and Koen had been held captive, or drugs…Damien just smiled as he relayed this information and let their imagination deal with the rest.

When Jenna asked how Damien was going to make sure Bull was there when they raided, he gave her a small, secret smile. Told her he'd put something in place, set up a meeting that would require Bull, as the vice-president, to be present. She had to believe him.

Dan had begged and pleaded with his old friend to be allowed to come along on the raid. Just to watch, he'd said. Or at least let them wait nearby, so they could see firsthand what went down. Damien had been polite but firm in his refusal. They'd been told to go back to their accommodation and wait for him to call. She knew he would, but the waiting was killing her. The Darwin police had only been told the barest minimum, on a need-to-know-basis, and the Senior Sargent had picked the men he felt were most trustworthy, but Jenna still worried word would somehow leak out. That Bull might be tipped off. If he wasn't there, then all this would've been for nothing. They'd be no closer to helping her daughter. Or herself and her mother, but her own safety was secondary in her mind to that of her daughter's.

The phone trilled loudly. Jenna gasped and stared down at the vibrating mobile like it might bite her.

'I'll get it.' Dan was already half-way off the bed and in one stride had reached the table and picked up the phone.

'Damo?'

Jenna watched his face intently, trying to decipher the small micro-emotions that flittered across it as he listened to Damien.

'Mmm hmm. That's good.' Dan's brows lowered. Then a grim smile played over his lips. 'That's great news.'

She wanted to shake him and scream at him to tell her what was going on. But she kept her mouth shut and tried to hear what Damien was saying.

'Really? Shit, that's not so good.' Dan's eyes widened in dismay and his free hand clenched by his side. 'Okay, yep, I understand. We'll come and meet you in half an hour.' Dan pressed the End button and laid the phone thoughtfully back on the table.

'What? What happened?' Jenna was on her feet, staring up into her husband's face. But she didn't like what she was seeing, something hadn't gone according to plan, she could tell.

He took her hands in his. 'It all went down pretty smoothly. There was very little resistance from the bikers when they went in,' he recited, as if making sure he got Damo's tale word-for-word. 'They found fifteen members in all, two of them women. The two blokes Bindi identified were there, a guy called Snake, and another one called Mongrel. So that's good they got what they went in for, Damo's quite relieved about that.'

'But,' Jenna said impatiently. He just needed to get on with it, because she could feel the but coming.

'But Bull and his girlfriend were nowhere to be found.'

Her heart plummeted. She let go of his hands and sat down with a thump. They'd failed. Bull was still on the loose. Now what were they going to do?

She hardly heard Dan's next words. 'Damo thinks even after all his efforts to keep it on the down-low, somehow Bull got tipped off. One of the club members said he'd left about mid-afternoon on some errand or other. He was due back for a meeting with a new potential club member at five, but never showed. That must've been the meeting Damien set up with him, to make sure he was there. Damo reckons he was tipped off three or four hours before the raid. Which was when the other police officers were briefed for the first time,' Dan finished darkly.

Jenna didn't really care how Bull had escaped their net, all that mattered was how to move forward from here. 'We need to go and get Rose from Kakadu. Get her to safety. Then we'll leave, go somewhere Bull can't find us. We'll leave the country if we have to.'

'Jenna.' Dan's strong arms came around her rigid shoulders, pulling her into his body. 'Come on, babe, it'll be okay,' he crooned. 'I agree, let's go and get Rose, make sure she's safe. Then we'll have a family meeting, with all of us and Damo and figure out the best thing to do from here. I don't think Bull is an immediate threat to us anymore, he knows the cops are on to him. He'll only be thinking about getting away from them. We have time to sort something out. We don't need to leave the country,' he chided.

Even though Dan's embrace was helping calm her racing pulse, she wasn't sure he was right. Something in her bones was telling her Bull was still a threat. A big one.

* * *

Rose was too shocked to move. For a few seconds, she was even too shocked to breathe. Her mind was trying to comprehend exactly what was going on. Bindi had come to tell them some news. But no, Bull had abducted her and forced her to bring him out here. How had he known? Why hadn't Bindi been more careful? Where were her mum and dad? Were they dead? All these questions circled around in her brain. But the only one that mattered was how they were going to get out of this.

Koen stood as still as a statue next to her, tension radiating from every pore. He was going to do something stupid, she just knew it. And then Bull would shoot him. She tried desperately to think of something to say to defuse the situation. But before she could open her mouth, another sound broke the quiet of the night. A familiar sound, one they'd been dreading. The low rumble of a Harley motorcycle winding its way down the narrow track. Rose strained to hear. It sounded like only one bike, not the whole gang coming to get them as she'd imagined.

'Move away from the car,' Bull growled as he pushed Bindi roughly.

She turned a venomous look on him and raised her fists in defiance. But all it took was for Bull to point the gun in Rose and Koen's direction, for her to lower them again.

'Just like I thought, you're all a pack of pansies, too eager to save each other. It's very commendable. But you're too stupid to see, it's the one weakness that gives me power over you.' He cast a quick glance over his shoulder to check on the progress of the Harley. The bright headlight lit up the woodland around them like it was day. The Harley came to a stop behind Bindi's car and a woman stepped off it. Alesha.

'Nice riding, babe,' Corey cooed delightedly at the figure coming toward them.

Rose was still listening for the telltale sound of any more motorbikes coming their way, but it seemed Bull and Alesha were on their own. Rose didn't have time to wonder why, because Bull handed the gun to Alesha, giving her a quick, lecherous kiss on the lips as he did so.

'Keep an eye on these two, will you, while I tie this bitch up out of the way.'

'Sure thing, babe.' Alesha sauntered toward them, her form a dark shadow against the bright headlights of the car. But Rose didn't need to see her face to know the woman was smiling perversely. She was enjoying this nearly as much as Bull was.

Or was she?

As the woman came closer, Rose read her aura. And she was giving off conflicting emotions.

'Don't move, handsome,' Alesha said as Rose felt Koen twitch beside her.

Koen bared his teeth, clenched his fists at his side, but did as he was told and remained standing still.

'Don't think for a second I won't hesitate to shoot you just because I'm a woman.'

But this wasn't completely true. Rose could feel a certain kind of steely determination coming from the woman. But there was also hesitation, she wasn't wholly committed to this plan of action. There was also another emotion. Was it frustration? But frustration at what? Or perhaps the question should be, at whom? Bull. Was she frustrated with Bull? There might be a chink in this woman's armor, if Rose could somehow use it against her.

'You two thought you were so smart getting away from us. But we get the last laugh. Ain't that right, babe?' she called over her shoulder, checking to see what Bull was up to.

'Shut up, woman. I'll be there in a second, no need for you to keep blabbering on.'

A shaft of blue passed through Alesha's aura, and Rose knew she'd been hurt by Bull's rudeness. Rose almost felt a stab of pity for the woman. Who in their right mind would put up with a bastard like him? He thought she was completely loyal to him, and he could treat her anyway he wished. And Alesha did love him, had loved him for a long time, but that love was being eroded, replaced by something else. Rose understood Alesha was starting to question her love for this man. There was a revulsion deep inside Alesha, a suffering beyond endurance. Rose wondered why she hadn't seen it before. Perhaps she could play to Alesha's weakness.

'Why do you let Bull speak to you like that? Like you're a piece of dirt?' She directed her low comment to Alesha, hoping Bull wouldn't overhear them. 'I wouldn't put up with that if I were you.'

Alesha shot her a startled look. Rose had never told Koen about her gift and maybe she should have, but now wasn't the time, and she hoped he'd just go along with her. But his

227

look of cross disbelief told her he didn't understand what she was trying to do.

'What are you doing to Bindi? You better not hurt her, you bastard,' Koen yelled, ignoring Rose. Bull had Bindi over by a tree, right on the periphery of the circle of light spread by the car headlights. He was tying her to the tree so she couldn't get away. And so she couldn't come to their aid, either. Bindi made a muffled noise. Bull had stuffed a gag in her mouth. Koen went to take a step forward, and Alesha raised the gun slightly, pointing it at his heart.

'Didn't you hear me? Don't try to be a hero.' Alesha's face was deadpan, but Rose could feel the anxiousness gnawing at the edges of her composure.

Maybe she should try a different tack. 'What are you gonna do with us now?' Rose demanded, yelling louder than was necessary to make sure Bull heard as he finished tying up Bindi. It might not be the right thing to do to provoke Bull. But if she could somehow get him angry enough, perhaps piss Alesha off as well, there might be another way for her to get through to his girlfriend.

'What I want to do is to kill you both fucking dead right now. But I'm not going to do that. I need you as bait. Your precious mother and her deadbeat husband did exactly what I thought they'd do. They came running to rescue you and now they're in town. But they're surrounded by fucking cops, and it's too risky to try and get them too.' Rose's heart skipped a beat at the information. They were safe, for now. 'But Jenna's not really the one I want, anyway. It's Ebony I want. She's the one who took away my life. She's the one who killed Alexander. And now she's been left vulnerable on the station. You're going to help me get her. Draw her out into the open.'

Alesha's face tightened at Bull's words and Rose felt a stab of pure envy come from the woman. She hated Ebony as much as Bull did. But for completely different reasons. She was jealous of Ebony. Jealous of her because she took up Bull's every waking moment.

'What's gonna happen once you kill Ebony, and then me, and then my mother? That's a lot of killing. What are you going to do then, Bull? Will it truly be over for you? You'll have to go on the run, the cops won't rest if you kill three innocent women.' Rose was facing Bull, but she was really directing her words to Alesha. Trying to get her to understand. Put the echo of doubt in her mind. Did Alesha really want to live like that? Perhaps she did. But Rose didn't think so. The tattoos and the leather were all a facade, most of it put there to please Bull. But pleasing him was starting to wear thin. 'What do you think, Alesha? Do you want to live like that?'

'What do you mean?' she snarled.

'Are you prepared to live with the death of all of us on your conscience? Live life on the run, constantly looking over your shoulder. You'll be charged as an accomplice. When they catch you, you'll probably spend the rest of your life in jail.' Rose knew Koen had glanced at her out of the corner of his eye, but she ignored him and continued to taunt Alesha. 'Is that what you want?'

The gun in Alesha's hands lowered slightly as she looked in consternation at Rose. Rose could feel her determination wavering. Good, she was getting through.

'He treats you with such disrespect, yet you're willing to give it all up for him. Why is that? It sounds a little one-sided to me.' Alesha's confusion grew stronger, her aura flickering between purple and blue now. Rose's heart lurched. Was she actually getting through? 'How many other people has Bull killed?' The thought struck her like a blow, and she knew instantly from Alesha's emotions that she'd hit the target. Bull had killed before. 'How many more people will he kill before he's happy, Alesha?'

'Shut the fuck up, you little whore,' Bull yelled, no longer concentrating on tying up Bindi, instead staring at her, his eyes full of hatred.

Alesha glanced over her shoulder to look at Bull, suddenly unsure, the gun dangling, forgotten in her hand.

Koen moved before Rose knew what he was up to. He lunged forward, covering the distance between him and Alesha at surprising speed. He was going to try and take the woman down while she was distracted. At the last second, Alesha turned and raised the gun. Aimed it wildly. Had Rose in her sights. Then Koen lunged at her, diving in front of the gun.

The sound of a single gunshot echoed through the night. Rose screamed. Koen crashed to the ground.

She'd shot Koen. He'd jumped in front of Rose to save her.

'Oh no.' The low keening sound came not from Koen, but from Alesha. Fear and adrenaline coursed through the woman, Rose could feel it through her aura. But she no longer cared about Alesha. All she wanted was to see if Koen was still alive.

'What the fuck have you done, woman?' Bull yelled in outrage from behind her, charging back from the tree.

Alesha swung around and pointed the gun at Bull.

'What the fuck?' Bull stopped in his tracks.

Rose took the chance and ran to Koen's side. Kneeling down in the dust, she felt for a pulse. He was still breathing, thank God. There was fresh, bright blood flowing from a wound in his head. Oh, no. Oh, no. She needed to get him to a hospital. Now.

'Look what you made me do,' Alesha screeched hysterically. The gun was shaking in her hands. 'I'm not staying here to pay for your crimes. To cover up your dirty work. You never loved me, not really. All you ever loved was yourself and your stupid need for vengeance. I don't know why I stuck around so long, I really don't.' Her voice shook with rage. Slowly she backed away, still pointing the gun at Bull, making her way toward the motorbike. 'You can stay here and clean up your own mess, I'm leaving.' With that, she stepped onto the bike and fired it up, the guttural engine ripping through the quiet of the night.

'You get back here right now,' Bull growled, not believing she would truly leave.

She aimed the gun at him. 'Don't give me a reason to shoot you too, Bull.' Then the engine revved, the back-wheel spinning in the dirt, and Alesha was gone.

It was just Rose and Bull now.

Bull turned around, and the look of bewilderment on his face was almost comical. His features soon turned hard again, however, as he took in the scene.

'See what the women in your family do, they take everything away from me, everything that's precious.' On the last word, Bull's voice broke. 'You turned my woman against me.' Bull swiveled his head to look in the direction of the disappearing headlight. 'She didn't think I loved her, but I did, in my own way.' When he turned back, Rose caught the glint of something metal in his hand. A knife—a large one—rested in his palm. Rose stood up, but hovered protectively over Koen. What was she going to do now? She needed a weapon.

'And you took away my father. The only person who truly loved me. Who truly understood me.' Was that tears she saw glinting in his eyes? Surely not. Surely this big hulk of a bearded man wasn't crying? In front of her. 'When he died, I lost my ability to hypnotize people. Did you know that? I not only lost the only man who gave meaning to my life, but I lost the one thing that made me special, gave me my power. Ebony took that away from me.'

Things were starting to make a horrible kind of sense now. In a twisted way, he blamed Ebony for losing the one thing that mattered to him. She wondered how she'd feel if she were to lose her gift. This guy was seriously damaged. She almost felt sorry for him. He belonged in a mental institution, not a jail.

'What you said before is probably true. I will live the rest of my life on the run. But it will be worth it, just to feel your blood running over my hands and knowing I got my revenge.'

Ice formed in Rose's veins at his words. He took a few menacing steps toward her, knife held easily in his right hand, a slow grin spreading on his face. She backed away, toward the edge of the billabong, leading him away from Koen. The water spread out dark and silken behind her, calm and peaceful. Would she dare go in there if he forced her?

Step-by-step she backed toward the billabong, down the dusty ramp they used to launch the boat, Bull stalking behind her.

'There's nowhere for you to go. You may as well give up and get it over with. I've waited so long to get my revenge. When your grandmother took my gift away, she made me into something less. I could hardly function without it. And those years I spent in jail...' He gave a nasty grimace. 'Well, let's just say, they weren't nice. It's taken me a long time to believe in myself again. To grow strong, to be a man. But I did it, I forced myself to lick other men's boots, to grovel, ingratiate myself. Until finally I made it to the top. It's gonna feel so satisfying, sliding this knife over your throat, watching your life ebb away.'

A shiver ran down her spine, and she could almost feel the knife against her skin. The sheer hatred Bull had for her was coming off him in waves so dark and menacing, his aura threatened to overwhelm her. It was his hatred for her grandmother and her family that had kept him going for all these years, she knew that now. There was a splash as her left boot landed in the water. Oh Jesus, she was right on the edge now. She stopped, not knowing what to do. Turning to her right, she started to skirt around the edge, feeling the mud sucking at her boots. Rose reached up and grabbed hold of her jet necklace, held onto it as if her life depended on it. The cool touch of the stone against her palm brought back a little clarity, helped her push down the naked fear his emotions were causing. Whether it was the magical properties of the jet, she didn't know, but her mind suddenly cleared, and a kernel of a plan formed in her head. That's when she noticed his feet were in the water, too. Did he realize the danger?

'Come on, Rose, come to Papa. I'm a good swimmer. If you dive into the water, I'll find you. Drowning isn't my preferred way of killing you, but it'll do, at a pinch.'

He didn't appreciate the danger. But how was she going to —

Bull lunged at her, knife pointing directly at her chest. She tripped and almost went down as her foot caught in the long sedge grasses at the edge of the water. But her almost-fall saved her, as Bull's blade went wide of the mark and he stumbled forward into her. They both went down into the muddy water. They were tangled together, everything was slippery and she couldn't seem to get a grip on the large man. Her face was pushed beneath the shallow water, and panic clawed at her insides. She was going to drown in less than two feet of water. He was going to drown her, just like he said he would. Heaving her knees upwards with all her might, she arched her back and tilted sideways. A gap opened up between their bodies, and she kicked out with all her might, hearing him grunt in pain as her foot connected with his large stomach.

She was free. Scrambling backward on her hands and feet,

she saw Bull's dark form struggling to rise up in the water behind her. She must've pushed him further out than she thought during their struggle. Paddling backward, trying to regain his feet, he was almost waist-deep now. But he still held the evil knife in his hand, and she caught the glint of pure hatred in his eyes. He wasn't done with her yet.

Suddenly, the water heaved and Bull fell forward, thrashing his arms at the water, as if fighting an invisible assailant. The look on his face was one of pure terror. Then he disappeared beneath the surface. The water boiled and frothed for a few more seconds until everything went uncannily silent.

Just like that. No time to utter even one sound. He was gone. A few seconds later, small waves formed by the turbulence lapped at her feet. Rose scrambled further backward, away from water's edge.

Holy fuck. Rose started to shake all over, tears streaming down her face.

CHAPTER TWENTY-TWO

The smell of disinfectant woke him. He hated that sterile smell. It reminded him of hospitals. And he hated hospitals, they were only for sick people and he was as strong as an ox. Except his head hurt like a bitch. He reached up a tentative hand to the side of his head and his eyes flew open.

What the hell? Why were bandages covering his forehead? Where was he? His gaze took in white walls, white sheets covering the bed in which he was lying, beeping instruments next to him. He let out a low groan. Bullshit, he was in a hospital. He shut his eyes again, as if he might be able to shut out reality at the same time.

'Koen?' It was Rose's voice.

Sweet relief flooded through him, and he opened his eyes to find her hovering next to his bed. She was here. She wasn't a figment of his imagination, as he'd feared. Her hand came to rest over the top of his, and he grabbed it and held on like it was his only lifeline. Her beautiful blue eyes gazed down at him. Jesus, she was a sight for sore eyes.

'Am I glad to see you, you gotta get me outta here.' Why was his throat so dry and his voice so raspy?

'It's okay, Koen. You're in the Darwin hospital. But you can't get up just yet.' A gentle hand landed on his chest and easily pushed him back into the pillows. He was as weak as a bloody kitten. What was going on here? Every time he moved his head, it throbbed like he'd been hit by a ten-ton truck.

'You were shot. Don't you remember?'

'What?' But at her words, images began to flood back into his memory. Images of him and Rose at the billabong. He and Rose in the hut, on the bed, making love underneath the mosquito net. He smiled as he remembered that. Then Bindi's car arriving down the track.

Bull stepping out of the car with a gun.

'Bindi, is she okay?' He sat up in alarm. Bull had tied her to a tree, put a gag in her mouth. God, if he'd hurt her in any way...

'Bindi's fine. I'm fine. And you're going to be fine,' she said soothingly. The machine next to him started beeping loudly. 'Lie back down, please,' she entreated, fluffing the pillows up behind his back.

He frowned, but did as he was told. 'How long have I been out of it? The last thing I remember was Alesha pointing a gun at us. At you. And then...Oh, I did something stupid, didn't I?'

'You've been unconscious for nearly twelve hours, it's Sunday morning now. You had me really worried for so long.' Her fingers stroked the back of his hand. 'The ride to the hospital in the back of Bindi's car was the longest thing I think I've ever had to endure.' Her eyes glazed over as she was lost in the memory. 'But the doctor said the bullet only grazed your skull. You were so lucky, if it'd penetrated...But it didn't so, you'll have a scar, but no major damage.' Her bright smile was back as she continued, 'And as for doing something stupid. Maybe it was. Courageous, definitely. You're a hero, Koen. You tried to save us, and you got shot. I've never had anyone throw themselves in front of a bullet for me before.'

'That's not what I did,' he said self-consciously. 'I thought I could take her down, knock the gun out of her hand and use it on Bull.' He gave a weak laugh at his own big-headed ego. 'It looks so easy in all of those cop shows. But you're really okay?' he asked again, scanning her up and down for any injuries. 'How did you get away? What happened to Bull, you have to tell me.'

'I think Alesha only shot you as a kind of reflex, on instinct, you know? Because after she shot you, she realized how being in love with Bull had turned her into a thug, just like him. She took off on his bike, left me and him standing there, staring at each other.'

'Wow. Didn't see that coming. And then what?'

'Well, then Bull said all these horrible things, he really is a sick puppy. He started threatening me with a knife, and we kind of ended up at the edge of the billabong.' She hung her head, no longer looking him in the eye, and he held his breath. 'We had quite a scuffle and I'm not exactly sure how it happened, but I kicked him into the water and then…' She finally lifted her gaze, showing him the fear and loathing that hovered there. 'Old Man Crocodile got him.'

'Bullshit!' he said in disbelief. 'You're kidding, really?' A large grin spread over his face as the truth hit him, and she nodded. 'How bloody ironic is that. He was killed the exact same way he wanted to get rid of us.'

'It is a little ironic. But still, not a nice way to die.'

'No, I guess not.' He sobered at the look of disquiet on her face. Even though he was her enemy, her nemesis, she still hadn't wished him dead. Hadn't wanted to watch him die in such a horrible manner.

'Thank God for that hard head of yours.' Koen looked up at the sound of a voice to see his sister standing in the doorway, watching him. She looked like she was still wearing the clothes he'd seen her in at the billabong, they were dirty and covered in mud. Her long dark hair was pulled up into a messy bun and there were deep worry lines he'd never noticed before etched around her mouth.

'Hi, Bind.' He kept his features neutral, he never quite knew what kind of reception he was going to get from his big sister, especially after he'd been the reason she was abducted and tied to a tree.

Rose broke the tense silence. 'Hi, Bindi,' she said, and went up and hugged the other woman. Bindi flinched at the unexpected vigor of Rose's welcome—much like him, his sister wasn't one for physical shows of affection—but then her face softened, and she returned Rose's embrace, gathering her up like a long-lost younger sister. 'Thank you. For everything. I can't believe we got you involved in all this. I don't even know where to begin—'

'Don't worry about it.' Bindi waved away her attempts at thanks. Koen thought he might've seen a glint of a tear in the corner of her eye. But no, his big sister was too tough for such sentimentality.

Rose finally let Bindi go, and she came up to the bed, scrutinizing his bandaged head. 'Not even a bullet can kill you, huh?' Her dark eyes were hard as flint as she glared down at him, and Koen had to steel himself not to shrink away from her. 'You bloody idiot. Trying to be a hero.' Then she surprised him for the second time that day and leaned in and pulled him to her breast in a quick, tight embrace. 'Don't you ever do that again.'

'I won't,' he mumbled, trying to hide the grin forming on his face. He'd been half-expecting his sister to rake him over the coals, lecture him for the next fifteen minutes on how stupid he was getting involved in all this. But instead of being angry, she'd showed respect.

'And you'd better go and see Mum. Soon,' she ordered. 'She just about went off her nut when I rang her last night and told her what happened. And Uncle Billy wants his motorbike back.'

And there it was. His sister always seemed to know how to bring him straight back down to earth. Bloody hell. The last thing he needed today was to have to face up to his mother's disapproving glare.

'I'll go with you,' Rose said, stepping up to the other side of the bed. 'We can face the music together. It was my fault you got mixed up in all of this, after all.'

He opened his mouth to argue with her, but then thought better of it. It might be good for his mum to meet Rose.

'Jon said he'd be in to see you later, too,' Bindi continued.

'Is he still mad at me?' Koen flinched at the thought of what Jon might say to him, as well.

'Nah, now that you're both safe and out of danger, he's even starting to see the funny side of it.' Bindi laid a hand on Koen's shoulder. 'Like the rest of us, he's just glad you're alive.'

Before Koen could reply, there was a light tap at the door, and he turned to see a man and woman standing in the doorway. 'Can we come in?'

One glance at the woman told Koen these had to be Rose's parents.

'Sure,' Rose said as she hurried over to meet them. After embracing each of them quickly, she said, 'I want you to meet the man who helped save my life.'

Koen grunted. 'No, I didn't, Rose, you saved yourself.'

'Whatever way you look at it, I'll be glad to shake your hand. I'm Dan,' the tall man said, engulfing Koen's hand in a strong, sincere clasp. 'I can't thank you enough for what you did to help my daughter.' Dan looked him directly in the eye, his other hand resting on his shoulder.

An unexpected lump formed in his throat. This praise from a man he hardly knew shouldn't affect him, but for some reason, he felt the significance of his words.

'Yes, and I second that.' Rose's mum, who was even more petite than Rose, if that were possible, had to stand on tiptoe to reach over the bed and kiss him on the cheek. 'You are our hero, and we can never thank you enough.' The light brush of her lips against his skin sent a small jolt through him. It was almost as if they accepted him, as if he were part of their family. 'Rose told us all about you, we're indebted to you.'

Didn't they know how far from the truth that was. Except both of them were staring at him, faith and appreciation showing on their faces. Perhaps he had done one good thing in his life in meeting Rose. And he thought he might be falling in love with her. Had that changed him? Could he be a better man for her?

Bindi had hung back in the corner, letting them get their introductions out of the way, the room was becoming a little crowded now. Both Dan and Jenna nodded in her direction in acknowledgement. They'd obviously already met. Now she came forward to the foot of the bed.

Her eyes glowed with something he didn't often see. Pride. 'Yes, my little bro. There is hope for you yet.'

What? He wanted to ask if this was a conspiracy. Were they all pulling his leg? So why were they all looking at him as if he were some kind of champion all of a sudden?

* * *

Rose stood waiting impatiently by the hotel reception counter. Where was Wanda? Koen sat in one of the reception chairs, looking a little pallid. She just wanted to get him out of here, get him home, where she could look after him. They'd kept him in hospital for three days, but finally the doctors had given him the okay to be discharged. The bell tinkled again under her palm as she pushed it for the third time.

At last Wanda's face, plastered with heavy make-up, her eye-liner so dark it made her look like Morticia Addams, appeared around the door from the back office. 'Be right with you, hon,' she huffed, as if she'd just run up the stairs. Except there were no stairs in this hotel. Wanda came out, patting at her hair and smoothing down her colorful kaftan. If Rose didn't know any better, she might've been tempted to think Wanda had a man in the back room.

'Hi, how can I...Oh, it's you,' she finished a little churlishly as she recognized Rose. Her face brightened when she noticed Koen in the chair, but then she narrowed her gaze speculatively at the bandages covering his head.

'You've got a hide, coming back here. Leaving with no explanation, and no one to clean my toilets. Leaving your room in such a mess, too. After I helped you out and all.'

There were many retorts hovering on Rose's tongue, but she kept them to herself. Wanda had helped in her hour of need, even if she was decidedly ungrateful.

'We were just wondering if you might have my stuff? I did leave in quite a hurry, you're right. And I'm very sorry.' She gave Wanda a bright smile, but it didn't seem to work, as the woman just glowered at her. Rose motioned behind her back at Koen, miming for him to come over.

She felt it the second Koen arrived behind her. Without even turning around, she knew he was there. The little hairs all over her body acted as a kind of antennae, letting her know where ever he was in the room. An internal compass that worked on him alone. It was both an odd sensation and a very comforting one at the same time. Koen's hand landed in the small of her back, warm and supportive.

'Hi, Wanda.' He flashed her that devil-may-care smile Rose was coming to love, the one that usually got him what he wanted.

The large woman brightened visibly as Koen kept his smile on her. 'Okay,' she said eventually. 'You're lucky. I did keep it, in case he...you came back. I'll go get it for you.' She got up from her chair and puffed her way across reception and disappeared into the back room.

As soon as she was gone, Koen's smile faltered.

'What?' Rose asked, aware of his change of mood. Even without her gift working on him, she was beginning to read his body language.

'I still can't believe I stole that money from you.' He hung his head in shame. It seemed like such a long time ago. In another world, when both she and Koen were two different people. He'd touched on this subject while he was still in the hospital and Rose had brushed it aside, saying the incident was forgotten. No longer on her radar. But it was obviously still on his. His shoulders hunched in anguish and he wouldn't look at her. How did she convey her feelings to him?

'Koen, look at me,' she demanded. 'I've forgiven you for that. Yes, I was mad at you to begin with.' Mad didn't really cover it, but he didn't need to know how devastated she'd been, because she'd thought she could trust him, and he'd betrayed that trust. 'But you brought it back. You did the right thing in the end.' And that's what matters, the fact he repented, felt so guilty he risked her wrath and perhaps her reporting him to the police, to bring it back to her. Teaching her she could trust him, after all. 'Now you need to forgive yourself.' And that was the crux of the matter. He needed to start believing in himself. Even her parents had absolved Koen, they understood that everyone made mistakes, but as long as you learnt from them, then there was always hope for something better. She could see what a courageous, bright, capable man he was. If only he would see it, too.

'Here you go,' Wanda said, struggling out of the office with the relatively small bag. She handed it to Koen. 'You be right with this, luv? You look like you've been in the wars.' Rose could see Wanda was itching to ask more, but she wasn't going to give her the pleasure.

'Thanks, Wanda. For everything.' On the spur of the moment, Rose reached into the back pocket of her jeans. 'Here's a little something to cover the mess we left in the room,' she said, placing a hundred dollars on the desk

'Oh, right. Thank you.' The woman seemed taken aback at the gesture. She finally found her fake smile and plastered it back on her face as she went around behind the desk.

Rose took her backpack out of Koen's hand, and he winked at her, but they both said nothing as they made their way to the door.

'Oh, by the way, hon.'

Rose drew in a breath and turned around. What did the annoying woman want now?

'That guy who owns the pub. I think his name was Todd,' she mused. 'He was down here the other day, looking for you. Said he wanted to offer you a job singing, or some such nonsense.' Even without her gift telling her that Wanda was more than a little disbelieving that Rose could sing, Wanda gave her a look that said it all. But Rose's heart thumped in her chest at the news. Todd thought she was good. He thought she could sing.

'Thanks, Wanda, I'll go up and see him right now,' Rose replied cheerily, and waved as they exited through the door. 'Is it okay if we pop past the pub quickly?' she asked Koen.

'Sure, girl, whatever you want,' he replied in his lazy drawl. She studied him carefully to make sure he wasn't covering up the fact he was in pain. But his eyes were clear and bright and even though his complexion was still a little sallow, she thought he was up to one more five-minute stop. They dumped her bag in their hire car, a 4WD tray-back her dad had organized for them so they could drive back to Shiralee, and walked the half-block to the pub. Her mum and dad were already at home, had left a few days ago, when it was obvious Koen was going to be fine. They were anxious to get back, mustering season was supposed to have already started, and now Bull was gone, they were anxious to get everything back on track. Guilt still ate at Rose's guts when she thought about it. She almost couldn't believe how selfish she'd been, running away, thinking only about herself.

The bar was nearly empty this early in the morning. Todd noticed her as she walked in and gave her a wave.

'I'll let you have a chat with him,' Koen said, veering off toward an empty table. 'I don't want to cramp your style.'

Ten minutes later she made her way over, carrying two soft-drinks and sat down, unable to keep the huge grin off her face.

'I told you, you were good,' Koen said. 'So now do you believe me?'

'Maybe,' she replied, still grinning like a maniac. 'He offered me a permanent gig, one night a week, as a sort of warm-up for some of the bigger bands he pays on Friday and Saturday nights. If I'm good enough, he might even stretch that to two nights. I can't believe it.' Her knees jigged up and down under the table with joy, she couldn't sit still. But she sobered when she remembered her reply. 'Todd was okay when I turned him down, he understands I have to go home. But he did say he'd give me a recommendation for any other gigs I might land.'

'That's great. Perhaps you could start up your own tour. Rose Simmonds Live and Exclusive,' Koen spread his arms wide as he drew a large imaginary banner in the air. Rose giggled. Perhaps one day that might be a dream of hers. But she had other things on her priority list right now. First, she needed to get Koen back to Shiralee, where he could recuperate.

It'd taken a lot of persuading to get him to agree to come with her. Her parents had talked to him, telling him how much they'd love him to come and stay. Even Bindi had weighed in, telling him he was an idiot if he didn't go. Rose said they could drive over and see his mother in a week or two, and so he could apologize to his uncle. Rose hoped if Koen liked it at Shiralee, he might even stay. Her parents would jump at the chance to offer him a job. And Ebony had already said she couldn't wait to meet Koen, she'd love to get his input on a new activity she wanted to put in place with the kids at the center.

Rose liked to think of a version of a future with Koen in it. But how did she convince him to stay? She was in love with him, of that she had no doubt. But if she told him, how would he react? If he didn't feel the same, he could conceivably turn and run the other way.

'That's good. You have something to look forward to. I'm happy for you. You're very lucky.' While his words rang with truth, she could hear an undercurrent of something else. Sorrow? Self-pity maybe?

'But…' she said slowly.

'But…' He shrugged and stared out the window of the pub. She kept silent, willing him to open up, tell her what he was really feeling for once. 'You have a wonderful life ahead of you. A family that loves you. But what do I have to show for my life up until now? All I seem to have done is squander my chances.'

His words hit her like a cold splash of water. He was always so cheerful, so full of life. Always had a joke or a wisecrack to lighten any moment, was seemingly unaffected by people's views of him. But they were all facades to cover up how poor his self-esteem really was. Her heart was breaking that he thought so lowly of himself.

'All of us deserve a second chance, Koen.'

'I'm not sure I do,' he replied.

She leaned over and took his hand. His fingers wrapped

around hers, white and brown, intertwined. 'Koen, I have faith in you.'

'Hmm,' he mumbled, but his stare was still directed out of the window, hiding his true feelings.

Damn, she really, really needed her gift right now, to help her mine the depths of Koen's issues. It was like driving a car down a road blindfolded, how did she navigate all the twists and turns? It was time she told him the complete truth, laid all her cards on the table.

'My life isn't nearly as perfect as you may think. The whole fact that Bull was trying to kill us all, might give you some inkling to that.' Koen smiled faintly at this and his gaze finally flicked toward her. 'I have something to tell you. About me, and my family. We're...a little different to most people you know. Well, at least the women in the family are.'

'Yeah, how?' His eyes brightened a little.

'We all have a certain gift. Something that no-one else can do. Or not anyone I've ever met, anyway.' She stopped, unsure if this was going to be a deal-breaker for Koen. But she had to tell him. So, for the next ten minutes, she talked, and he listened as she told him her whole family's life story, including how her mother could communicate with animals, and how her grandmother had a special healing ability. He listened quietly, his hand still clasped tightly in hers.

As Rose finished her story, Koen laughed out loud. 'That's not so strange, girl. The elders in my community could tell you tales a lot stranger than that. About a woman who can talk to snakes, for instance. And you know, our wise-women have rituals that have healed things white-man's medicine can't explain. I can't wait to take you to meet some of them.'

'I can't wait to meet them, either.' Telling him about her family's problems had shown him that no-one was perfect. Would he take that on board? And perhaps change his own self-view? Only time would tell.

CHAPTER TWENTY-THREE

'Hey, all you handsome boys, I brought you some lunch.' Rose placed a tray covered with a dish-cloth to keep off the flies on a table in the corner of the shed.

Koen gave her a secretive wink and bent back toward the bench. 'Be there in a sec,' he said. Fingers resting lightly on the plank of wood, he looked down at the two dark heads hovering over the bench below him. 'Okay, Dade, tell me where you need to cut this piece of wood. I've given you the measurements, now how would you do it?'

The boy scratched his head and gave a quick, wary glance up at Koen, as if he were expecting some kind of trick. Dade was nine years old, a new kid at the Ironbark Center. He'd only started coming six days ago, made the trip every day from Smokey Creek on the special bus Ebony had organized. Any of the kids in the area were welcome to come to the center whenever they wanted. And stay for the day, or a night, or as long as they liked. Dade was still plagued by many issues. Trust being a major one. But he would come around, eventually. With care and compassion, they almost always did.

'I know how to do it, Koen,' a cheeky voice piped up.

'I know you do, Samuel, and I'm very proud you learnt so quickly.' Koen's heart swelled, so it was almost painful as he watched the eagerness in Samuel's face. The boy looked up at him, almost jumping up and down on the spot with enthusiasm. Samuel was only eight and had been coming to the center for over six months. Ebony told him Samuel was one of the trickier kids to handle, still overly defiant and disruptive and talking back to all the adults. Until Koen had arrived and shown him how to form a set of clap-sticks out of wood. The boy had taken to Koen straight away, followed him around like his own personal shadow most days now. He was still disruptive and annoying, but he was starting to learn to respect. Learn that there were people in the world he could put his faith in, and who wouldn't let him down, no matter what he did or said.

'But I want Dade to try it today. You can do the next measurement, after lunch, okay?' Koen said, giving the other boy an encouraging nod. He watched as Dade brought out the tape measure and pencil and then checked the numbers he'd scrawled on a bit of paper. Koen drew in a deep breath, still a little overawed when he thought about what he was doing with these boys. The responsibility of it all.

When Rose had brought him back to Shiralee—supposedly to recover from his head-wound, which apart from some ongoing nasty headaches and a scar along his hairline, had almost completely healed—he'd fallen in love with the outback cattle station immediately. The country so similar to that of his own community in Balgo. The country folk also so familiar with their tough, no-nonsense attitudes and ready smiles, no matter the weather or the hardship they faced. It felt like he'd come home. And her step-brothers, Rodney and Tallow, were a breath of fresh air, too. He'd thought they might be wary of him when he first arrived, they were obviously fiercely protective of their older sister. But it hadn't taken them long to work out he was no threat to them or their sister and embraced him the same way they embraced the rest of their lives, with gusto and enthusiasm. It was an honor to watch the two boys, so full of self-assurance and vitality. Koen just hoped they knew how lucky they were to have step-parents and grandparents who loved them so unconditionally, allowed them to flourish and grow into their potential on the station.

Even with all this to take up his time, it'd only been a week or so before he found himself spending more time at Ironbark Center than on the station. Ebony and Jay owned the adjoining property, but the house was only a fifteen-minute drive from the station house. At first Rose had driven him over, so he could watch what she and Lex did with the boys, teaching them horsemanship. But then Jay called him to ask his advice on a project they were building with the kids in the carpentry shed. They wanted to make a large totem pole, completely carved out of wood, to put at the main gate of the center. Jay's calls became more frequent, and Koen would hop on one of the motorbikes and drive over to give guidance.

One night, around a month ago, Jay called him up to the main house and handed him a beer and asked him to sit with him for a few minutes. Koen respected Jay. Rose told him Jay was ex-army, and it showed in the way he ran the center, with precision and organization. But there was also a deep compassion in the man, he was so calm, even with the unruliest of kids. Even if they were yelling and cursing at him, he never lost his cool. And it was so obvious how much he loved Rose's grandmother. A deep, abiding love that sometimes had Koen in awe. Would he and Rose ever be like that?

That night, Jay offered Koen a job. It'd taken Koen by surprise. The thought never crossed his mind before. He'd been happy drifting through the past couple of weeks, not thinking much about the future. The idea of moving away, of perhaps checking out Tasmania had slowly faded. He was only going to do that to protect his family, so he couldn't hurt them anymore. But those days of being a screwup were also fading. For some strange reason, everything he did out here was good. Could he accept Jay's offer with good faith? Did he want to work here? Help these kids? Help them feel like they were worthy again?

If only Mack had a chance to come to this youth center, or something like it. Perhaps he would still be alive today. In a way, it was almost like a penance. Koen could never bring Mack back, but he could try and help other kids like him, so they didn't end up going the same way.

His answer had been a resounding yes. Jay had shaken his hand, and he'd moved over to the center the very next day.

Koen could feel Rose's eyes on his back, so when Dade finally made his first hesitant measurement, Koen said, 'That's great, you got it right. Now let's go celebrate and have some lunch.' Both boys shot off with a whoop toward the little table, where Rose was uncovering a pile of thick-cut sandwiches full of cold meat and salad. She poured them each a big glass of ice-cold water from a thermos, filling a glass for herself and Koen as well. Koen watched her as she moved, talking easily to the kids. She was wearing the eternal pair of faded blue jeans, the ones he loved to watch her walk in as they hugged her luscious hips.

The boys wolfed down their sandwiches in record time, and then Samuel said, 'Can we go and visit Lex in the stables? Please, Koen, can we?' The stables held a close second in Samuel's world, next to the carpentry shed. Dade looked up with expectant eyes, still afraid to say anything, but hoping.

'Sure, I'll call you in twenty minutes. We've still got lots to do here,' he warned. Then was silently shocked at how fatherly he'd just sounded.

'Thanks, Koen,' Samuel called, already dashing around the

side of the shed, Dade hot on his heels.

'Those two are a handful,' Rose said as she watched them disappear. 'Fast becoming inseparable too, according to Ebony.'

'Yeah, it's good. Dade found a friend. If anyone can help bring that kid out of his shell, it's Sammy.'

'And thanks to you, Samuel is coming along in leaps and bounds as well.'

Koen grinned at Rose's praise. It still felt odd to have people applaud him, but he was beginning to learn to accept it, even if he didn't always like it. 'Let's go sit out the back,' he said, grabbing her by the hand and stuffing the rest of his sandwich into his mouth. There was a single plastic chair huddled in the shade next to the trunk of an old casuarina tree. It was very hot outside, the midday sun beating down upon the desert with its usual ferocity. But Koen liked the view from the chair, stretching out over the paddocks of red earth, the clumps of green tussocks forming some relief to the never-ending outback. And he was going to make the most of having Rose all to himself for a few minutes of blissful solitude.

He sat in the chair and pulled Rose down onto his lap, where she sat giggling like a schoolgirl. 'One of the kids might see us,' she said, half-pretending to stand up again.

'Nah, hardly anyone ever comes back here. We're safe from prying eyes for a while.'

'Well, what are you waiting for? Kiss me then.' She wriggled in his lap, and he felt himself harden as her appealing butt ground into his thighs. It reminded him of what they'd got up to two nights ago. A few nights a week, if Rose could get away from Shiralee, she would come and spend the night with him at the center. Last time she'd come, they snatched some fresh bread and a hunk of cheese from the kitchen and thrown a swag in the back of her ute and driven out into the desert. They'd made love under the stars, with the sound of wild dingoes howling their mournful tirade to the moon. He still couldn't believe how much the woman turned him on. She only had to glance in his direction, and he was hard. That night had been extra sweet, reminding him of their first night in the hut in Kakadu. Afterwards she'd lain in his arms and he'd listened to her breathe, watching the stars revolve through the night sky, and he knew he'd never been this happy. Ever.

Rose's lips were soft, and her tongue found its way into his mouth. She was so warm and giving and spirited. And she was his. In all of her different ways and complicated layers. Including that special ability she had. He'd seen it at work, when she'd been able to tell a kid was going to lose their shit even before he could, and then she'd know exactly what to say to soothe the child, bring them back down to a calmer state. He was bloody glad she couldn't read his emotions, however. It gave him time to figure out how he was feeling without her knowing first.

And now it was time. He withdrew a few inches so he could look into her eyes.

'Rose?'

'Hmm.'

Koen licked his lips. He'd never said the words to any other woman. Ever. Jesus, why was this so much harder than he imagined. He'd known for weeks now, turning the idea over and over in his head, trying to find any justification to prove his feelings wrong. But he kept coming back to the same solid truth. It was a fact, she'd etched herself across his heart, across his soul. There was no turning back, she was the one and only woman for him. For now and forever.

'I love you.'

'Oh, Koen, you don't know how I've been hoping you'd say that,' she breathed.

'I love you, too.'

* * *

Rose's heart felt like it would pound right out of her chest. She wanted to dance. Sing the words from the rooftop. Rip his shirt off right here and have him show her how much he loved her.

She'd been waiting so long to hear those words. Months. The whole time she'd been keeping her own words of love hidden. Hadn't wanted to say them before he did. Little warning bells in her head told her he needed to figure it out for himself first. He needed time to come to terms with this thing between them. Would only say those words when he felt worthy of being able to receive love. Worthy of her. When he finally valued his own self-worth enough to let her in.

And now her waiting had paid off.

She kissed him, and he returned her passion, his mouth strong and intense with wanting.

Then she laughed. 'This actually works out really well. I was going to tell you my news tonight. But I'll tell you now instead.'

Now that Koen worked here full-time, Rose could as often as not be found hanging around the center. Forsaking her duties over at Shiralee to come and visit him, finding the weakest excuse to run an errand over to her grandparents. She smiled at the thought of her parents' forbearance. They were just so happy to have her home and in one piece. She'd had a long talk with them a few nights after she got home. Her mum apologized for the way she'd been so overprotective with Rose. Acknowledged they probably should've handled it differently, and they were as much to blame for Rose running away as she was. Her parents had given her their blessing for complete freedom from now on. No more telling her what to do or keeping her imprisoned on the farm. Jenna had broken down and wept, saying she had only ever wanted to protect her daughter. Rose had wept right alongside her mother. And they'd both forgiven each other. And with Bull out of the picture, there was no more reason for their vigilant safety precautions. Rose was free to do whatever she liked.

And she was about to exercise those rights.

'I talked to Ebony this morning.'

'Hmm,' he replied, running a finger over the jut of her collarbone beneath the neckband of her shirt, only half-listening to her.

Rose touched her necklace beneath the fabric of her chambray shirt. Not for good luck, but more out of habit, as she took a deep breath. 'Ebony asked me to come and work here full time.'

'What?' He looked up, his full attention on her once again.

'I'm going to take over from Lex with the horses. He was really only on loan from Shiralee until they could come up with a better solution. And it looks like I'm the solution.'

'But what about your job as station-hand at Shiralee?' He was shocked. Probably thought she would never leave her parents' farm. Owed them her allegiance and her loyalty. Which she did, but she was determined to live life on her own terms now.

'They can hire a new station hand. I'm not indispensable, you know. I'll still go over and help out if they're ever short-handed. And I'll probably see them every day or so, anyway.'

'Wow, that's great news.' His eyes lit up with delight as the implications sunk in.

'Ebony said we could have the married quarters. If you want to, that is.' Oh God, she hadn't really thought about it before, had just been so excited by her grandmother's offer. It was almost like they were moving in together.

'Of course I do,' he growled, and nibbled at her neck playfully.

'I'm also going to play one night a week at the pub in Smokey Creek.'

'Well, you are full of surprises today, girl.' He drew back so he could stare into her eyes. She could drown in those dark, chocolate depths. 'My mum's coming to visit in a few weeks. I'll bring her along to watch you sing.'

'That's great news.' She knew Koen wanted his mum to be proud of him, of what he'd achieved now. And she would be. Rose just knew it.

'I love what I'm doing here. Maybe we could start something like this in Balgo? In a few years' time. What do you think?'

'I think that's a great idea.'

They both turned to stare out into the desert as the heat haze shimmered at the edge of the horizon. Rose knew she belonged here, the outback was in her blood, just as it was in Koen's. She wanted to stand by this amazing man's side forever. He was her home. And she was his. Together, they would make a wonderful life. Perhaps change a few children's lives for the better at the same time.

'I'm glad it was me who picked you up in the desert that day,' he murmured.

'Me too.'

Was it fate, bringing two lost souls together? Who knew? One thing Rose was certain of, she'd never let him go again.

If you liked Shadows of Red Earth, you'll love;

Shadows in the Dust

Her heart's been broken by tragedy, but will a cowboy's courage be enough to save her when there's a killer on the loose in the outback.

Shadows in Deep Blue

Pulled out to sea by a rip-tide, Ebony is drowning. Ex-army Corporal, Jay risks his own life to rescue her. But that's just the beginning of her secrets and lies and soon they're both caught up in a fight for their lives.

The books in this series can be read as stand-alone novels, but are enhanced if you read them together.

Also by Suzanne Cass
NEW
Stormcloud Station Series
(A Stargazer Spinoff Series)
Small Town Romantic Suspense
Clear Skies
Starlit Skies

Stargazer Ranch Romance Series
Small Town Romantic Suspense
Books are better read as a series
Combustion: Prequel Novella
Wildfire
Firelight
Snowbound: A Christmas Novella
Snowfall
Cloudburst

Island Bound Series
Mystery Romance (on an Island)
Books can be read as stand-alone
Bound by Truth
Bound by Silence
Bound by the Stars

Colors of the Earth Series
Small Town Romantic Suspense
Books can be read as stand-alone
Shadows in the Dust
Shadows in Deep Blue
Shadows of Red Earth

Romantic Suspense
Single Title
Island Redemption

Glass Clouds
Chasing Bullets

Love in the Mountains Novella Series
Small Town Short Romance
Novellas can be read as stand-alone
Rain on a Tin Roof
Lost and Found
Rescue his Heart

Please Leave a Review

The greatest gift you could ever give an author is to leave a review. You will be helping other people to discover this book and making a difference to me as an Independently Published Author. If you liked this book and want other people to read it too, please leave a review.

Connect with the Author

I really hope you enjoyed reading Shadows of Red Earth. For more action romance info, upcoming release dates, and access to free books join the exclusive Suzanne Cass reader club. As an added bonus, you'll get a copy of my FREE STORY.

Solar Flare

http://www.suzannecass.com/contact/

Or you can stay in touch via my website
www.suzannecass.com

Or

About the Author

Suzanne Cass is an Australian author who writes rural romance and romantic suspense abounding with passion and danger.

Her debut novel, Island Redemption, won the Romance Writers of Australia Emerald Award in 2016. Suzanne was also a finalist in the 2019 Romance Writers of Australia RUBY award.

She had always had a fascination with the tough resilience of people who live in our amazing red-dirt outback country. When not writing about the characters that inhabit her head, Suzanne can be found roaming the Perth beaches with her border collie, or encouraging from the sidelines as her two sons play sport.

Stay in touch via my website

www.suzannecass.com

Or

Acknowledgements

This book, the third in the Colours of the Earth Series, was in some ways easier to write than the first two. The characters, Rose and Koen burned bright and vital in my imagination right from the start and I loved telling their story of two souls who were always meant to be together.

This book is dedicated to my family, who've read every one of my books (whether they like to read romance or not) and helped me feel special and valued right from the start. Thanks so much for your continued encouragement.

To my author friends, Rachel, Jillian and Rose, there are not enough words (or hugs) to tell you how much I value your input and support. Thank you. We are all on separate journey's in our writing career, but the best part of it is we are sharing those journey's.

I also want to thank Rebecca, for her help in shaping Koen's character and his Indigenous heritage, making sure I treated him with truth and sensitivity that honored the Aboriginal people and their culture.

There is a team of people who I also couldn't do without, other beta readers (special thanks to Rebecca) and my ARC team, who are essential to an Indie Author like me.

I am so very grateful to all the readers who have bought and enjoyed my books and who will continue to do so. Writing for you is what keeps me focussed and motivated.

And last but never least, to my husband who lets me follow my dream of writing, while he supports me and our family. Thanks Gaz.

www.ingramcontent.com/pod-product-compliance
Lightning Source LLC
Chambersburg PA
CBHW030636110726
47901CB00002B/468